PRAISE FOR KATHLEE~

"*The Chisholm Trail Bride* is an exciting read that kept me g___
each page as it led me into unpredictable twists. Kathleen has a talent
for writing the unexpected!"

–Hannah Alexander, author of the Sacred Trust series

"I've always enjoyed Kathleen's vivid descriptions and page-turning
romance. No matter the time period or setting, Kathleen works hard
to bring the story alive through her characters and passion for God."

–Tracie Peterson, best-selling author of over 100 novels including
the Heart of the Frontier and Song of Alaska series

"[*The Pirate Bride*] was a fresh and interesting read. I loved the twists
and turns in the plot. A lot surprised me. It kept me turning pages as
fast as I could read them. I highly recommend this novel for all readers
of historical fiction."

–Lena Nelson Dooley, author of *A Heart's Gift,* winner of the 2017
Faith, Hope, and Love Reader's Choice Award for Long Historicals

"Kathleen Y'Barbo knows how to write adventure-filled historical
romance that will keep the pages turning! *The Alamo Bride* was packed
with action, danger, adventure and of course, a bit of romance! I loved
it! It kept me on the edge of my seat, yet still managed to have plenty of
warmth and humor from the characters. Fantastic read!"

–Ashley Johnson, book blogger and reviewer at BringingUpBooks

The Chisholm Trail Bride

The
Daughters
of the
Mayflower

KATHLEEN Y'BARBO

BARBOUR BOOKS
An Imprint of Barbour Publishing, Inc.

Print ISBN 978-1-64352-287-6

eBook Editions:
Adobe Digital Edition (.epub) 978-1-64352-289-0
Kindle and MobiPocket Edition (.prc) 978-1-64352-288-3

Cover Image: Magdalena Russocka / Trevillion Images

Published by Barbour Books, an imprint of Barbour Publishing, Inc., 1810 Barbour Drive, Uhrichsville, Ohio 44683, www.barbourbooks.com

Our mission is to inspire the world with the life-changing message of the Bible.

ecpa Member of the
Evangelical Christian
Publishers Association

Printed in the United States of America.

Daughters of the Mayflower

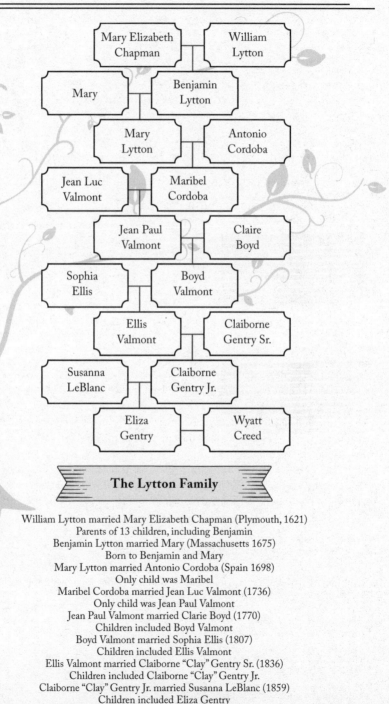

Mary Elizabeth Chapman — William Lytton

Mary — Benjamin Lytton

Mary Lytton — Antonio Cordoba

Jean Luc Valmont — Maribel Cordoba

Jean Paul Valmont — Claire Boyd

Sophia Ellis — Boyd Valmont

Ellis Valmont — Claiborne Gentry Sr.

Susanna LeBlanc — Claiborne Gentry Jr.

Eliza Gentry — Wyatt Creed

The Lytton Family

William Lytton married Mary Elizabeth Chapman (Plymouth, 1621)
Parents of 13 children, including Benjamin
Benjamin Lytton married Mary (Massachusetts 1675)
Born to Benjamin and Mary
Mary Lytton married Antonio Cordoba (Spain 1698)
Only child was Maribel
Maribel Cordoba married Jean Luc Valmont (1736)
Only child was Jean Paul Valmont
Jean Paul Valmont married Clarie Boyd (1770)
Children included Boyd Valmont
Boyd Valmont married Sophia Ellis (1807)
Children included Ellis Valmont
Ellis Valmont married Claiborne "Clay" Gentry Sr. (1836)
Children included Claiborne "Clay" Gentry Jr.
Claiborne "Clay" Gentry Jr. married Susanna LeBlanc (1859)
Children included Eliza Gentry
Eliza Gentry married Wyatt Creed (1889)

To Andrew.
My son.
My heart.
When I look up at the stars, I see you.
I'll meet you at the gate, sweetheart.

In one of the stars I shall be living. In one of them
I shall be laughing when you look at the night sky.
—Antoine de Saint-Exupéry, *The Little Prince*

PART I

The old Chisholm Trail wound its way over the hills and through the valleys. Wildflowers grew in the greatest profusion everywhere and there were many rare varieties that I had never seen before. I was fond of flowers and it afforded me great pleasure and helped to while away the long, lonely hours to gather them in armfuls. Sometimes, I would fill my buggy and decorate my horses' bridles and harness with the gorgeous blossoms, then I would weave a wreath for my hair and a chaplet of flowers for my shoulders.

— Mary Taylor Bunton, *A Bride on the Old Chisholm Trail in 1886*

Chapter 1

April 1880
On the Chisholm Trail
north of Waco, Texas

The stars at night were big and bright. Eliza Gentry sighed. Was there any more beautiful sight? There couldn't possibly be.

A wisp of cloud drifted lazily over a nearly full moon while cattle lowed in the distance. Eliza lay back on the pile of quilts she'd made into the most comfortable bed in the entire encampment and stared up at those beautiful Texas stars.

Tonight they were the canopy beneath which she would sleep, and tomorrow the blazing sun would take its place. The cowboys would rise before dawn to complain about the coffee and each other, but never would they complain about riding all those miles under the big blue sky.

Much as they grumbled about other things, the men who drove cattle from the Gentry Ranch—halfway between San Antonio and Austin—up toward the Red River land and beyond to Kansas lived the whole year for the spring drives. Chief among them was her father, William Gentry.

While his fellow ranchers were turning their herds over to contract drovers, Papa had resisted. She'd heard him talk with his foreman, Red, about giving in next year.

"One last drive," he'd said to the red-haired giant. "Just one last drive."

The fact that Mama had allowed her to go along with Papa and her brothers this year was a miracle in itself. She'd threatened to bundle Eliza off to New Orleans for the annual visit with the Gentry and Hebert cousins.

"The girl needs finishing," she'd heard her mother say. "She needs the companionship of fine young ladies and the company of young gentlemen."

Papa's chair legs had scraped the kitchen floor at that statement, causing Eliza to gather closer into the shadows behind the kitchen door lest Papa come strolling past and find her.

"There may not be a next year. She's got time for finishing," he'd said gently.

"My mother would disagree. At twelve I already knew my place as a young lady. I had been taught how to carry myself in society and was already planning my trousseau. Meanwhile, our daughter is doing nothing of the sort."

"I do not recall asking your mother for her opinion of how our daughter should be raised."

Mama's voice rose. "Do you know I caught her on the roof of the springhouse again? When I asked her what on earth she was doing, she told me she'd only just determined that it might be possible to land in the saddle of her horse from that angle if she were to wait until the wind blew just right. Can you feature it?"

Papa's chuckle drifted toward her. "Sounds like the work of her brothers, Susanna. Boys tease, especially their sisters. Likely Trey put her up to it. Zeke, he's a rule follower and aims to be just like me someday, so I don't see his hand in this. Yes, Trey it likely was. He'd have thought it funny."

"I don't find it funny at all," her mother said. "And no, this time the culprit was that Creed boy. I can find no fault with that Ranger, W. C. Creed, other than perhaps his background, but the younger

Creed is trouble. You mark my words."

Eliza's lips twisted into a smile as she recalled the conversation and the dare that precipitated it. Mama spoke the truth when she told Papa that Wyatt Creed was involved, but what she did not know was that Eliza had never planned to try landing in that saddle.

As with every other conversation she had with Wyatt, if he thought Eliza would do it, he'd have to do it too. And better. Or faster. Or whatever else it took to best her.

Sometimes he did, and sometimes he didn't. This time they would never know whether Wyatt might have landed that jump into the saddle thanks to Mama's interruption of what would have been a perfectly good idea.

And of course that traitor Wyatt saw Mama heading for them and cut out for home before she spied him. That left Eliza on the roof with no good explanation other than the truth.

The reverend said the truth would set her free. This time the truth almost sent her into exile.

Only Papa and his insistence on taking her along with the purpose of talking sense into her kept her off the steamer that was currently heading east. For that she was eternally grateful.

Mama's sister, Eugenie, had just given birth to a baby girl she'd named Justine. All Mama had done from the time the letter arrived until she'd left on the stage was to sew up dainty baby girl clothes for her new niece, all the while rattling on about how in no time it would be Eliza's turn to marry and have babies of her own.

As much as she loved Mama, she did not value her opinion on this subject. From what she could tell, growing up and marrying meant giving up riding alongside Papa on the trail and sleeping under the stars.

A life without that was no life at all. And babies? They fussed and made messes and were a general source of disruption. She had Wyatt for that.

Eliza shifted positions and kicked off her quilt. It was a warm night for late March and the breeze was nice, so Papa had pulled back the canvas that covered the wagon to allow Eliza and her brothers to slumber there while he took up his turn keeping watch.

Ezekiel Gentry, who at nearly sixteen was the eldest of the Gentry children, had curled up in the corner and taken to snoring as soon as Papa rode away. Not that she blamed him.

This year he had joined the menfolk and taken on full duties as a ranch hand. That meant he'd be chasing strays and keeping watch just like the rest of the men.

A few days ago, he'd driven the wagon across the big suspension bridge over the Brazos at Waco, and he was still telling anyone who would listen what that was like. As always, Eliza had craned her neck to look down at the brown water rushing beneath them and marveled that it was all happening and she needn't worry about wet clothes.

Poor Zeke had bragged about his upcoming adventure in the weeks leading up to their departure. Now her big brother could barely keep upright on his horse most days for the exhaustion.

Beside her on his own pile of quilts was Claiborne "Trey" Gentry III, the middle brother with the fancy-sounding name who'd nearly caught up to Zeke in height and surpassed him in strength and general bullheadedness. Namesake of both Papa and Grandpa Clay, Trey was an old soul who rarely complained and, for that matter, hardly commented unless there was something worthwhile to say. He wore his heart on his sleeve and, despite Mama's objections, a shark's tooth he'd found on the beach in Galveston on a leather string around his neck

Oh, but he did love to tease, and Eliza was his favorite target. Now that Wyatt Creed's father, WC, had joined them as far as Fort Worth, both father and son had taken up places on the drive, and Wyatt and Trey had become fast friends and partners in the crime of irritating Eliza to distraction.

"Close those eyes, girlie."

Eliza tilted her head to see Papa standing near the wagon. "I'm not tired. Besides, the stars are so beautiful," she told him. "How can I sleep when God has given me something so entertaining to study?"

His low chuckle made her smile. "There'll be plenty of time to study the stars someday. Tonight is not that time. Besides, I don't want to have to send you home because you cannot keep awake."

Trey shifted positions beside her but did not awaken. "I'll try," she whispered. "I truly will."

"Why am I suspicious of your sincerity?"

Eliza giggled. "The same reason I am suspicious of yours. You wouldn't send me home."

He lifted his dark brows, but even in the moonlight she could see the beginnings of a grin. "Wouldn't I?"

"Why am I suspicious of your sincerity?" she said with her own grin firmly in place.

Papa was the youngest child and only son of Claiborne Gentry Sr. and his bride, Ellis Dumont. Born into a family of sisters whose hair was as red as the curls Eliza tried to hide under her bonnet, her father was dark and handsome and had to be the smartest man alive.

All her life Papa had told stories of her grandmother, the quiet woman who'd done brave and amazing things in her life, and of Grandpa Clay who'd descended from pirates and fought bravely for the independence that Eliza took for granted.

Eliza's response to these stories of battles fought, lost loves found, and treasures buried but not forgotten was always to question whether Papa told the truth. So this question, often bandied about between them, was one that held humor as well as meaning.

Tonight it appeared her father intended a bit of both. "Eliza Jane," he said slowly, "do not try me. Your mama will have my head if I bring you back in worse shape than I took you, and you know it."

She did. It was likely that Mama was already looking for an excuse to say no to her accompanying Papa and the boys on the spring trail ride next year.

"I have not yet seen a shooting star," she protested. "Once I do, I promise I will sleep."

"That is a wish, not a need," Papa said as he leaned down from his horse to tuck the quilt back over her legs. "Sleep is needed tonight, else you will be wanting the stars tomorrow."

Eliza closed her eyes but opened them again once the sound of Papa's horse faded away. Overhead stars twinkled while Zeke continued to snore. She counted the points of light that made up the Big Dipper, Orion, and—

Pssst.

She glanced over at Trey, who was still sleeping soundly, and then returned to her study of the heavens above. If her brother wanted to tease her, she would show him. Ignoring Trey was one of her favorite pastimes.

Maybe she ought to snatch that shark's tooth off his neck and hide it. No, he was far too suspicious of removing that necklace ever since Zeke told him taking it off would bring him bad luck.

She glanced up. Oh, but the heavens above. Studying them was infinitely more enjoyable.

The Lord had made each star—that she recalled and believed from the Bible—but how many were there? Perhaps one day she would be the one to give that answer.

If only she could light a lamp and continue her attempt to read *The Heavens* by Amédée Guillemin. Wyatt had secretly delivered a copy of the book to her after he discovered he'd gotten her in trouble with Mama regarding the jump from the springhouse, but the words were difficult and the ideas hard to grasp.

So she'd been reading it slowly to make sense of it all. Mostly she just admired the beautiful illustrations, especially the illustration of Donati's Comet from October 4, 1858.

Pssst.

A movement to her right caught Eliza's attention. She turned on her side and spied a pair of sage-green eyes watching her from beneath the brim of a battered straw cowboy hat.

Wyatt Creed. Of course. Eliza stifled a groan.

"What are you doing here?" she whispered. "Go back to wherever you're supposed to be and leave me in peace."

She knew of course that he'd probably come about the meteor shower tonight. Watching the Lyrids together had become somewhat of a tradition ever since she read about them in a book three years ago. Before that, she'd just assumed that every night on the Chisholm Trail was dusted with falling stars at bedtime.

"You're not still mad at me, are you?"

"I am," she told him. "You got me in trouble with Mama and almost caused me to have to go to New Orleans with her instead of coming out on the trail with Papa."

He rose and stretched out to his full height, then rested his bony elbows on the edge of the wagon. Though the two of them had been the same size for years, Wyatt had suddenly shot up almost a foot since last year's spring trail ride. At just past fourteen, he was now two heads taller than her with legs long enough to cause her to have to run to keep up with him.

If she were to want to keep up with him. Which she wouldn't, of course.

After the jumping-into-the-saddle incident, Eliza was done with Wyatt Creed. Well and truly done. Even if she did very much appreciate his peace offering of the book.

One of these days Wyatt was going to have to figure out how to tell Eliza Gentry that he was getting too old to have a girl following him around like a lonesome pup. He still tolerated her—enjoyed her company if the truth be told—but soon he'd be grown and she'd still be a child.

And a distraction.

If he was ever going to become a Texas Ranger like his pa, who could track a man like nobody's business and sleep in the saddle if he had to, then he had to avoid all forms of distraction. Pa was with them on this drive, but he'd leave at Fort Worth to meet up with Captain Junius Peak and take on his next assignment for Company B.

He gave the obstinate female one more look, then shrugged. "I was going to invite you to watch the meteors tonight like we've always done, but it looks like you have other plans."

Her eyes narrowed slightly, indicating he'd struck a nerve. Though he hadn't always had an interest in falling stars and such, he'd learned enough from Eliza and those books she was always reading to appreciate the science behind them.

"The moon is mostly full," she whispered. "There'll not be much to see whether here in this wagon or out there away from the campfire."

Wyatt shrugged. "Suit yourself. I'll go alone. Bet I see more falling stars in an hour than you ever have. What's your highest amount?"

"Why should I tell you? You'll just brag tomorrow about besting me with some made-up number."

Rather than take offense, Wyatt laughed. That had indeed been his plan.

"I'll be too busy to bother about that tomorrow," he told her. "I'm the wrangler on this drive, and that's kept me occupied."

Occupied was an understatement. Any wrangler who hired on to a cattle drive was going to be working hard to take care of the remuda of horses that were required. With every man needing three horses and there being a dozen men on this ride, he had plenty to do.

More than he'd expected. Not that he'd tell Eliza's pa that. Mr. Gentry was the boss of this trail drive, and as such he'd hired Wyatt on to be a responsible member of his team.

He wouldn't let Mr. Gentry down. Or his pa.

Another shrug. "All right then. I'll just let you turn the tables on me and best me tomorrow for whatever amount I see tonight. Good evening to you, Liza Jane."

She hated when he called her that. Thus, he did so regularly.

Wyatt left the Gentry wagon behind and returned to the circle of firelight where Pa and a half dozen other men had gathered. The men were deep in discussion and ignored him as he joined them.

"Rumor is these cows ain't going to bring us enough to make all this worth the trouble."

Red Pearson, Mr. Gentry's right-hand man on the drive and his foreman back at the ranch, spat into the fire. Wyatt had heard tell that Red used to be a circuit-riding preacher before he settled down and took up the job with the Gentrys. Right or wrong, Wyatt knew him to be a good man.

The fellow beside Red, a cowboy known only as Concho, spoke into the silence. "But it sure beats being at home and having to listen to my wife."

The men guffawed. All but Pa.

He looked across the fire at Wyatt. Pa reached down beside him and pulled up a bottle and took a swig, never breaking eye contact.

Mama wouldn't allow alcohol in her home, so Pa quit it altogether out of love for her when they married. But Pa had hated living without Mama since she passed on last fall, which meant he'd gone back to drinking.

And when he was drinking, he was mean.

Mr. Gentry didn't allow any sort of alcohol consumption on his trail rides. But the boss was out guarding the cattle tonight and not here to witness what his old friend was up to.

Wyatt rose and made for the bedroll he'd stashed not far from the campfire. He figured Pa might follow but never thought he'd move so quick.

When the hand closed on Wyatt's neck, he knew Pa had caught him.

"I saw that look you gave me," his father said, his voice ragged and his breath smelling of the rot-gut whiskey he preferred lately. "You ain't no better than me, Son, and if you don't know it yet, you will."

Wyatt stood stock still. He was easily as tall as Pa but not nearly as heavy or strong. The old man's fist might hurt, but his legs weren't sure enough to carry him far. At least he hoped that was the case.

In one quick motion he slid under his father's arm and lit out into the night.

CHAPTER 2

The drive was well under way the next morning before Eliza spied Wyatt. He was hunched over his saddle with his head dipped low and his hat shading most of his face. If she didn't know better, she'd think he had spent the night wide awake.

In past years when they'd watched the Lyrids, it hadn't taken long for Wyatt to grow bored enough to start snoring. Why he tagged along was a mystery to her, though he claimed it was to keep her safe from any sort of beast that might be lurking in the dark.

She turned her attention back to the trail. Trey held the reins tight as he guided the wagon over the rutted trail. Just ahead were the cowboys who brought up the rear of the drive.

The purple sky at sunrise had given way to full daylight. Eliza shaded her eyes against the sun and looked beyond the sea of cattle and cowhands to study the gray clouds gathering on the horizon.

Spring showers were always expected but rarely welcomed on the trail. Lightning and thunder could spook just one or two of these simple-minded bovines and send them all skittering in different directions.

Now that he was fourteen, Wyatt had charge of the spare horses—the remuda as the cowboys called them. This meant he had moved up in ranking from previous years when he was relegated to doing odd jobs and helping out Cookie like Eliza was.

Other than the Gentry children, seeing anyone but cowboys on a drive was rare. This much she had learned from her father.

Despite her mother's objections, he had insisted that his children not grow soft with the easy life they had on the ranch. He required the same chores that had been required of him, and each year he brought any of his children who had reached the age of ten along with him.

When Eliza's first year arrived, she had been stunned that Mama expected her father would not require her to go along with him as her brothers had. To her mother's surprise—and Eliza's delight—Papa decreed that his daughter would have the same opportunity as his sons to experience a cattle drive up the Chisholm Trail.

The opportunity to experience that privilege was gained by hard work. And that hard work was beneath no one.

Not even Eliza Jane Mirabel Gentry, a descendant of Spanish royalty, Texas pioneers, and one particularly enigmatic pirate whose treasure may or may not have been found depending on who was telling the story.

Bringing up the rear of the drive several yards behind the Gentrys' wagon, Cookie's chow wagon clanged along. Between the pots and pans hanging from the hooks inside the wagon and the provisions stacked in tins and trunks sliding about in the back, the cook's wagon was nearly as loud as the lowing of the cattle and the racket that the horses made when agitated.

Eliza's job was to jump down as soon as the wagon stopped and hurry over to attend to whatever chore Cookie had for her. The old man had been on countless drives—Papa said when he was a boy Cookie was already feeding the men—and his face bore the evidence. Wrinkles as deep as the ruts in the trail were etched across his tanned cheeks and forehead, but his blue eyes twinkled with mischief as if he were somehow still a boy inside.

Cookie's clothing was a combination of military attire so faded it could have come from either side of the combatants in the War between the States, but his boots shone as bright and new as if he'd just purchased them before he hit the trail. What was left of his gray hair was tied back in a strip of leather that had seen better days.

He mopped at his forehead with the old bandanna he kept in his back pocket. Anyone who didn't know Cookie might have decided he wasn't much to take notice of. Eliza knew better.

From where he rode at the back of the drive, Cookie could see everything. And from his position next to the stew pot at mealtimes, he heard everything.

So when he spoke, which wasn't often, Eliza listened. "He's a good man, that one."

Eliza looked over in the direction where he had nodded and spied Wyatt tending the remuda horses under the watchful eye of his father. "Yes, he's a Texas Ranger and a war hero," she said as she turned back around to face the cook.

"Ain't him I'm referring to," he said. "But I reckon you'll figure that out eventually. Now come make yourself busy stirring the beans. I see that Barnhart fellow, and I don't intend to allow him to hold up the line trying to impress you with his vocabulary."

She shook her head. "I am not impressed by Benjy Barnhart. Never will be. He's a braggart. I don't know why Papa brought him along."

"Same reason he brought you and your brothers. Folks who've been given much ought to see what it's like to work for something."

Eliza took over the stirring from Cookie. "I don't disagree with that," she told him. "But why can't his own papa teach him that?"

Cookie looked over at the men who were ambling toward them. "Because his papa ain't learned it yet. Now look alive. We've got hungry mouths to feed." He clanged his bell and the ambling became a stampede. "All right now," he called to the men. "Form a line and act like you've got manners. We may be out on the trail, but we aren't savages."

It was the same speech Cookie gave at every meal, but Eliza never grew tired of hearing it. Or of watching the expressions on the cowboys turn from eager to polite in the length of time it took the old cook to shout out the warning.

Not only did he require the men to stand still and wait until he prayed before each meal, Cookie also insisted on a thank-you from each cowboy once his plate had been filled. Though Pa could have used his status as boss to take first place in the line, he always stood back and watched until each of his men had been fed.

Unlike Benjy Barnhart. He would have been the first one to grab for a plate at every meal if Cookie hadn't shamed him for it the first time he tried it.

"Respect your elders," he'd told him. "And that's all of us. You'll eat once we're all done."

That cured Benjy of elbowing his way to the front. Unfortunately, it appeared that nothing short of a miracle would stop him from pausing to brag to her about something he'd seen or done since he last spoke to her.

Eliza saw him watching her from behind Papa's foreman, Red. "Thank you, Miss Eliza," the gentle giant told her as she ladled beans over his cornbread. "I'm going to have to tell your mama that you're doing a good job on the trail."

She beamed and slid him an extra dollop of beans. Red returned her grin with a wink, then moved on.

Benjy presented his plate. "Hello, beautiful. You gonna give me extra like you gave ole Red?" he asked.

Eliza answered him by spooning a meager portion over his

cornbread. "Don't forget to say thank you," she told him.

"There's not enough to thank over." Benjy leaned close. "I'm gonna marry you someday. Don't you think you ought to treat me better?"

"Get on out of here, Barnhart," Cookie told him. "That girl is too smart for you, and she sure won't be taken in by promises of marriage at her age, will you, Miss Eliza?"

"Not the least bit interested," she said as she looked past Benjy to the cowboy waiting in line behind him. "Next!"

Benjy moved forward, but his eyes followed her until he found a place to sit nearby. A few minutes later, Mr. Creed stepped in front of her. He'd looked out of sorts all morning, but now he just looked mad.

After she served him, he mumbled something that might have been a thanks and walked away. Eliza cut her eyes toward Pa, who was watching her. He shook his head and looked away.

Next up was Wyatt. She dipped the ladle into the pot and looked up at him. His left eye was smudged black and purple and was swollen nearly shut.

"What in the world happened to you?" she gasped.

He shook his head. "Nothing."

"Wyatt Creed, that cannot possibly be true. Nothing doesn't look like that. Tell me what happened. Did you fall asleep and tumble off the rock? Last time we watched the stars, you might have done just that if I hadn't poked you with a stick."

His laughter held no humor. "I guess that's what I get for looking at stars without you." Wyatt nodded toward the spoon. "Do I get beans or are you just airing them out for the next man?"

Eliza hurried to pour what was in the ladle over his cornbread. Her eyes met his, and he held her gaze for a moment. Then he grinned. "Thank you, Liza Jane."

Finally, it was Pa's turn to be fed. He accepted his beans but shook his head when she offered a second helping. "I'll not be a bad example to my men," he said.

"No, of course not, Papa."

"You look troubled." He glanced past her, presumably to Cookie, and then returned his attention to Eliza. "Did that Creed boy tell you something you didn't like?"

"Wyatt? No." She paused. "His eye looked terrible though."

Pa worked his jaw like he did when he was thinking about something that upset him. A moment later, he shrugged.

"That situation will be handled," he said before walking away. Then, as if recalling he hadn't completed the requirements to be fed by Cookie, he turned back around. "Thank you," he called. "Best beans in Texas, and Cookie, your grub can't be beat." He turned back to his men. "Isn't that right, boys?"

Every man except Mr. Creed shouted his approval. Cookie beamed, and Eliza smiled. Mama might not have wanted her to go on this ride, but she wouldn't have missed it for the world.

Benjy caught her attention and grinned. When she didn't return his smile, he made a face that caused her to laugh.

Cookie stepped in front of her to take the ladle from her hand. "I've done had this conversation with your pa, and now I'll have it with you. You'll have nothing but trouble with that one."

"What one?" She shook her head. "I don't know what you're talking about."

He studied her a moment then dropped the ladle into the pot. "No, I don't suppose you do at that. But one day you will. And I'll be the one reminding you, if not in person then in your memory, that Ben Barnhart will bring you nothing but heartache."

Eliza turned her back on the gathering of cowboys. "Oh, for goodness' sake. I'm not the least bit interested in him. If I get my way, I'm leaving Texas to go study the stars somewhere back east at a college with a telescope."

"You won't get your way," he said. "You ought to know your mama wouldn't have none of that."

She did, but she also knew that Mama's wishes could be thwarted. If that wasn't so, she'd be sipping tea in a drawing room in New Orleans wishing she was with Pa and her brothers on the trail.

Glancing back over her shoulder, she spied Pa chatting with Wyatt and Red. Red had just said something, and the other two threw back their heads, laughing. Eliza's smile rose.

The key to getting her way was always to get her father to agree with her. That was how she had landed on a trail drive again this year, and it was how she would make her dreams of studying the stars and discovering new galaxies come true.

She would do all of these things because Papa always said yes.

And of course he always would.

The moon was full and the wind had ceased. Yesterday's rain had soaked into the Central Texas prairie and left the ground soft enough to be comfortable. Even the cattle seemed to be enjoying the evening. Not a sound came from where they were grazing.

Wyatt looked across the broad expanse of land. The moon had cast everything in a silver light, making the familiar horizon look strange and unfamiliar.

He had just put his rifle down and settled with his back to a rock when his companion for this watch arrived. Stifling a groan, he ignored the greeting.

"One of these days I'm going to marry that Gentry girl," Benjy Barnhart declared as he took up a spot beside Wyatt and eyed the rifle. "You watch. She's got it bad for me. Anyone who looks at her can see it."

Wyatt had spent most of their shared watch tonight looking for falling stars and ignoring the irritating braggart. He'd heard the rich fool talk about everything under the sun, always adding something about him besting someone else. But when he brought Eliza Gentry into the conversation, he finally had Wyatt's attention.

Red told him Barnhart's father had called in a favor in order to get Mr. Gentry to agree to bring him along. The hope was that being out with men might teach him to act like one.

So far it hadn't worked. Not that he could see, anyway.

His fists balled up, but Wyatt kept them at his sides. Though the moon was almost full, a cloud had slid over it, rendering the landscape nearly pitch dark. He considered picking up the rifle that lay between them on the ground and taking a walk, but Mr. Gentry would have his hide for leaving his post.

"She's just a kid," Wyatt said. "She likes everyone."

"What?" Benjy said. "You like her too? Well, you can't have her. She's mine."

He slid Benjy a sideways look. "I doubt she knows that." Wyatt grinned when he realized his comment had struck a nerve. "No, I'm sure of it," he added.

"Oh, she knows it. You're just jealous."

"Eliza is just a kid," he repeated, his temper rising. "I don't think about her like that. She's my friend."

"Maybe so, but from now on you leave her alone. If I catch you with her, you'll answer to me."

That did it. Wyatt stood and looked down at the braggart. "I'm answering you now, Barnhart. Stand up, look me in the eye, and say that again."

He did, although he kept just out of reach of Wyatt's fists. His face had gone as pale as his straw-colored hair. "All right, I'm standing," he said.

Benjy swallowed hard but kept his eyes on Wyatt. Even under the moon's light, Wyatt could see the fear in his eyes.

"Say it again," Wyatt snapped.

"Don't need to." He squared his shoulders and straightened his back but still couldn't manage anything near Wyatt's height.

A limb cracked in the distance. Could be nothing. Could be trouble.

The remuda was quiet and the cattle gave no sign of a reaction.

Wyatt returned his attention to Benjy. "Scared to," he taunted. "Try one more time to tell me I cannot be friends with Eliza Gentry and see what happens."

"I don't have to tell you to stay clear of her, Creed," he said. "Won't be long until she will see you for the sorry son of a drunk that you are. She won't have anything to do with you then."

Rage blinded him. When Wyatt came to his senses, Benjy was on the ground, his nose bleeding and his eyes wide. Had he kept on with the beating he was giving Benjy, who knows when he might have stopped.

Wyatt took two steps backward. Benjy was smaller and slower and had no experience with defending himself. Wyatt hadn't cared. Hadn't been the better man and just ignored him.

He swiped at his forehead with the back of his hand and let out a long breath. There was no doubt that he was no better than his pa.

Benjy sprang up, fists flying. Wyatt easily avoided his attempts to fight back. Finally, he snatched one arm and threw him backward. "Stop. I don't want to fight you anymore."

"Coward," Benjy spat at him. "You're a coward just like your pa. My pa told me how he ran off from his boys in the last gunfight."

Wyatt's jaw clenched. "You take that back."

His opponent stood a little taller. "I won't because you know it's true. You're a coward now, and you'll be a drunk later. Did you know he's with us on this ride because the other Rangers don't trust him anymore?"

"That's not true."

"It is. My pa and Mr. Gentry were talking about it. He ain't getting drummed out of the Rangers because they don't do that to one of their own, but he ain't trusted and he ain't going to ride with them much longer."

He reached out to snatch Benjy up by the throat. "You're a liar. A braggart and a liar."

"Let him go," a familiar voice said. "He's right."

Wyatt's blood ran cold. "Pa?"

His father swayed into the clearing. "Be glad it was me and not an outlaw bent on stealing cattle." He waved his pistol. "If I was, you two idiots would be dead. Good thing I'm not the excitable sort."

Wyatt released Benjy, who dropped to his knees. For a second Wyatt thought he might be begging for mercy. Then he came up with Wyatt's rifle and aimed it at Pa.

"Get on out of here, you old drunk," Benjy said. "You couldn't hit the broad side of a barn in your condition."

Pa's smile chilled Wyatt to the bone. He'd seen it too many times just before a thrashing or, worse, before Pa took up his gun and started shooting. He never knew whether he was still alive because the Lord had more for him to do or because Pa was a lousy shot when he was drinking.

Pa stood silhouetted in the moonlight, his right hand at his side and his left clutching his pistol. He hadn't raised his weapon to aim, but he could at any minute.

"I could, and I will," his father said, his voice low and even. "Want me to show you?"

"Is that a threat?" Benjy demanded, matching Pa's tone.

"It's a promise. Just ask Wyatt. That's how he got that scar across his neck. If I'd been aiming to kill him, I would've, but I was just looking to get his attention. Ask him."

Ben looked over at him.

Silence. Then his father laughed.

A moment later, a shot rang out. Benjy stumbled backward. Pa crumpled. A wisp of smoke rose up in front of him.

Wyatt ran toward his father. Benjy was shouting, but the words refused to register. Pa looked up at him, eyes cloudy and barely blinking.

"Don't die," Wyatt said on the cusp of a sob.

Pa responded with a cough and a shudder. "I ain't in charge of deciding that," he said on a ragged breath. "Just remember you ain't me but you could be, so watch yourself."

Wyatt sat back on his heels and looked up at the sky. Overhead a star fell. At his feet, blood fell. Behind him, he could hear Benjy's ragged sobs.

He looked back down at his father, the man he'd loved and hated all at the same time, and something inside his heart twisted. All the times he'd wished this man dead, had prayed that God would take him, and now. . .

No. The old man was too tough. Too mean.

Pa lifted his bloodstained hand to press it against Wyatt's chest. "Your mama's heart is in there, not mine."

Then he was gone.

CHAPTER 3

Eliza sat bolt upright. *Wyatt.*

He was on duty tonight. She knew because Zeke had told her when he stumbled into the wagon after his watch ended and Wyatt's began. It had to be him who'd fired the shot.

Or Benjy, though it was well known on the ride that Mr. Barnhart had left instructions that his son not be granted the use of a firearm unless it was an emergency. No one needed to ask why. Benjy was Judge Barnhart's only heir and his successor not only in the cattle business but also in his law practice.

She'd been on enough trail rides to know that the sound of gunfire meant trouble. Never had she been so thankful that on the trail a person slept in the clothes worn the day before. There were no ribbons to fumble with so as to exchange a nightgown for a dress, and she didn't bother to do anything about the braid that had likely come undone during the few hours of sleep she'd managed tonight.

It took her seconds to leave the wagon and her slowly awakening brothers and less than a minute to find Wyatt leaning over a man on the ground and Benjy standing a short distance away looking like a scared rabbit about to bolt and run.

"What happened?" she asked as she stumbled to a stop.

Neither answered, so she moved two steps closer. Wyatt's back was to her. She looked down at the man on the ground and could only see the bottom half of his face because his hat had been placed over it.

"Who is that?"

"It's his pa," Benjy said, his voice low and shaky.

Eliza moved to kneel next to Wyatt. If he noticed, he showed no sign of it. His head was bowed and his eyes closed as if he was praying.

Gently she leaned over to move the hat away from Mr. Creed's face. She had seen one dead person, her little cousin who had died of the consumption just before her seventh birthday. Abigail had looked like she'd fallen into a peaceful sleep. W. C. Creed looked like his face was frozen in anger.

His eyes were open and staring straight up at her. Eliza quickly returned the hat to its former position and sat back on her heels.

"How did this happen?" When Wyatt remained unmoved and silent, she nudged him. "Quick, tell me, Wyatt. The men will be here in a minute, but I want to know."

Her friend's eyes opened. After a moment, he turned his face toward her and swiped at his cheeks with the backs of his hands, leaving dark smudges of blood behind.

Wyatt's mouth moved, but he seemed to have trouble finding the words. "It happened so fast," he finally managed. "Before he died, he warned me not to be like him. Told me I had. . ."

His words trailed off as he shook his head.

Eliza leaned close, aware that the answer to her question might be something she did not want to hear. She looked down at the blood-stains on his shirt and up at his face again.

"Did you do this, Wyatt?" she said quietly enough that he alone could hear.

Wyatt stared at her as if he didn't know who she was. She looked at those sage-green eyes and wondered if it was true that a man's guilt could be seen there.

She saw nothing that would tell her the answer. Then he opened his mouth to speak.

Before he could answer, one of the cowboys jerked Wyatt backward. Another hauled him to his feet.

Red parted the crowd with Pa following a step behind. "What happened here?" Then he caught sight of Eliza. "And what, pray tell, are you doing here, young lady?"

"I heard the shot," she said as she stood and faced her father. "Just like the rest of you. I just got here."

Benjy looked over at Wyatt and then back at her father. "I saw it all, sir. Wyatt there killed his pa in cold blood. He busted my nose when I tried to stop him. That's what happened."

"He's lying," Wyatt managed, panic rising on his face. "Pa was drunk and mouthing off, and Benjy took exception to what he said and shot him."

"Don't believe him," Benjy shouted. "He's been sore at his pa ever since the old man punched him. You all see his black eye. He didn't get that tending the remuda."

Eliza gasped. How had she not realized?

"You did it," Wyatt shouted, his voice ragged. "It was you, not me. I never wanted him dead. He was all I had."

"He was a drunk, and that makes you the son of a drunk." Benjy puffed up his chest. "My pa is a judge."

"That's enough," Pa told him. "There's no cause for that kind of talk. We're all judged on who we are, not whose blood flows in our veins, and none of us is better than the other."

"What reason would I have for killing a man I hardly know?" Benjy demanded. "I don't even have a gun!"

"You took my gun and shot him because he insulted you," Wyatt said. "Everyone knows how much you care about being important.

That's why your pa made you ride the trail with us. He hoped you'd get knocked down a peg."

"All right," Pa said. "That's enough from the both of you." He looked around. "Did anyone witness the shooting?"

All around him, men shook their heads. "I heard it," one of the cowboys called. "I was over there seeing to the remuda, what with Wyatt on watch. There was a fuss of some kind. I heard WC but couldn't tell who he was arguing with. Everything got quiet. Then I heard a shot."

"A shot from Wyatt's gun," Benjy added.

"Wyatt?" the boss said. "How did Benjy come to have your gun?"

"Benjy took it off the ground where it was lying between us."

Pa studied him for a minute, then turned to Red. "Send a few of your men off to find shovels. These two will dig the grave, and there will be a burial at sunrise."

"But what about the killer?" Benjy said. "What are you going to do with him?"

The boss stared at Benjy for just a moment, then looked over at Wyatt. Her friend stood with his back straight and his shoulders squared. He waited for Papa's pronouncement of his future in silence.

For the first time in a long time, she didn't think of Wyatt as annoying or irritating. She didn't hold it against him that he got her in trouble regularly. Rather, she wondered how she would ever manage without him.

The boss on any trail drive was the law when there was no other law around. The man with the Ranger badge was dead, which meant that Wyatt was staring at the person who held his fate. His knees shook, but he stilled them through sheer determination not to show weakness in front of Mr. Gentry.

Or, more importantly, Eliza.

"Red," Mr. Gentry finally said, "after we offer up a proper burial to WC and eat our breakfast, I want you to take these two back to Waco. Let the Rangers sort out who killed one of their own. In the meantime, I want them together all the time and supervised."

Red's expression soured. "My men are busy, sir, and they'll be busier now that Wyatt's not taking care of the remuda." The ranch foreman caught Wyatt's attention and held it. Was that admiration he saw in the older man's eyes? "You did a fine job, son."

"Thank you, sir," Wyatt told him.

"We'll already be shorthanded by two, boss," Red continued. "Who do you want to watch them?"

"I'm turning them over to Cookie until after breakfast. He can keep them busy, and he still shoots straight enough to discourage either of them from running off."

"Sir," Red said. "Miss Eliza works with Cookie. Are you sure you want her around them?"

Mr. Gentry's eyes narrowed. "I'll find something else for her to do." He turned to Wyatt and then looked over at Benjy. "I don't know what went on, and I don't need to know because the Lord saw it all, and He will repay for that life that was taken by one of you."

Wyatt slid a glance at Benjy. He was acting awfully unbothered for a man who had just heard that God would smite him for what he'd done.

Mr. Gentry cleared his throat. "What I do know is that neither of you will have anything to do with my daughter. Ever. I'll have your agreement or you'll both be shot as murderers. You have my word on that."

He could easily make good on that promise, and not even Judge Barnhart could raise a complaint about it. Justice was swift on the trail, especially when it concerned murder.

Punishment for the murder of a Texas Ranger was swifter still.

"Papa, no," Eliza exclaimed, though her father's stare presumably kept her from saying anything else. Her brothers made their way through the crowd to stand on either side of her. Trey looked away when their eyes met.

"You know the terms. Do I have your word on it?" Mr. Gentry looked first at Benjy, who quickly nodded.

"I understand, and you have my word," Benjy told him.

Wyatt turned his attention away from the boss to watch Eliza. She swiped at a tear, and his heart broke. That girl was the only friend he had left in the world.

"Wyatt?" the boss said. "What will it be?"

"I'd rather die than agree to that, sir."

The boss's expression gave away nothing of what he was thinking. However, he turned to face his men.

"Red, clear this area. See that every cowboy is back in his bedroll and my children remain in the wagon. Pick a man to supervise Barnhart while he digs a grave. Make it big enough for two."

"Papa, no!" Eliza broke free of her brothers to rush past the boss and fall into Wyatt's arms. "He is my friend. He wouldn't hurt anyone."

Wyatt carefully extracted Eliza from his embrace to hold her at arm's length. It was the most difficult thing he'd ever done outside of saying goodbye to his mama at her grave site.

"Listen to your pa," he told her.

"Wyatt, no," came out on a ragged breath.

"Look here," he said. "You're just jealous because I'm about to go where all the stars are and you're stuck down here where you just see some of them. That means I win the count and you don't." He leaned down to press his forehead to hers. "Don't be a sore loser, Liza Jane. And don't forget me, okay? I'll be riding the tail of every star you see."

He took a step back and put his arms down at his sides. Eliza crumpled onto the ground in a puddle of blue calico and began to wail.

"Red," Eliza's pa said. "You know what to do."

"Yessir," Red said, his eyes on Wyatt. "You sure you don't need me here with you?"

"I can handle this," Mr. Gentry said as he removed his revolver from his holster. "You'll watch the remuda tonight. Zeke, take your brother and sister back to the wagon."

The eldest Gentry child stepped forward. Avoiding Wyatt's gaze, he scooped Eliza into his arms and carried her off into the night, her cries trailing in their wake.

Trey moved toward him, seeming unsure what to do. Wyatt stuck his hand out to shake, but Trey wrapped him in a bear hug, then walked away without saying a word.

"You heard the boss," Red shouted to his men. "Off with you."

They did as he asked, leaving only the three of them standing there. Eliza's cries could still be heard over the lowing of the cattle off in the distance.

The boss squared his stance. "Wyatt Creed, I believe you're a man of your word, and I am a man of mine."

"Yessir," Wyatt managed. He wouldn't cry. Not here. Not in front of these men he respected. "I try to be."

The boss leaned over and said something to Red. The foreman nodded, then walked over to shake Wyatt's hand.

He pulled out his bandanna and swiped at Wyatt's cheeks. Smears of dried blood dirtied the bandanna when the foreman stuffed it back into his pocket.

"You're more of a man than your pa ever hoped to be," Red told him. "We all know it. I hope you do too."

He looked up into the older man's kind eyes. "Thank you, sir."

A moment later, Red was gone. Mr. Gentry now held his firearm at his side.

"It's just you and me here, Wyatt. Tell me one more time what happened, and this time I want details."

"It don't matter," Wyatt said. "I'm ready to go. I don't have anyone else but Eliza. When a man loses his family and his only friend, there's not much reason to stay if he's offered the chance to go." He shrugged. "Plus a man's word is his word, and I'm standing by mine."

"So you don't want to offer detailed testimony against Benjy?"

"He done it. My pa was full of rotgut and spoiling for a fight. I suspect he came looking for me, thinking to use his fists on me again. Instead, he found the both of us, and Benjy did the work for me."

Mr. Gentry's expression softened. "You mean to tell me you intended to shoot your father?"

"I didn't plan it, sir, but after the thrashing he gave me the other night, I swore I'd shoot him before I let him do that again. I said it out loud too, although there weren't anyone around to hear me except the horses, and they didn't seem to take any interest in it."

He was rambling, and a man never rambled. The less he said, the more a man knew. That was his father's philosophy.

There were few things Pa was right about, but that was one of them. So Wyatt clamped his mouth shut and waited to be shot for the crime he wished in his heart that he had committed.

"You got any last words, son?"

Wyatt stifled a sob. He would not cry. He just would not.

"Tell Eliza she was a friend to the end and that didn't go unnoticed. And tell her to keep up her studies and learning about the stars. Oh, and to stay away from Benjy Barnhart because he's got designs on her, and I don't trust him."

"Nor do I," the boss said. "I'll be sure Eliza knows."

"Thank you, sir. I've tried to watch out for her, but I guess that responsibility will go to someone else now."

"I'm not sure I would call the saddle incident watching out for her," he said with the slightest hint of a smile. "Although my daughter is able to find trouble on her own without anyone's help, so I cannot fully blame you." He paused. "My wife, however, holds a different opinion."

"Then maybe I ought to amend my last words to offer my apology to Mrs. Gentry for the concern I have caused." He nodded. "Yessir, that would be what I'd like. It wouldn't do to leave that sort of thing unsaid."

Wyatt shut his mouth. He was rambling again.

"Consider it said then. Anything else?"

He swallowed hard. In all the adventures on the trail that he'd considered, dying there had not been one of them. "No, sir," he said as his throat tightened.

"All right. May God have mercy on your soul, Wyatt Creed."

The boss lifted his pistol. Then he fired.

PART II

CHAPTER 4

May 1889
Coliseum Street, New Orleans

B*ut I love him."*

Three words that had sent Eliza into banishment. And for
what? So Mama could host teas in her honor with her New Orleans
friends buzzing about and offering up their sons as a substitute?

Hardly a fair trade for either of them. But that was Papa. Send
out the edict and order the punishment before hearing what anyone
had to say.

What happened to the days when she had her father wrapped
around her pinkie? When all she had to do was run to him and anything Mama said would be overturned in favor of what Eliza wanted?

To the days when she could talk her way into or out of anything,
including a trail ride. The thought of that last ride, of what happened,
ripped a fresh wound in her heart.

As she always did, Eliza sealed the wound and tucked it back
where it belonged in the deepest recesses of her heart, returning her
mind to the topic at hand. The topic of her parents and their ridiculous determination to live up to a command that Papa had issued
nine years ago on a night that all of them would like to forget.

She sighed. Eliza loved her mama and papa dearly, but neither of
them cared to hear what she had to say when it came to Ben Barnhart.

Benjamin Franklin Barnhart had one foot in the traditional world
of the Old West and the other solidly on the trail back east where he

would surely be inaugurated as president one day.

"Only you would turn down a man with more money than you, and the political clout to make even more," Eliza had thrown at her father in their last argument. "And all because of what happened on the Chisholm Trail nine years ago."

Those words had her bundled up and hauled off to New Orleans before she could even get word to Ben that she was going. She'd been here the better part of two months, and the man hadn't made a single attempt to find her or to get past the security in the form of a rotating pair of deputies Papa had secured through a local agency. Not only did they protect the Gentry home, but the men also shadowed the Gentry women whenever they left the house.

That stung.

It also made her realize that maybe what she thought was love actually wasn't. Not that she was ready to admit that to her parents.

Plink, plink, plunk.

Eliza whirled around to face her cousin, who was once again treating the ivory keys on the harpsichord as if they were bugs in need of smashing. "Justine, truly, must you make such a foul racket?"

The girl, barely out of the nursery, offered an expression that told her exactly how she felt about the criticism of her musical abilities. "Why are you so mean?"

A fair question. She hadn't been herself since arriving in the city of her grandparents' birth, but that was no reason to treat Justine so poorly. The child had followed her around like a shadow ever since her arrival with the only aim, as far as Eliza could tell, of becoming a friend as well as a cousin.

Ever since Justine's papa had died, his much younger wife had spent more time touring the Continent than she did with her only daughter. Mama complained to her sister about leaving the girl to be raised by a governess, but apparently those complaints fell on deaf ears.

Eliza ought to have more patience with the girl. She did try, but Justine was just so persistent and always underfoot.

Eliza let out a long breath and put on a smile. "Forgive me," she said. "It's not your fault. I am just feeling out of sorts. I haven't seen a falling star in months. In fact, you cannot see the stars at all here in the city. It's an abomination."

Instantly Justine matched her grin. "I know just the thing for that. When my governess was out of sorts, she sent me to the kitchen for something sweet."

"Why you?" Eliza said as she settled onto the chair beside the floor-to-ceiling window that overlooked the balcony facing Coliseum Street. "She is the governess. Shouldn't she be fetching her own sweets?"

Justine shrugged. "Apparently she and Cook don't get on, so she's banished from the kitchen. Something about a gentleman."

"Isn't it always?" Eliza mused as she spied a maid hurrying toward them.

"For you, mademoiselle." The girl handed her a letter and hurried away.

"Is it from that man in Texas?" Justine asked in a singsong voice. "I've heard all about him, you know. He's no good but he'll be president someday. That's what my mama says. Doesn't matter if he is president. His family is the sworn enemy of our family. That's what your mama says."

"Sworn enemy?" Eliza's chuckle held no humor. "That's an awfully dramatic way to describe a disagreement between my father and his. I do hope Mama isn't actually saying that."

"I might have exaggerated slightly," Justine admitted. "But that was the general idea. Something about a vow your pa made that the judge took exception to. Your pa thinks he ought not to be considered as a suitable husband, and his pa thinks he'd be marrying beneath him to wed a Gentry. Or something like that." She paused to look up at Eliza. "I bet he's handsome, isn't he?"

"Very. And Ben is going to be a politician, so he is quite charming." She turned the letter over to reveal the name of the sender. *Beatrice Cunningham?*

How odd. Though the Cunningham family owned land adjacent to Eliza's family home back in Texas, she hadn't seen Beatrice in ages.

Eliza settled onto the settee near the window and broke the seal on the letter. Three lines in, she stopped reading as anger rose along with the twin pains of disappointment and disgust.

She crumpled the page and then stared down at it. So that was why Ben hadn't come charging after her to pledge his undying love. He'd been pledging it to Beatrice. And to who knew who else, according to the letter.

"Bad news?" Justine asked.

"For Ben it is." Eliza rose and walked to the foyer. "Mama!" When there was no answer, she shouted again. "Mama, where are you?"

And then she did what Papa always did when he was looking for her out on the ranch. She whistled. After that, things happened quickly.

Mama practically flew down the stairs with several maids trailing in her wake. By the time she finished lecturing Eliza on the impropriety of loud noises in polite society, her face was flushed and she'd exhausted herself to the point where she plopped down in a most unladylike manner on the settee.

"If you ever do that again," she managed as two of the maids fanned her, "I will. . ."

"Banish me until I've learned my lesson?" Eliza supplied. "You and Papa already did that. Well, guess what I have. Now I want to go home."

Mama sat bolt upright. "I promised your father you'd stay a full three months, maybe more. I cannot just take you home now."

"Of course you can." Eliza put on her best smile and settled beside her mother, causing the maids to scatter. "You have my word that I am absolutely not interested in Ben Barnhart. In fact, I don't care if I ever see him again."

Her beautiful mother, so at home in these fine surroundings, gave away nothing of what she might be thinking. Though Eliza had longed to look just like her with glossy dark hair and eyes the color of coffee laden with cream, she had inherited the fiery red hair and, according to Papa, the fiery temperament of his people.

When Eliza had a thought, there was no hiding it. At least she had not yet figured out how.

"I don't believe you," Mama said.

She shrugged. "I got a letter today from Beatrice Cunningham. Remember the strange girl who was always madly in love with cousin Travis?"

"The little blond?" At Eliza's nod, her mother continued. "Yes, I do remember her. She certainly wasn't cut out for ranch life, and neither was her mother. The two of them moved north ages ago. Why in the world would she be writing you now?"

Eliza handed Mama the crumpled remains of the letter from Beatrice. "Read it. You'll like the part about how she is no longer in love with Travis."

Mama unfolded the letter carefully. Too carefully. It was all Eliza could do not to pull it out of her hands and complete the job for her.

"For goodness' sake, Mama. Don't be so delicate. I can summarize by saying that Travis's loss is Ben Barnhart's gain." She paused to shrug. "It appears that Beatrice and Ben have fallen in love. She's forgiven him of his philandering—including his momentary flirtation with me—and is to marry him in the spring in Washington, DC.

Pending my approval, that is?"

Mama's dark brows rose as her eyes scanned the page. "Of all the. . ." She shook her head and returned the letter to its crumpled state and tossed it onto the rug.

"I take it you have an opinion?" Eliza said.

"My opinion is that girl doesn't want your approval at all. She just wants to gloat. It certainly wasn't a momentary flirtation that landed you here. Had your papa not intervened, you'd be the one wed and Beatrice would be crying in her teacup in Boston or Baltimore or wherever it is she and that mother of hers escaped to."

Oh my. Mama did have an opinion.

Though it was true that Mama was a fierce defender of her three children, even to the point of standing up to Papa when she felt one of his edicts was unfair, it had been a source of much irritation to Eliza that her mother had actually agreed with her father on this banishment. Or perhaps Mama had just wanted a nice visit with friends and family.

None of it mattered now. The ferocity with which her mother defended her was enough to sway Eliza.

"Honestly, Mama, she can gloat all she wants. I cooperated with you and Papa, but only because Ben promised he'd come and fetch me as soon as he could manage it." She shrugged again. "It seems he got distracted. Or never intended to follow. Not that it matters now. I just want to go home."

Plink, plink, plunk.

Mama's brows rose again as Justine ignored them both to bang the keys into submission. "What is she playing?" she whispered.

"I have no idea," Eliza told her.

"Beethoven," Justine said as she continued to massacre the tune.

Mama's face took on a sympathetic look. "Eliza, I know your father had strong opinions about Ben and the judge, but I never really had much objection to him, nor did his mother dislike you as a match for her son."

"You never said a word about that," Eliza said.

"Nor, I doubt, did Sally Barnhart." Mama shook her head. "Someday when you're a wife, you'll learn when to speak and when to keep quiet. Men like to stomp about and make noise, but eventually they calm down and become reasonable again."

"Is that what you and Mrs. Barnhart thought would happen with Papa and Judge Barnhart? Because unless it's happened and we don't know about it yet, I am skeptical that it ever will. Not that it matters now."

Mama smiled and reached over to pat Eliza's arm. "Whether you were to wed Ben or not, those men just need time and a reason to stop being angry with one another. God will provide both. After all, they were once friends."

Until that night when Wyatt's father died and Papa had Benjy hauled back to Waco to face his father.

Eliza leaned her head on Mama's shoulder. The words she'd read in that letter stung, but if she were truthful, she had known a month ago that Ben must have turned his attentions elsewhere. A man in love wouldn't wait two months to claim the woman he swore he couldn't live without.

And a woman in love wouldn't give up so easily on her man. But she had. Completely. So what she felt for Ben Barnhart never was love. In that moment, she was certain of it. She was also certain he had never loved her in return.

All at once she felt tired. Very tired. And lonesome for Texas.

"Can't we just go home, Mama? We can get there just as quickly as any letter."

"Your father would be furious with me," Mama said. "But I do miss him."

"And I miss the ranch. I miss my horses, and most of all, I miss the stars."

Plink, plink, plunk.

"Justine, do find something else to do, please," Mama and Eliza said in unison.

"The adults are having a conversation," Mama added in a soothing tone. "Perhaps you might find a treat in the kitchen while they continue talking?"

"No, Mama." Eliza rose and pulled her mother to her feet. "The adults are busy packing. Come on. If we start now, we can be on our way in a few hours."

Justine skittered out of the room, presumably to find the treat that Mama mentioned. Or perhaps she would just wait out in the hall and listen in on this conversation as she apparently had with many others.

"Truly, Eliza," Mama said when the child was gone, "that just isn't going to be possible. We have obligations. Until you got that letter, you were excited about the masquerade ball tonight."

Excited was absolutely not how she felt about the event that Mama had been chattering about for weeks. However, the fact that her mother thought so gave Eliza hope that she at least had managed her thoughts.

"Mama," she said. "Please. I just want to go home."

"Tomorrow," she said firmly. "Today is for arranging the trip and packing. And for attending the ball. Your costume is absolutely stunning. Have you seen it?"

The maid had brought in a pale blue gown dusted in feathers and some sort of iridescent silk overskirt, but she'd barely given it any notice. The mask, wrapped in a matching blue fabric and lined with jewels and more feathers, was waiting for her on the dressing table.

The cost of that mask and its matching gown was likely twice that of a good horse. And she would take the horse over the baubles and finery any day.

"Eliza?"

"Oh, yes, I did see the dress and it is beautiful."

"It must be," Mama said. "You'll stand out above all the young ladies there."

"Mama?" Eliza said slowly as suspicion of her mother's motives in attending the ball tonight rose. "What are you up to?"

"Why are you so suspicious?" Mama said. "The Heberts are old friends. If they have anyone special on the guest list, I am sure it would be a surprise to both of us."

Which of course meant it was absolutely no surprise to Mama who this special guest was. "Are you matchmaking?"

"Me? Not at all." Her expression of innocence was almost believable.

"Then it must be Papa."

And there it was. The tiny crack in the armor. Eliza might not know this mystery man who would "accidentally" be thrown together with her, but Papa did.

She sighed. It would be all too easy to throw a fit and storm out. To complain that at the age of twenty-one she should not be subject to her parents' attempts at finding her a husband of their choosing and not hers.

A thought occurred. Was it possible that Papa's aversion to her engagement to Ben Barnhart was solely due to the fact he had not arranged it?

"I am not sure I want to know what you're thinking," Mama said.

She shook her head. "No, you probably do not. Just one question: Will Papa always require that I marry a man of his choosing, or will I ever reach an age where he will trust me to choose for myself?"

Though she expected a spark of irritation from her mother, instead

Mama shrugged. "I suppose that is a question for your father. I will say that you will never reach an age where he doesn't love you enough to choose what he knows is right for you over what you want."

"What does that mean?" she snapped.

"It means that you may never know the things that have happened to make your life what it is," she said. "And you may never know how difficult those choices were for your father."

Still not an answer that made sense. She could have pressed for more. Could have insisted on an explanation. Instead, Eliza kept her thoughts to herself as she gave her mother a curt nod and swept out of the parlor.

CHAPTER 5

It would not happen until tomorrow, but at least they were going home. Tonight Eliza could endure anything, even yet another of her parents' attempts at matchmaking.

Justine caught up before she reached the stairs and then fell into step beside her. "I'll tell you if she actually buys the tickets and sends the telegram," she offered. "Because I know things."

"Because you eavesdrop," Eliza corrected. "I would, however, appreciate that information."

She entered her room at the top of the stairs, and Justine slipped in behind her. "What a beautiful gown. May I try it on?"

"You're just a little girl," she said. "And the gown is far too big for you."

"I don't care," Justine protested. "Someday I will be of a size to wear a gown like that, but I do not like waiting."

"Nor do I." Eliza shrugged and then rang for the maid. "Justine would like to try on that costume," she told the girl when she arrived. "Please help her but also see that she doesn't ruin it. Unfortunately I am wearing it this evening."

If the maid thought the request was odd, she did not say so. Rather, she nodded and then went about the business of dressing up an enthusiastic child in a gown made for an adult.

"The mask too," Justine insisted. "I want to wear it. And put the diamonds in my hair."

"Enough of that," Eliza said. "There are no diamonds for hair or for any other purpose."

"There are indeed." She nodded to the dressing table where an envelope had been hidden beneath the mask. Justine showed her the contents: a comb featuring an array of sparkling diamonds set in the image of a comet and its tail.

"There was a note too." She thrust the folded paper, written on stationery from the Hotel Monteleone, toward Eliza. "It says—"

"I see what it says," she interrupted.

Wear this in your hair tonight so I will know it is you.

"How very odd." Eliza dropped the note onto the dressing table and examined the hair comb. There was nothing out of the ordinary about it other than the way it arrived.

Justine reached for the comb and Eliza stepped back. "Not this," she said. "And it's time to give me the dress back."

"What if I could tell you where the letter came from?"

"It came from the Monteleone," Eliza said. "Now if you could tell me who wrote it or even who delivered it, that might be helpful information."

She looked up at Eliza through the mask. "How helpful?"

Eliza kneeled in front of her. "Very helpful. Do you know either of these things?"

The girl blew at a feather that fell from the mask and landed on her nose. "No," Justine said. "But I will let you know if I learn anything helpful."

"Thank you. Now let the maid help you take that dress off before you crease it."

Justine complained for a moment and then fell silent. Once the dress was restored to the peg on the dressing room wall, the girl lost interest altogether.

She went to the window to look out. "That man is here again."

"What man?" Eliza followed the girl's path to join her. The view of the walled courtyard was blocked by the black iron railing that spanned the second-floor balcony, but the street beyond the gates was visible.

"That one." She pointed to a lone figure dressed in black leaning against the wall across the street. "He's there a lot."

Her first thought was that it might be Ben. Even if it was, her mind was unchanged. What she had thought was love was something entirely different. Something she did not want anymore.

But this man was too tall, too broad at the shoulders to be him. He must be one of Papa's men.

Eliza shrugged and turned her back to the window. "My papa has hired men to watch Mama and me. I assume it is to keep a certain unwanted man away." She moved back toward the dressing table. "Apparently it's working."

"Oh," Justine said. "You mean your man friend from Texas?"

"Yes," Eliza said. "He hasn't made any attempt to storm the castle." She shrugged. "Is it awful that I have realized I am relieved about that?"

"Truly I do not know," Justine said. "I only listen to grown-up things. I rarely understand them."

Eliza laughed. "I fear I have the same problem. I have a lovely dress and a nice party ahead of me this evening, and I would rather watch the stars or be back home on horseback."

"Again, I do not understand grown-up things," Justine said. "But the idea of wearing that dress on horseback under the stars does appeal."

Another laugh. "Actually, it does to me too, although I couldn't possibly keep a horse under control with the limited vision that mask offers."

"Oh, but the mask is the best part," the child said dreamily. "Well, that and the lovely hair comb with the diamonds and stars."

"It is lovely," she agreed. "But a mystery."

"I shall have my treat now," Justine announced as she hurried toward the door. "Thank you, Eliza," drifted back in her wake.

The maid finished her examination of the gown and pronounced it fit for the evening ahead. "Is there anything else you'll need before it is time to dress for the ball?"

"No, and thank you." She shook her head. "I'm sorry. I've been here for months and I don't even know your name."

"Opal," she said. "And thank you for asking."

"Opal, did you deliver the dress?"

"I did." Her brows gathered. "Why? Is there a problem?"

"I'm not sure. Probably not. But I wonder, was this letter with the mask when you brought it up here?"

Opal looked down at the letter and then back at Eliza. "No, miss. Just the dress and the mask."

"And that fellow Justine showed me? Have you seen him lurking around? I wonder if he is one of the security detectives my father hired."

She shrugged. "What man?"

"Go and look out the window. There was a fellow in a black coat, hat, and trousers leaning against the wall across the street."

Opal did as Eliza asked. "I don't see anyone odd."

"Thank you," she told the maid. "That's all."

With a nod, Opal hurried out of the room. Eliza moved to the dressing table and sat down in front of the mirror. Her finger traced the words written on the elegant paper. Finally, she placed the comb in her hair and examined her image in the mirror.

The diamonds caught the light and sparkled. She smiled. Perhaps tonight's event might hold some enjoyment after all.

She shook her head, and again the comb caught the light and sparkled. Then a thought occurred. Of course. Papa was behind this.

The potential husband he'd chosen for the evening would know her by the diamonds in her hair. She reached up to remove the comb but then thought better of it. It was a beautiful piece. Why ruin the fun?

No matter who Papa had chosen for her, she would decline his offer of marriage. She always did. And unless God changed her heart, she always would.

There were so many more things she wanted to do with her life. Eliza sighed. How could she possibly have thought she wanted to be married to Ben? She had been foolish, impetuous, and a tiny bit rebellious in accepting Ben's offer to wed.

Papa saw that. Mama too. How had Eliza missed it?

The answer to that question was neither appealing nor worth concentrating on. She *had* missed it. She *had* nearly made a disastrous choice.

"But I am wiser now," she whispered as she removed the comb and returned it to the dressing table. "I will know love when I see it. And I have not yet seen it."

Or perhaps she was looking for something—or someone—that did not exist.

A few hours later, she'd been fed, dressed, and fluffed into a presentable party guest. Opal did her magic on hair that refused to behave, leaving Eliza baffled as to how she'd managed the feat.

"Will you wear the hair comb?" the maid asked, a slight twinkle in her eye.

"I believe I will," she said. "I've never been one to shy away from an adventure."

"Discovering who your gentleman friend is ought to be quite the adventure." She positioned the comb in place and then stepped back. "There, it ought to hold."

"Thank you, Opal." She offered the maid a smile. "I very much appreciate your help."

The girl grinned and left in a hurry, crimson coloring her cheeks. A few minutes later, Mama came in to do her usual inspection.

"Perfect," she said as Eliza spun around. "But what's this in your hair?"

"Don't be coy, Mama," she said. "I know you and Papa did this. Now the latest chosen future husband will be able to find his quarry."

Her mother shook her head. "I have no idea what you're talking about. I did nothing of the sort."

Eliza studied her for a moment. "No," she said slowly, "I don't think you did."

"If not me, then who?" she asked.

"Papa is still a suspect," Eliza offered. "But beyond him, I suppose I will just have to wait until the dance to find out."

"Oh darling," Mama said. "You're terrible at waiting. Perhaps we should go and have some fun. And if you're that worried about the comb, then don't wear it."

She laughed. Her mother knew her too well.

"And miss the fun of solving the mystery? Absolutely not."

Mama shrugged. "Then there's nothing left to do except call for the carriage. The drive out to River House is a long one."

This she knew from her childhood when the endless carriage rides were part of their visits to the city of Mama's birth. Though he might get away with bringing his daughter on a trail drive, when Papa was in New Orleans, he had to abide by Mama's rules.

And Mama's rules meant ladies rode in a carriage. They certainly did not arrive by horseback.

"Or we could stay home and supervise the packing of our bags so we can leave early tomorrow." She shrugged. "I prefer that over another night of dancing and smiling."

"Darling," Mama said as she wrapped her arm around Eliza's waist, "you are far too young to have such a pessimistic attitude. Yes, your father does have a young man in mind, and no, he won't tell me who he is."

Eliza gave her a sideways look. "You truly don't know either?"

"I don't. He refused to say in his last letter, and it's quite annoying." She took a step away and nodded toward the door. "The only solution is to go to that party and find out exactly what your papa is up to."

She gathered up her mask and followed Mama out into the hall. "Fine, but tomorrow we go home. If this man wants to court me, he can court me back in Texas."

CHAPTER 6

Every window in the beautiful home on River Road blazed with light, and carriages were lined up out front, waiting for their passengers to alight.

As was Mama's custom, she took her maid and Eliza in the carriage while the two security officers rode behind. Wouldn't it be lovely to be on horseback tonight?

She glanced back at the men who were following them. She couldn't tell if either of them was the man she'd seen across the street.

Neither looked familiar, but then, Papa's arrangement stipulated that no two officers would remain in place long enough to become complacent or, worse apparently, to get too comfortable in the presence of his daughter.

One of the men—a pale-haired fellow of middle age and stocky build—nodded a greeting when he caught her watching. The other, a tall fellow with broad shoulders and an affinity for hiding his face beneath his hat, ignored her.

She smiled at him anyway.

"Darling, are you flirting with the security officers?"

Eliza gave her mother a sideways look that told her exactly what she thought of such a ridiculous question.

"No, of course not," Mama said. "My daughter does not flirt."

"I don't," Eliza said as she shifted around to look over at her mother. "It's pointless. I'm not interested in romance, so why pretend?"

"Maybe you should pretend. And maybe you should flirt. It just might be fun."

"Hardly. Unless perhaps I found a man who wished to count falling stars. Now that would be fun."

Mama shook her head and looked away. Eliza leaned back toward the window and craned her neck to look up at the sky.

It was a warm night in late May. Too late for the Lyrids that held such deep memories for her and too early in the evening for the waning Eta Aquarids that would peak just before dawn.

Still she looked up at the stars, much more visible here than in the city, and thought of that night on the trail. Of the boy who irritated her and then broke her heart. The boy she imagined rode on the tail of every falling star—which of course she now knew not to be a star at all but rather bits of solar dust and rock streaking toward earth.

"Eliza. Stop your woolgathering."

Mama's voice shook her into action just as the door to the carriage opened and a fellow in a smart-looking uniform helped her down. Though she longed to remain out here under the stars, Eliza allowed herself to be swept along the path beside Mama toward the house, with the protection officers walking a respectful distance behind.

She'd lost count of the times she'd visited River House, the lovely home of Mama's distant kin. The parties were legendary, but Eliza's best memories came from childhood when she and Louis, the eldest son, made a game of spying on the adults as they danced.

It seemed so long ago now. Mama brought her here to forget that awful day on the Chisholm Trail. To distract her until the memory of the crack of a gunshot splitting the air disappeared.

Eliza shrugged off the rest of the thought, for she would never forget. That memory would never disappear.

Not like Wyatt had.

The front doors opened, and the sound of music and laughter spilled out into the night. She cast one last, longing look up at the sky, adjusted her mask, and then stepped inside.

It was too early in the season for Mrs. Hebert's prize roses, so clusters of irises, magnolias, and daylilies provided a riot of color and a pleasant scent in the foyer. Eliza walked past the floral display toward the sound of an orchestra playing Johann Strauss Jr.'s "Blue Danube."

Instantly she was engulfed in a sea of beautifully costumed people. Jewels sparkled beneath the glow of chandeliers, and feathers bobbed and swayed as ladies and gentlemen paired up and moved about. A bank of french doors had been opened to the night air, and a soft breeze ruffled feathers on the masks as it floated past.

The theme for the evening was a rainy night in Louisiana, ironic since the area was in the throes of a rare drought. Much care had been taken to mimic rain showers with dark puffs of silken clouds hanging from the ceiling overhead and sprays of candlelight seemingly falling from the heavens.

Water splashed in the courtyard fountains while guests mingled. Servants carried bright-colored umbrellas in one hand and trays of food and beverages in the other. The effect was both exotic and comical as the poor servants were quite limited in what they could accomplish with both hands full.

Mama and her friends had planned their costumes together and thus easily recognized one another. Now they were busy guessing the names of each guest.

The protection officers had moved into position near the door where they would remain until the Gentry women were ready to leave. While it was tiresome to be followed by such intimidating men, it also came in handy when she was dodging a potential suitor.

Around her the ladies of mama's group squealed and laughed and generally made a fuss about each other's elaborate costumes. They fussed over Eliza too, although their interest waned when they realized they'd get no decent conversation from the Gentry daughter.

Thus, Eliza easily slipped away after a few moments of smiling and nodding. The ladies wouldn't miss her. Mama might eventually.

For now, however, she was free to roam about and enjoy the evening. The protection officers would keep a discreet watch, but they need not follow. She was safe here.

Though her feathered mask kept her vision limited only to what was in front of her, there was certainly plenty to see. As she strolled through the crowd that had gathered on the edges of the ballroom, Eliza studied each face and watched for a reaction as she passed by. Thus far no one had given her pretty hair comb a second look.

A waltz ended and another one began. Someone brushed past her, but when she turned to look, no one was nearby. She moved toward the dance floor where women in brightly colored gowns with matching feathered masks whirled around in the arms of men dressed as their opposites in dark suits and ebony-colored masks.

Someone tapped Eliza's shoulder, and she turned to see Louis Hebert smiling at her. "Welcome, Eliza. *Allons danse?*"

She returned the smile. "I would love to dance with you, Louis."

The fact they were family kept him from the list of potential husbands, making Louis a safe choice for the dance floor, with the added benefit of his being an excellent dancer.

A thought occurred. Was her host behind the gift of the celestial pin? He certainly knew of her penchant for gazing at the heavens.

"How did you know it was me?" she asked as the first dance ended and the second began.

"Your mother told me," he said with a grin. "Now stop talking and pretend you're infatuated with me. I am trying to make Adelaide Duchamp jealous."

"Abominable Addy?" she said with a giggle. "I thought she was back in Paris with her father's family. Something about refining her education, I think Mama said."

His grin broadened. "Her education was not the only thing that was refined during her time in Paris."

Louis whirled her around in time to see Addy glide past in the arms of Albert Fontenot, one of Papa's top choices for son-in-law. Indeed, Abominable Abby, the scrawny girl with the unfortunately splotched cheeks, was nowhere to be seen. In her place was a lovely young lady with a peaches-and-cream complexion wearing french couture that fit her figure like a glove.

Eliza's eyes widened. "How long was she away being refined, Louis?"

"Just long enough, apparently." Louis's expression went serious. "Eliza, you have to help me. I was awful to her before she left. I always liked her, but I tormented her mercilessly."

"As did most of the other boys," she offered.

He frowned. "She's dancing with Albert. After you turned him down cold, he's likely turned his eye toward Abby."

"Louis, dear," Eliza said with a chuckle, "every man in the room has turned his eye to her."

"Not that one." He tilted his chin to the right. "That one."

Eliza followed his gaze. Through the maze of dancers she spied a man dressed all in black leaning against the wall with his arms crossed and studying her openly. His chin was covered with a dark trimmed beard, his suit looked expensive, and a stylish hat covered his hair.

Either this was the current candidate on the husband hunt or he was simply audacious. "Who is that?" she asked Louis.

"I have no idea, but isn't that the point?" He shrugged. "I would tell you to go find out, but you are far too busy right now."

"Dancing with you?" she said with a chuckle.

"No. Plotting with me. Abby will be passing by again soon. When she does, follow my lead."

She gave him a sideways look. "What are you scheming, Louis?"

"Just follow my lead, please."

Eliza nodded. "All right, but am I going to regret this?"

"Only if you don't want to be related to Abigail," he said as he swept her up into the rhythm of the next dance. "Remember, you're following my lead. My apologies in advance for what I am about to do."

He whirled her around twice, and then just as Eliza managed to catch her breath, the horizon tilted. Louis swept her backward into an embrace directly in front of a couple waltzing toward them.

The two couples collided, and Abigail somehow landed in Louis's arms. Of course, Louis had to release Eliza to catch Abigail.

She landed harder than the last time her horse kicked her off. Grimacing, Eliza took the first hand offered to her and climbed to her feet.

Their collision had not stopped the other dancers. They moved past as if nothing had happened. Meanwhile, Eliza stumbled forward on the arm of a gentleman whose mask hid not only his identity but also most of his face. Glancing over her shoulder, she spied Louis and Abigail huddled together near the edge of the ballroom; she placed her hand on his arm and looked up into his eyes adoringly.

The desire to go over and give her distant cousin a talking-to rose, but she ignored it. There would be plenty of time to let Louis know her opinion of his tactics later.

Besides, as much as she didn't care to be courted, she appreciated the effort when it was extended to others. And Louis was definitely making the effort.

Eliza turned to thank the man who'd helped her off the dance floor, but he was gone. She dusted off her skirts and straightened her shoulders as she glanced around to see if anyone else had witnessed her humiliation. Apparently no one had, for no eyes were turned her way.

She looked around the room and spied Mama and her friends gathered near the door. Behind her a short distance away were the two security detectives. Both were wearing masks so as not to stand out in the crowd.

The taller one regarded her solemnly. The other man had his attention focused elsewhere.

The music stopped and Louis's father stepped up to stand beside the orchestra. The elder Hebert was famous for his lengthy and sometimes colorful speeches welcoming his guests, so his presence sent the remaining attendees hurrying toward the dance floor to witness firsthand what would likely be written about in tomorrow's society column of the *New Orleans Picayune*.

Eliza took the opportunity to move toward the open doors leading to the courtyard and make her escape. Outside the air was warm, and the sound of Mr. Hebert's voice was muted by the chorus of frogs and other night creatures rising up from the river.

A roar of laughter from inside chased her into the shadows. She moved swiftly across the tiles that covered the courtyard, her feet sure and her destination certain due to so many years of making this journey in her childhood.

Avoiding the rear kitchen and the gathering spot for the staff, Eliza reached the river's edge. She glanced over her shoulder. Streams of lamplight spilled out of the windows on the lower floor of River House, and a light came on in one of the upstairs bedrooms.

Something cracked behind her. Eliza jumped and turned around to see nothing but darkness and the glint of moonlight dancing off the river. Up ahead a small dock suspended over the river was fitted with two benches. She found it easily and settled onto the bench that gave the best view of the night sky.

Mama had brought her here that summer after the last trail ride to distract her. To make her forget. When it did not work, Papa came for them and she went home.

Where she wanted to be now.

Another crack and she knew she wasn't alone. "Who's there?"

"Hello, beautiful."

Eliza's heart lurched. "Ben?"

The man she had almost married stepped out of the shadows and removed his mask. He was easy to look at and had a way of making a woman feel as though she was the only person in a crowded room.

In that moment Eliza knew for certain that she felt nothing for him. What Ben had offered was freedom from Mama's rules and Papa's overprotective nature.

"I was about to ask you to dance when I saw you slipping outside."

He was standing between her and the riverbank. To get back to River House, she would have to get past him.

"Why are you here?" she asked. "Aren't you supposed to be marrying Beatrice in Washington, DC?"

"Oh, that," he said with a smirk. "Sweet girl, but she misunderstood and assumed a relationship that did not exist."

"She assumed more than that, Ben. She is planning a wedding. I have the letter to prove it." Eliza allowed her gaze to sweep the length of him before returning to his face. "I doubt she misunderstood that."

"Sweetheart," he said as he took two steps toward her. "I came for you. That's what matters."

"First, I am no longer your sweetheart." She rose to face him. "And second, you are way overdue for coming for me. It is too late."

A momentary look of surprise crossed his face. Then it was gone.

"It is never too late. You've been meant for me since we were children. You knew that and so did I."

"No, Ben. You never asked me if I was interested in you. You *told* me and everyone else who would listen." Eliza paused, hands on her hips. "Just because you say it, Ben Barnhart, does not make it a fact."

"But you were ready to marry me. That is a fact."

"It is," she admitted. "I let you charm me with promises of taking me all over the world. Of allowing me to study the stars wherever I wished. But it was all just to make me believe you cared, wasn't it?"

"I do care," he said.

"All right, but tell me the truth. What took you so long to come for me?"

Ben shrugged. "I got here as soon as I could. That's what is important. And I've got a plan."

Eliza's chuckle held no humor. "You always do. What is it this time?"

"Your mother is here. There's no one at home but the servants, and they won't say a word. You can pack whatever you cannot live without and we can be gone before anyone figures it out."

"Like last time?" she said. "We know how well that plan worked."

"Your father isn't here, Eliza. I know better than he does what you need."

"You have no idea what I need, Ben. I think we're done here," she said as she made a move to leave.

Ben stepped in front of her. "We were meant to be together. Just stop making this so difficult."

"No, Ben. I'm not going anywhere with you. Please just leave."

"You always say that right before you change your mind. Stop playing games, Eliza. I didn't come here to leave without you."

He advanced on her. She ducked under his arm and ran.

CHAPTER 7

Something big and dark stepped in front of Eliza. A man. She sidestepped but he was quicker.

His arm wrapped around her. She looked up to see Papa's security detective. The tall one who'd been watching her earlier. Instantly Eliza relaxed. She was safe with him.

The detective's attention was focused behind her. He said nothing and his expression remained neutral. From her vantage point, however, she could see the detective's free hand rested on the revolver strapped to his side.

"Let her go—she's mine," Ben shouted as he caught up to them.

A moment passed, just a second though it seemed longer, and then the larger man spoke. "I doubt she knows that." The detective paused to sweep his gaze over Ben before he looked down at Eliza. "No, I'm sure of it. Now go."

Ben faltered a moment and shook his head. His attention went to the detective. "Eliza does this, you know. She pretends disinterest and then changes her mind. Just when it appears she will commit, she runs. Then she comes back."

When the detective did not respond, Ben turned his gaze to Eliza. "You always do. So when it happens again, I'll be waiting. But just know that I won't wait long."

With that warning, or what she figured he thought was a warning, he stormed off. Eliza watched him disappear inside River House and then exhaled a long breath.

"Thank you," she told the detective as she stepped away. "He's harmless, mostly, but very annoying."

"I can see that." The detective nodded toward River House. "It's best you go back inside now. Unless you think that fellow will make a scene."

"I have no idea what he'll do," she said as she removed her mask and adjusted her hair. "But I would prefer to just go home. Would you mind?"

The man seemed at a loss for an answer. His mask remained in place beneath his hat, and his beard covered his chin so she could not see what he looked like. But there was something in those eyes.

Something distantly familiar. And oddly unfamiliar.

"My partner and I are under orders to remain on-site together," he finally said. "I'll have him check with your mother to see if she is ready to leave."

"I can save you the trouble. She is not." Eliza shrugged. "What are your orders when my mother and I are not together?"

Again he looked perplexed. "Actually, miss, that has never happened, so there are none."

The truth of that statement stung. She and Mama had done everything together for the past two months. Any visit Mama made, Eliza went along. Any entertainment or ball, lecture or luncheon was attended by the both of them.

No wonder she was pining for Texas and her horse.

An idea occurred. Eliza grinned and set off walking.

"Miss," the detective said, "where are you going?"

She decided not to answer. Long ago Eliza had learned that sometimes it was best to act first and apologize later if necessary. The policy hadn't always served her well, but tonight she could see no other option.

The detective had no trouble keeping up. But then, he was a head taller with legs that were unencumbered by a ridiculous ball gown. By the time the carriage house and stables neared, he was wise to her plan.

"Oh no," he told her. "You'll need to come with me back into the house now, miss. I've got orders to keep you safe tonight and to deliver you back home in one piece, and I intend to do that."

"I have no intention of impeding you in your assignment." Eliza offered the poor man a grin. "I also would like to return home safe and in one piece. The difference between us is when that will happen."

The groom, a young man named Étienne whom she recognized as the cook's eldest son, met them at the stables. Eliza leaned in and made her request and then watched the boy hurry away.

"Miss, truly, whatever it is you're about to do, you cannot do it." Moonlight slanted over his worried features, and for the first time since he'd saved her from Ben's temper, she wondered what was under that mask, the hat, and the beard.

Though her fingers itched to snatch away at least the two things she could remove—the hat and mask—Eliza decided she would be making enough poor decisions tonight without adding another to them.

Wandering out alone at River House was something she'd done without thinking as a child. Looking back, however, she was never truly alone here in Louisiana. There was always a governess, a member of the staff, or one of her grandfather's or her father's men lurking about to keep her from harm.

Another reason why Texas appealed. The ranch was the only place Papa believed her to be truly safe. Thus his hired hands were kept busy minding their own tasks rather than minding the ranch owner's daughter.

Étienne returned leading two horses. "I wasn't sure which was which," he said.

"Neither of them belong to her," the detective said. "They are the property of my employer."

"Apparently I am as well; thus I will have the roan." She deliberately chose the horse she'd seen the irritating detective riding earlier. "Étienne, help me up."

"Étienne, you'll do no such thing," he told the boy.

"Ignore him," she said. "He has no authority to make decisions for me."

"I have the authority to make decisions on behalf of her father." He moved to stand in front of the horses, his attention fully on Étienne. "I will have the reins, please."

Étienne quickly complied and then disappeared into the stables. The detective turned the horses back toward their stalls.

"Fine," Eliza said. "If you will not allow me a horse, then I will have to find another way home."

"Groom, come and get these horses," the detective called.

She set off walking down the path that led to River Road. It skirted the grounds and kept her away from the main house and the chance of seeing Ben or her mother while she made her escape.

Attempted escape, as it turned out, for a moment later, she heard the sound of hooves behind her. Eliza ducked into the nearest foliage and was immediately rewarded by catching her sleeve on the thorns of one of Mrs. Hebert's prize rosebushes.

The detective, now on horseback with his partner's horse trotting behind, stopped just shy of where she was caught and looked down at her. "I can offer a better alternative to your thorny situation."

She opened her mouth to offer a sarcastic response. The answer died in her throat as she moved and was yet again stuck, this time in the posterior.

"I didn't realize security detectives were allowed to be funny," she said as she reluctantly nodded. "I will accept your help."

He landed on the ground in one swift move and studied her. "We are trained to respond to a variety of situations," he told her. "Humor sometimes helps."

"It isn't helping at this moment," she told him.

"Be still," he commanded. "I am giving you the reins to the horses so I can use both hands to remove you from the rosebush. If you make any sudden moves or loud noises, they'll spook. Then, depending on whether you're still holding the reins, you will either come out of those bushes faster than you'd like or we will be chasing horses in the dark until we catch them."

He stood there, tall and dark, menacing and still a little endearing. "I prefer we do this my way, but it all depends on you. I don't see you as a rule follower, miss."

Eliza squirmed. "I'm willing to try if it gets me out of this predicament."

"All right," he said evenly. "The rule is to do as I say. Nothing more and nothing less. Hold tight to the reins." He handed them to her, and the horses shuffled a bit before settling again. "Now wait just a minute while I move the branch you're caught on."

"Be careful," she warned him. "Those thorns hurt."

He looked up from his work long enough for his eyes to collide with her gaze. "Unlike your gloves, mine have a purpose."

A moment later, the branch was no longer jabbing her. "That's already better," she told him.

"Now take a step forward."

She did and felt something snag her dress. Eliza swatted at it out of instinct and was rewarded by a yelp from the detective.

"Why did you do that?" he demanded, blood trickling from a wound that slashed across his cheek just above his beard.

The horses protested but she held the reins tight. With her free hand, she used the back of her glove to swipe at the wound. "I'm sorry. I reacted. I shouldn't have."

Again the detective looked as if he would respond and then seemed to think better of it before going back to the task at hand. A few minutes later, that impediment was removed too.

"Okay, step carefully forward. Slowly," he said against her ear. "I think I've got you unstuck."

Eliza did as he said and found she could easily walk away from the branches without being caught again. "Thank you," she told him when he stepped in front of her. "Now can we go home?"

He stood there looking every inch the security detective that he was. In that moment she was absolutely sure he was the man who had been watching the house from across the street earlier today.

"Not until your mother is ready to leave."

"Tell me your name," she said in hopes she could turn the conversation in her direction.

The demand failed to distract him. "No."

"Then at least take off your mask."

Again he merely said, "No."

She shrugged. "All right. Suit yourself. It just doesn't seem fair that you know who I am but your identity is a mystery."

He stood there saying nothing. Waiting him out crossed Eliza's mind, but she was far too interested in leaving River House and going home to endure any sort of exercise in patience.

So she thrust the reins to one of the horses into his hand. "Fine."

"The other one," he demanded.

"Sorry," she said as she hitched up her skirt just enough to put her foot into the stirrup and climb into the saddle.

She was off. The horse wasn't hers, but it was a well-trained beauty that swiftly adapted to her commands. Together they traversed the path that followed the river until River Road appeared up ahead.

There the path widened and an irritated security detective appeared in her peripheral vision. A moment later, he was beside her.

Eliza didn't have to look at him to know he was displeased with her. She also didn't care.

It had been far too long since she had been on horseback. Far too long since she gave a good horse free rein to race across the land toward someplace she wanted to be.

Toward home. Or at least the next best thing.

So Eliza did just that. Somewhere along the way, perhaps when she dodged the slow-moving horse and cart just outside of the city, she lost her hairpins, but she never slowed her pace. The detective kept up with her but, to Eliza's surprise, did nothing to try to stop her wild ride.

Finally, when she reached the gates of her New Orleans home, Eliza reined in her mount. She glanced over at the stranger and found him grinning.

Yet another surprise.

The gates swung open, and she rode through to the carriage house where the groom met them. The detective followed her but remained in the saddle until she handed the reins over.

She looked over at him and laughed. "Did you think I might change my mind?"

"According to your friend, that's what you do," he said as he swung one long leg over the saddle and then dismounted.

All her good humor soured. Several responses occurred.

Then the detective reached up to help her down. His hands grasped her waist. Her eyes locked with his. Only then did she consider that the fellow had ridden the entire way from River House with the mask still in place.

Only then did she wonder why.

Eliza reached to remove it and he dodged her attempt. "I want to see your face."

Something passed between them. Eliza couldn't say what it was or why it happened, but she knew this moment would remain fixed in her mind for quite some time.

He set her on her feet, and she wobbled so he caught her. "I'm just out of practice," she told him, though that was only part of the reason.

His hand remained on her elbow, his eyes watching her carefully. It all felt so very familiar.

"Eliza Jane Gentry, what have you done this time?"

She jolted at the sound of her father's voice, the moment shattered. The security detective took two steps back.

"Papa? What are you doing here?"

Papa stepped into the circle of light. Oddly, he looked more curious than upset that she'd returned home from the ball on horseback in such a bedraggled condition with a masked security detective in tow.

"I'd say I arrived just in time." He looked past her to the detective. "Does she know?"

He shook his head, his expression unreadable.

"No, I suppose not." Papa returned his attention to Eliza. "I suppose you've got an explanation for all of this?"

Now that was the father she knew. The father she could easily cajole out of almost any irritation he might feel toward her.

"All of this?" she asked innocently. "I am home safe, and that's the point of having a detective follow me, isn't it?" She paused only a moment. "And what is it you're wondering if I know? I just might. I have my sources."

"Justine doesn't know either," Papa said. "And don't be impertinent. It isn't how you were raised." Again he looked past her to the detective. "Anything else I should know about tonight?"

"Why not ask me?" Eliza demanded.

"Because I am asking him." Papa nodded. "He found her, didn't he?"

"He did, sir." The detective looked only to her father, not sparing a glance in her direction. "The subject followed her to the river and tried to corner her when he thought she was alone. I intercepted him and defused the situation."

"Where is he now?"

"I was alone with Miss Gentry, so I sent him back inside with the idea of alerting my partner so that we could detain him." He paused. "Unfortunately, Miss Gentry found a horse, and what happened after that, as you can see, is obvious."

"I'm right here," Eliza snapped. "I can hear both of you, and guess what—I could also answer questions if they were directed at me."

"They aren't, Eliza. In fact, why don't you go upstairs? I see no further purpose for you to stand out here when you're in such obvious need of a maid's attention."

She stood her ground and stared at her father. "As soon as I find out how long you have been keeping Ben Barnhart away from me."

CHAPTER 8

Wyatt Creed stood in the shadows, his hat pulled down low over his brow. Between the heat and the mosquitos, New Orleans had long ago lost its charm.

So had spying on Eliza Gentry.

He tucked the idiotic mask in his pocket and gave thanks that the party Eliza had attended required them. Otherwise she might have figured out that her dead childhood friend was very much alive.

Or maybe she wouldn't have. When he looked in the mirror, he hardly recognized the skinny, scared kid with the gun aimed at him out on the Chisholm Trail.

Eliza and her pa had gone inside after her comment about Barnhart, and he could still hear their raised voices out here in the stables. What he couldn't figure was why Eliza was so dead set against accepting Barnhart's advances out at the river and now was defending him.

It made no sense. But then, there was much he didn't understand about women.

Especially this woman.

And she had grown to be a beautiful woman. A woman who, no matter the feelings from his youth that he hadn't managed to shed, was very much off-limits to him.

That part of his deal with the boss was ironclad and nonnegotiable. If he was found consorting with Eliza Gentry, her papa would contact the authorities in Texas and have him tried as a murderer.

And this time there would be no mercy. No second chance.

Wyatt shrugged off the thought. There was no need to worry.

His arrangement with Mr. Wyatt was to keep watch until he was no longer needed here. He'd already been informed that Mrs. Gentry was planning to return to Texas as soon as possible.

Though Mr. Gentry's appearance here might delay that return, eventually the family would go back to the ranch, and he could go back to doing what he did best: being a hired gun with no home and no name.

Father and daughter were still arguing, and it seemed likely that wouldn't change anytime soon. There was no sense in remaining here at the Gentry house when his partner was back at the party alone.

He found the groom and sent him for a fresh horse to ride back out to River House. There he could rejoin his partner and see what had become of Ben Barnhart.

His fists curled at the reminder of Barnhart coming after Eliza. He might never be able to have her or even to allow her to know he was alive, but he certainly was not going to stand by and let a liar and a murderer anywhere near her.

When Mr. Gentry had told him that the pair were threatening to run off together, he hadn't needed to hear more. It would never happen. Not on his watch. He'd agreed to the terms and trained the rest of the security team himself.

Thus far they'd done a good job of keeping Barnhart away. Until tonight.

That breach would need to be investigated. Jim Bryant, the fellow he'd taken with him to River House tonight, was a good man he'd stolen away from his job at the Secret Service. Bryant was relatively new to this type of work. If Barnhart had gotten to him, there would be consequences.

Wyatt's hand went to his vest pocket where the hair comb he'd found on the dance floor rested. He smiled when he recalled how her cousin Louis had used Eliza to capture the attention of the woman he wished to court.

Clever man, though he had no interest in the pretty but empty-headed type. No, give him a smart woman any day. A woman with whom he could match wits.

Or stare up at the heavens with and count falling stars.

It was the stars on that hair comb that had caused him to purchase it for Eliza. Diamonds for a woman who never left his thoughts but would never be his.

"Your horse, sir."

Wyatt jolted. Somehow he'd completely missed the fact that the groom was leading a horse toward him until he arrived with it.

Yet another reason to avoid Eliza Gentry at all costs. The woman was dangerous.

Around her he forgot all safety procedures. He could have stopped her wild ride, but the sorry truth was he'd enjoyed every minute of it.

"Well, no more of that."

"Sorry, what was that?" the groom asked as he accepted the coins Wyatt handed him.

"Nothing. Just a reminder to myself." He climbed into the saddle and rode away before he could make a bigger fool of himself than he already had.

He got halfway back to River House when he spied a carriage coming toward him down River Road. The night was dark but the lamps made it easy to spot.

He checked his weapon and then reined in his horse to wait and see if this might be Mrs. Gentry. It was.

His agent was seated next to the driver looking none too happy. From his expression it was obvious he knew there would be a conversation between them once the Gentry woman was deposited on her doorstep.

Eliza's mother ordered the carriage stopped as soon as she spied him. "I do hope my daughter has returned home safely," she called to him.

"She has, ma'am," he told her.

Her smile was much like her daughter's. "Drive on then," she said to the man at the reins. "But be in no hurry."

"Might I have a word with my man before we depart?" he asked.

"By all means." Again she smiled. "As I said, I am in no hurry."

Wyatt climbed down from his horse and motioned for the agent to follow. Bryant stepped down and trailed Wyatt as he led him away from the carriage.

"Keeping track of Barnhart was the objective. What happened?"

Bryant shrugged. "I never saw him, Boss, and that's the truth. I kept watch, but everyone looked alike with those blasted masks on."

The truth, yet he couldn't allow that as an excuse. "He got to Eliza. Would have harmed her if I hadn't stopped him. I know it's hard to tell who is who with masks on, but it is essential to keep eyes on Miss Gentry if we can't determine who the men are."

He ducked his head. "I did, sir, but then Mrs. Gentry asked me to dance with her friend, and what was I to say?"

Wyatt hid his grin by looking away. He'd been on enough assignments to know that this sort of thing sometimes happened. And when the boss's wife asked, the employee complied.

As long as the request was reasonable.

"I'll do better." He straightened. "I saw Barnhart light out of here in a buggy about a half hour ago. He aimed his horses toward the city, but I figure he's not stupid enough to try to go to the Gentry place, so he must have been headed elsewhere." He paused. "He likes to gamble. And he has a lady friend."

He gave Bryant a sideways look. "And when were you going to tell me this?"

"Once we finished for the night, I swear, Boss. I only just found out for sure this afternoon. I caught him coming out of the same house on Magazine Street a few times, but I wasn't sure who lived there until earlier today."

Wyatt thought a moment. "All right. Take the horse. I'll get Mrs. Gentry home. I want you to find Barnhart and see that he leaves New Orleans."

"How am I going to do that?" Bryant asked.

"I'll leave that to you, but I don't need details. Two rules though. Don't break the law, and don't fail."

"That doesn't leave many options."

"You've already figured out which one you'll use."

"I have."

He clamped his hand on his employee's shoulder. "I want confirmation that he's gone."

At Bryant's nod, Wyatt handed him the reins. He watched his new employee ride off toward the city and wondered if he'd placed too much trust in him. Only time would tell.

And this was not a job Wyatt would trust himself to do. Not without breaking the first rule. For what he wanted to do to the man who killed his father was definitely not legal.

So as much as he could, he stayed away.

Wyatt strode back to the carriage. He was about to take his place next to the driver when Mrs. Gentry waved him over.

"Join me, please," she commanded.

Wyatt shook his head. "With all due respect, it wouldn't be right to do that, ma'am. I'm an employee."

"Nonsense. Get in, Wyatt."

His eyes widened and cut toward the driver for just a heartbeat, and then his face went neutral again. Mrs. Gentry laughed.

"It's all right. Martin has been with my family since I was a young girl, so he is discreet. He is also quite deaf. It's one of the requirements I have of my drivers." She shrugged. "I value my privacy but find it difficult not to speak my mind."

He let out a long breath but complied with her order. Once he was situated across from his employer's wife, the carriage set off again.

Wyatt sorted through his responses to Mrs. Gentry's choice to call him by name but came up empty. He elected to continue to keep silent.

While Eliza got her red hair and curls from her father, everything else came from her mama. Looking at the dark-haired Mrs. Gentry was like peering into Eliza's future.

That raised a smile.

"You're wondering whether it's safe to admit your secret, aren't you?" She shifted positions and toyed with the feather mask lying next to her on the seat. "I assure you it's quite safe. I want what you do."

"And what is that?" he asked carefully.

"To see you and my daughter together."

His gut tightened. Again he elected to say nothing.

"No, I don't suppose you feel safe enough with me to admit to any of this. I understand that." Her fingers stilled, and then she met his gaze. "I know you're the one who convinced my daughter to try that ridiculous jump into a saddle. I used that to try to keep her off the trail that year so she could come with me to New Orleans. I wish I had succeeded."

Part of him agreed. The other part was glad he'd had that one last trail ride with Eliza.

A look of vexation crossed her pretty features. "Do you intend to sit there and say nothing the remainder of the trip back to the city?"

He leaned forward and rested his elbows on his knees. "Ma'am, I mean no disrespect."

"No, you wouldn't. You were always a very respectful young man."

They rode in silence for the better part of a quarter hour. Then he caught Eliza's mother watching him again.

"It is unlikely that you and I will have another opportunity to speak frankly. Much as I will miss New Orleans, I miss my husband even more, so my daughter and I will be leaving tomorrow for Texas. I would very much like to finish this conversation."

"Ma'am," he said easily, "I have good news. Mr. Gentry arrived this evening and is waiting for you at home."

She laughed. Not at all the response Wyatt expected.

"So he was there when Eliza rode in like a heathen with her braids and her security detective trailing behind her? Oh, that is priceless."

He hid his grimace by turning away. When he returned his attention to her, Mrs. Gentry was still studying him.

"Which of you took the brunt of his temper?"

"That would be Miss Gentry," he said. "The boss was particularly peeved that she had returned in such a state."

"As I expected." She shrugged. "And then what happened?"

"When I left to return to River House, she was giving him as much grief as he'd given her. Maybe more."

This time her laughter was expected. "They're perfectly matched, those two. I wouldn't be surprised to return home and find the battle still waging."

"Nor would I, ma'am," he admitted.

He sat back and looked beyond her to the night sky. He found Orion and the Little Dipper. Somewhere not too far away, Eliza might be looking at those same stars.

"Was Ben Barnhart at the party tonight?"

The question took him by surprise. "He was," Wyatt told her. "He made an attempt to speak with your daughter. I was able to divest him of that notion, but unfortunately, Miss Gentry took our horses before I was able to do anything further."

"Of course she did." Mrs. Gentry shook her head. "That girl and her horses. Or should I say that girl and her determination to do what she wants to do?" She paused. "Did you come upon the two of them in conversation?"

"I did. Barnhart did not realize she was being shadowed." He paused to recall the conversation he'd overheard. His fists curled. "She was not receptive to his advances."

"Well, good." She let out a long breath. "I wasn't completely certain that she was sincere about being over her silly romance with the Barnhart boy. He was never the right one for her, no matter what transpired between my husband and the judge."

Wyatt could imagine what had transpired. Mr. Gentry would have had the responsibility as boss to report the loss of Pa to the authorities upon his return to Texas. He also might have told said authority—Judge Barnhart—exactly what happened.

Or maybe not, considering who actually did the killing.

In either case, there was likely an argument that made his fussing with Eliza look like nothing at all. Judge Barnhart's only son never could do any wrong. Not in his father's eyes, anyway.

"Young man," Mrs. Gentry said, diverting his attention, "there has never been a fellow who could stand up to my daughter other than Wyatt Creed. I've missed him over the years."

Then he spied a falling star. "So have I, ma'am, but I assure you that Wyatt Creed is dead."

"Wyatt. . ."

"Ma'am, with all due respect, please don't call me that. The man you miss—the boy, actually—is buried on the Chisholm Trail next to the man he killed."

"He didn't kill anyone," she said, never breaking eye contact with him. "He wouldn't have. Not under those circumstances. Not ever."

Wyatt said nothing.

"What name do you go by now?" she finally asked.

"The name I was given at the beginning of my life, ma'am. John Brady."

His maternal grandfather's name. Anything he had learned about being a man had come from the years when his grandparents lived nearby.

And though he hadn't been born with that name as an infant, that night on the Chisholm Trail he'd been given a new life. He stepped into that shallow grave as Wyatt Creed and walked away later—after the men had seen him covered up with dirt like his pa—as John Brady.

"Well, John Brady," she said as the carriage turned onto the street leading to the Gentrys' New Orleans home, "it's a pleasure to meet you properly. You and your associates have taken good care of my daughter. I would like it very much if that arrangement continued."

"That is up to Mr. Gentry, ma'am."

The carriage stopped to wait for the gates to open, and Wyatt took the opportunity to say his goodbyes and climb out.

"Mr. Brady?" she called, drawing him back to the carriage.

"Yes, ma'am?"

Mrs. Gentry offered a smile that touched her eyes. "Your mother would be so proud of you. So very, very proud."

She tapped on the carriage and was gone before he could respond. It took three times around the block before he could return to his post across the street without the telltale sign of the tears he'd shed.

As he leaned against the wall, he looked up at the stars and prayed that Eliza's mama was right.

Chapter 9

Papa glared at Eliza across the breakfast table. Their conversation last night hadn't ended well, and apparently a good night's sleep had not changed his opinion.

She'd overheard him tell Mama last night that he'd left for New Orleans the same day the telegram from John Brady arrived warning him that Ben Barnhart was in the city.

"Who is John Brady?" she asked.

After a quick sideways glance in Papa's direction, Mama responded. "He is that nice young man who escorted me home last night." She paused. "I understand he also escorted you."

So the masked detective had a name. John Brady.

"Not so much as our daughter led John Brady on a merry ride through the city," her father said. "I appreciate that he managed to keep up with her on horseback. Many don't."

Eliza sighed. "You act like this happens all the time, Papa."

"It has happened enough." He slammed both palms on the table, and Mama jumped. Eliza, however, just allowed another sigh. "I have two sons who have given me no grief whatsoever, but this daughter of ours. . ." He shook his head. "I am at a loss."

"You did this, William. If you hadn't insisted on taking her along with her brothers every year on those ridiculous cattle drives, she might have turned out to be a proper lady."

"Those 'ridiculous cattle drives' paid for all of this and more, Susanna," he snapped. "And she learned valuable skills out there."

"Like how to ride and shoot like a man," Mama said. "Not exactly what makes a woman a good wife."

"I beg to differ," Papa told her. "I come from a long line of women who could stand alongside a man and defend her home and who could ride a horse as well as any of their menfolk. That is a benefit to a marriage, not a hindrance."

"Maybe when wars are being fought, but this is 1889 and a woman's place is not with a rifle in one hand and a saddle in the other."

Crimson climbed into Papa's cheeks, and his fingers curled on the table. "Where we come from, it is."

"Where I come from, it is not. And remind me, dear. What sort of woman did you choose?" Mama's tone was smooth as silk, but her expression told another story altogether.

"I am right here. Please do not talk about me as if I am not." Eliza stood. "And Papa, I understand you want to see me taken care of. It's your job as my father. But if you truly want that for me, settle some money into an account and allow me to get an education."

He sat in mute silence. This was a battle that had been waged more than once. Never had she won.

"Darling," Mama said. "If you were to marry, perhaps your husband would allow it. Have you considered that?"

"Allow it." She kept an even tone. "Mama, I do appreciate your attempt at encouraging me, but I only want to do what makes me happy. All my life I have counted stars and read books about the heavens. Haven't you realized that what I miss about the ranch is seeing the stars at night?"

Papa let out a long breath. Before he could offer yet another counterargument, she hurried to continue.

"I am still young. If you would just allow a few years of study, I could show you that it is a worthy calling. I do want a husband and children, but I also want something of me to give to them."

"Something of you?" her father asked. "Where do you think you got this love of the night sky, Eliza?"

"From you," she said softly.

"Exactly. I learned what I know without having to go off and take lessons, and you can do the same." He shook his head. "I am trying to be understanding, and I do appreciate that you are a smart woman with a desire to learn more than this old man can teach you. But a woman of your age needs a husband. Not years from now but soon."

"I am twenty-one years old, Papa. I am hardly an old maid."

"At the rate you're going, you will be," he said, his tone icy.

"That is quite enough, William," Mama told him. "Eliza has had her share of offers."

Her temper flared. "Including the one I had last night. Perhaps I will tell him yes."

Papa shook his head. "What offer? I had a man in mind for you, but I've been told the two of you never met. Am I wrong?"

"I don't know who you thought you would push me off on this time, but no. I did not meet any man who had been told he was approved by you."

She balled up her fists and resisted the urge to storm out of the room. Instead, Eliza decided to allow her anger full rein. "The offer of marriage last night came from Ben Barnhart."

"You said you were over him," Mama protested. "Did you lie to me about that?"

She spared her mother a quick glance. "Oh, I am, but Papa apparently does not care about that. If he wants me wed, I can make that happen this very day."

With that threat, idiotic as it was, she turned and stormed out.

"Eliza Jane Maribel Gentry, come back here. This conversation is not over," her father shouted. "Not over by a long shot. I forbid you to go anywhere near the Barnhart boy."

Eliza turned around and stared at her father's reddened face. "He's a man, Papa, not a boy. And I am a full-grown woman. You cannot ignore that fact anymore, and you can no longer treat me like a child."

"And yet you are acting like one. Stop the empty threats," he told her. "You're too smart to run off with a man you don't like just to prove a point to me."

He was right. Yet her temper pushed away any reasonable response.

"But I am not smart enough to make a life with my brain instead of my ability to run a household and produce children."

Mama held up her hands. "That is quite enough. You are both well beyond reasonable discourse." She nodded to Eliza. "Come back and finish your breakfast as well as your conversation."

"It is finished, Mama. Papa and I will never agree."

"I never said you should agree." She nodded to the chair Eliza had just vacated. "I only said you should finish what you started."

Eliza remained rooted in place. Her mother rose.

"Think carefully before you answer," she said. "Were you telling me the truth when you said you no longer had any desire to marry Ben Barnhart, Eliza?"

She took a long breath and let it out slowly. "I was."

"So you tried to run off with the Barnhart boy and then you changed your mind?" Papa said. "Now you've changed it again just to prove a point to me. Eliza, really, if you want to be thought of as an adult, make a choice and stick to it."

Her father's statement echoed the same words Ben said to her last night.

"Do you want me to choose between a life of freedom married to

Ben or a life back at the ranch being constantly matched up for that husband I require? Then I want neither. But if I must choose, I will."

She got her temper from her father. Eliza had heard this all her life. They had skirmished off and on for more than a decade, but never had she seen him sit in stony silence.

His silence was much more frightening than all the noise he made when he was arguing his point. Worse, his silence was deafening.

Mama, however, felt no compunction to keep her thoughts to herself in that moment. "You are not marrying Ben Barnhart, Eliza. I forbid it."

"You too, Mama?"

Her mother looked over at Papa. "Just tell her, William. It is the only right thing to do."

A look passed between them. For a moment, the only sound in the dining room was the ticking of the massive grandfather clock in the corner.

Finally, Papa stood. "Eliza, we have our disagreements, but I do hope you realize I love you with all of my heart."

"I do," she said.

"Then I want you to understand that if I did not have very good reasons to say this, the words would never be said."

She nodded. "All right."

"Think very carefully before you pledge your life to become a Barnhart," he told her. "To choose him is to walk away from this family."

"William," Mama said on a sharp exhale of breath. "You do not mean that."

"I do," he told her before returning his attention to Eliza. "I will always love you. Nothing you do will change that. But if you marry him, you will be a Barnhart, not a Gentry."

Her heart raced. Never had she seen this side of her father.

"Papa, I will take the name of whatever man I marry. What makes the Barnhart name particularly offensive to you?"

"Tell her," Mama repeated.

"Tell me what?" she demanded.

"Susanna, you do not know what you're asking. You weren't there."

Her mother moved to stand between Eliza and her father. "But she was. Even if it didn't happen in front of her, she was there."

He seemed to be considering her statement. Then he nodded. "Walk with me, Eliza, while your mother supervises the packing."

"But you only just got here," Mama protested.

"And already I am ready to go." He gestured toward the door. "After you, Eliza," he told her.

She followed him out into the front courtyard where the groom hurried to open the gate. "Will you need the carriage, sir?" he asked.

Papa glanced across the street and then shook his head. "No, Eliza and I will walk." He linked arms with her and strolled out through the gates.

Eliza spied the detective, now free of his mask. At the sight of them, he crossed the street to acknowledge first Papa and then, a moment later, Eliza.

She studied his face, its pleasing lines and angles, and the green eyes that watched her with what appeared to be great interest. Then he abruptly returned his attention to her father.

"Would you like an escort, sir?"

Papa dismissed the detective with a curt nod. Eliza fell into step beside him.

They walked for quite a while in silence with only the noise of the city to keep them company. Finally, her father led her away from the street and into the park that had once hosted the World's Fair.

Though the drought had turned some of the foliage a dull brown, enough greenery remained to almost make Eliza forget she was still in the city. After a few minutes, her father paused to look down at her.

He seemed to be studying her, and then he shook his head. "Eliza, you are me in female form, and that confounds the daylights out of me."

She wasn't sure how to respond, so she kept quiet.

"My mama used to tell stories of the women in my family and how they had backbone enough to stand up to anything that came their way." He glanced around the park and then returned his attention to her. "We come from royalty, from pioneers, and from pirates. Our people are proud—too proud sometimes—and we are tough. But there is one thing we do that is sometimes our downfall."

"What is that, Papa?" she asked.

"We love too easily and too hard." He shook his head. "We're fiercely loyal. We're smart." He paused. "But we love too easily and too hard."

A leaf brushed her sleeve as it fell. "I don't understand what that means."

"You know our family history, sweetheart. From Maribel Cordoba and her pirate Jean-Luc to your Ellis Dumont and her solider hero—also part pirate, I should add—to your mama and me, once we set our sights on love, we do anything to have it." He let out a long breath. "Are you in love, Eliza?"

"In love?" She shook her head. "No, Papa. I thought I was, but I was wrong."

"When you truly are, you will know." He reached down to brush his index finger along her cheek. "And when you know, there is nothing that can keep you from the one you love. Not even me."

She smiled and he joined her. Then his expression sobered.

"I want you settled," he told her. "A father always wants that for his children. I want a protector for you to care for you when I no longer can."

Eliza opened her mouth to offer an explanation of just how well she could care for herself. Then she thought better of it and nodded. "I understand."

"Good. Then we are agreed."

"Agreed?" She shook her head. "On what?"

"Ben Barnhart is neither the man you love nor the man you will marry."

She frowned. Papa knew her too well. How had he managed to make a case against Ben so easily? Yet she couldn't deny it. "We are agreed."

He let out a long breath. "Good. Now let's go home. We've worried your mother long enough."

Once again she matched her strides to his as they traversed the length of the park to emerge onto the street. There she stuttered to a stop. "Papa, what was it that Mama wanted you to tell me?"

Her father gave her a searching look and shook his head. "I have no idea."

"Stop," she said. "You do."

"Eliza, someday you will realize we just talked about much more than you think we did. I've told you. You just don't know it yet."

She frowned. "What does that mean?"

"That means as long as you remember you should have nothing to do with Ben Barnhart, now or ever, that's all you need to know."

One week later, June 1, 1889

The Gentry assignment had come to an end, as had the month of May, but there was much more work to be done elsewhere. Work that would pay well and would go far to keep his detective agency's name on the lips of important people.

Wyatt had letters of request waiting from two senators, a governor, and a very well-placed member of Spanish royalty, yet all he wanted to do was stand in front of that house on St. Charles Street and watch for Eliza to ride past in a carriage with her mama. Or spy a glimpse of her in a second-floor window.

He was like a whipped puppy when it came to that woman. Pained in her presence yet ever aching to see her again.

Wyatt paid his men too well for them to comment on the fact that their boss was acting like he was one of them. Still, they had to wonder why.

The family had set off for Texas this morning. He ought to be securing his own passage to Galveston where he now made his home, but Bryant had sent a message that he had news about Ben Barnhart.

News that might involve something illegal.

That put a smile on Wyatt's face. He might never be able to see justice done for his pa, but he could certainly put the man away for something else. If he could catch him at it.

Barnhart and his father had powerful friends. They'd gone well beyond the influence of their circle in Texas. The judge had tired of his local brand of popularity and had already seen his boy elected to the state house. The next step was to put him in the White House.

Wyatt, however, preferred to see him in the jailhouse.

He met Bryant at an establishment near the wharfs where decent people wouldn't be seen. The room was poorly lit, and only a fool would step inside unarmed.

But the regulars knew Wyatt, and they left him alone. In turn, he'd been known to toss the occasional rowdy patron out the door on behalf of the management.

Rodrigo was behind the bar, but he left his place to greet Wyatt with a warm embrace and usher him to a table in the back of the room. Wyatt sat with his back to the wall, facing the door.

Bryant waited until Rodrigo returned to the bar to report his latest findings. "He ran, Boss," his detective said. "Just two steps ahead of the cops. Another hour and he would've been there when they raided the place."

"Start at the beginning," Wyatt said as he watched two men step inside and close the door behind them. They looked as if they were fresh off the ship and spoiling for trouble.

"The lady friend was a dead end. No idea what the arrangement was, but she stopped coming around three days ago. I tracked the subject to a warehouse near the river. I was able to get inside when nobody was around, and that's where I found them."

Wyatt tore his attention away from the river toughs to focus on Bryant. "Found what?" he asked.

"Plates," he said with a satisfied smile. "Stacks of them. And not the kind your wife puts on the table for roast and potatoes. These were counterfeiter's plates. They were making counterfeit money in there. Or they were making plates and selling them to someone who did. I did some investigation while I was at the Service. These are good. Not amateur. We're not dealing with street thugs on this."

So Barnhart was dabbling in making money. Literally. He smiled. "Good job, Bryant. You're certain no one saw you?"

"Absolutely certain." The detective paused for just a second. "And I made sure to leave everything like it was except for this." He retrieved a folded piece of paper from his pocket and handed it to Wyatt.

After examining it, he shook his head. "This doesn't look like paper a counterfeiter would make money out of."

"I thought the same, Boss. And there were stacks of it." He shrugged. "Not as much as the paper they would use to make dollars, but they had plenty. I snagged that one because I thought you'd maybe know what it was."

Wyatt tucked the paper into his pocket and retrieved an envelope.

Inside was a pay draft and the detective's next assignment. He'd also added a bonus.

"Good work, Bryant." He slid the envelope across the table and the detective quickly put it away. "Watch for those two on your way out."

He grinned and patted the knife hidden beneath his vest, then stood. "Already saw them."

Wyatt climbed to his feet and followed Bryant toward the door. As expected, the two river toughs stood in a pitiful attempt to block their exit. Rodrigo moved to help them, but Wyatt shook his head.

Bryant took the first one out with two punches. Wyatt finished the second one off with one well-placed blow to his ample belly, then bid Rodrigo goodbye and stepped out into the sunshine.

He patted his vest to be sure the paper was still there and felt something else there. Retrieving the comb, he held it up to the light and watched the diamonds sparkle while he recalled how beautiful Eliza looked with the comb in her hair.

Someday he would put this comb back where it belonged. For now it would remain safe with him.

Chapter 10

June 13
Gentry Ranch

Eliza opened her eyes to the sun shining on her face. She blinked against the blinding light as she sat bolt upright.

She'd dreamed she was at River House on the dance floor. She was spinning and spinning beneath the candles and silken clouds and couldn't stop. Even now as she shook away the cobwebs of her dreams, Eliza felt the slightest bit light-headed.

As it had since she returned from New Orleans, it took a moment for her to remember where she was.

Home.

Texas.

Letting out a long breath, she threw off the quilt and stood. Sleep had eluded her since her return, and she'd fallen into bed exhausted and without bothering to braid her hair. Now she paid the price with tangles that fell all around her face and into her eyes.

What she wouldn't give to be able to ring for Opal to come with hot tea for her to sip while the maid combed through the tangles.

Comb.

She frowned at the reminder that she'd somehow lost that lovely celestial comb the night of the masquerade party at River House. So far it had not been found on the property. That meant it likely flew off somewhere between River House and her home in the city.

If that was the case, then the comb was lost forever. And without ever discovering who sent it to her. Papa said it wasn't him. Mama declared she would have purchased something more feminine like flowers or a fleur-de-lis. If Ben had sent it, he would have mentioned it first thing in their conversation at the river.

That left the name of the giver as mysterious as the comb's location.

She sighed and padded over to her dressing table to retrieve her brush. By now Ben was probably back up north marrying Beatrice. Or perhaps he was still in New Orleans, chasing a pretty planter's daughter.

Either way, he was out of her life, and that was just fine with her.

Her mind settled briefly on John Brady. Papa refused to allow any discussion of him, even to the point of forbidding the topic. Perhaps that was part of why she remained so curious who this fellow was.

The other part was those eyes. A memory floated just out of focus, and as hard as she tried, Eliza couldn't see it.

But there was something familiar there.

She pinned up her pitiful excuse for a braid, donned her riding clothes, and set off. Giving thanks that both Mama and Papa were away this morning, she snatched up a piece of toast from the kitchen and headed off to the stables. Since Mama had plans to go into Austin today, surely Justine had gone with her.

While Eliza was happy to have the little girl under their roof, even just temporarily, she had already tired of Justine following her around like a lost puppy. Certainly the child was out of her element and missing her friends back in New Orleans, but couldn't Mama help with that?

Red met her at the door with a grin and a saddle slung over one broad shoulder. He looked past her and nodded.

"Look out. Here comes your shadow."

She cast a glance over her shoulder and spied Justine hurrying toward her. Today's ensemble included a yellow floral dress more suited to city tea parties than a Texas ranch, a pair of braids tied with matching ribbons, and a fancy hat she certainly must have taken from Mama's wardrobe.

"What am I going to do with her, Red?" she said on an exhale of breath. "She follows me everywhere and refuses to wear the clothes Mama bought for her. Apparently they aren't pretty enough."

Papa's oldest employee chuckled. "Sounds like someone else I know."

Eliza watched Justine stumble over the hem of her dress and lose her hat. Or rather, Mama's hat. The wind picked up the headpiece and sent it rolling like a tumbleweed toward the pasture. Justine gathered her skirts and chased after it.

"Me? Hardly. If I had done any of those things, do you think Papa would have allowed me out on the trail? I doubt it."

"Girlie, your pa would have taken you to the moon and back if you'd asked him to." He hitched his hat back a notch with his free hand, revealing a thick shock of gray with a few strands of red still visible. "It just so happened you wanted a trail ride instead."

Her smile was bittersweet. "I miss those rides."

"Well, you're the only one. The rest of us are glad for the droving company your pa sends the herd off with nowadays. They make money, your pa makes money, and we all sleep in our beds every night instead of on a bedroll under the stars."

"I miss sleeping under the stars too."

Another chuckle. "I'm sure you do. I told your pa to watch out or you'd be trying that here. You haven't, have you?"

She shrugged. "Not yet. It's not as fun when you're alone."

"Nothing much is, I reckon, but then, I've worked on this ranch since I was younger than you, and I don't recollect a single day when I was alone." He chuckled. "You ought to go help that child. She's got no idea how to conduct herself out here."

Eliza let out a long breath. "She's a sweet child, but I am not her governess."

"No," he said, his voice uncharacteristically stern. "But you're family. Family helps one another. Do they not?"

"They do, I suppose," she said reluctantly as she thought about the old hand's comment on loneliness. While Eliza agreed with Red, Justine probably knew exactly what it was like to feel lonely.

"Well, I cannot tell you what to do, but I do know how you've been raised. Enjoy your ride, girlie. I've got a saddle to work on."

"I'll send Justine to help you," she said to his retreating back.

Red neither responded nor acknowledged her statement. Instead, he just kept walking.

Eliza turned around and quickly closed the distance between her and Justine, arriving just in time to keep her from tripping over a tree root. "Careful," she told her. "You're not in New Orleans anymore, sweetheart."

"I know." She looked up at Eliza with tears in her eyes. "I don't like it here. It's scary."

"Oh honey. It's not scary here." She embraced the girl then held her at arm's length. "Things are just different than in New Orleans. You'll learn to love it in Texas, I promise."

"I don't want to love it here," she said in a pitiful tone. "I want my mommy."

According to Mama, Justine's mommy could be anywhere between Nairobi and New York City, Boston and Bombay. But it wouldn't do to tell the child that.

"I know you do, but what if we do something fun today?"

"There's nothing fun to do in Texas." She looked around and then back up at Eliza, causing Mama's hat to slip back.

"That's not true." Eliza took her hand and turned her back toward the house. "We just need to get some supplies and then we can go on an adventure."

"What kind of adventure?"

"You'll have to wait and see." Eliza stopped and shrugged. "Unless you'd rather do something else. I mean, maybe you're too busy to come with me. You do look like you're dressed for a party."

For a moment, Eliza thought the girl might not answer. Then she regarded Eliza with a serious expression. "I would rather go on an adventure today."

"All right. That means we have to prepare. I'll see to a picnic lunch. You'll need to put on your adventure clothes like me."

Justine looked horrified as she took in Eliza's boots, shirt and trousers, and straw hat that made up her summer riding attire. "You mean I should dress like the stable boy?"

"Justine, just trust me. Wearing a party dress would not make this an adventure." They arrived at the back door, and she held it open for the girl to go inside first. "And when you return Mama's hat, make sure you put it back exactly where you found it. She's very particular about her things."

"Your mama has beautiful gowns," Justine said. "She doesn't dress like the stable boy."

"Neither will we all the time. But today we're having an adventure, so we are dressing for the adventure. Now hurry!"

"I will!" she said as she raced toward her bedchamber.

Eliza was packing the picnic basket into the carriage when Justine burst through the door. While she had deigned to dress in the trousers and shirt that she'd been given when she arrived, the braids and bows remained in place. She had exchanged Mama's yellow hat for a pink bonnet, and she'd tied a blue satin ribbon around her waist.

"Well, that's better," Eliza said, stifling a grin as Justine joined her in the buggy. "Let's go."

A flick of her wrists and they were off. Eliza headed north under a bluebonnet-blue sky toward the grove of live oak trees and the thicket that lined the creek. It was a beautiful early summer day with just enough warmth in the breeze to give a hint of the heat to come.

She stopped the buggy beneath the trees and jumped down. "What are you doing?" Justine demanded.

"I thought you might like to dip your toes in the creek," she said as she walked around to Justine's side of the buggy to offer to help her down. "I used to love that when I was a little girl."

Looking past her to the creek, which was no more than ankle high at the moment, the girl made a face. "I don't like water."

Eliza laughed. "Since when? You were always the first one to jump at the chance to walk down to the river to watch the boats, and you've sailed to Europe and here to Texas many times."

Justine's lower lip quivered. "That was before."

"Before what?"

She sighed. "Before I heard your papa and your mama talking about how the water destroyed a whole town in Pennsylvania two weeks ago. It was just awful what they said about the water rolling through town and taking homes and families with it."

Her eyes shimmered with tears as she told the story. Eliza glanced down at the creek and then back at Justine.

She reached up to take Justine's hand. "It was a terrible flood and a horrible situation for the families who lived there. I'm sorry Mama and Papa had a discussion like that in front of you."

The girl ducked her head. "They didn't, actually."

"I see." Eliza reached over to lift Justine's chin. "So you were eavesdropping again?"

A defiant look surfaced. "I don't like that word."

"Yet it is what you were doing." She paused. "Perhaps you've learned that sometimes grown-ups speak privately because the topic they're discussing is not one that should be heard by little children."

"I am nearly grown," she said.

"Fine." Eliza turned her back on Justine and slipped off her boots and set them on the grassy bank beside the buggy.

"What are you doing?" Justine demanded.

"Never mind." She rolled up her trouser legs. "Just sit up there like a grown-up. I'm going to enjoy myself. And then you and I are going to have a serious conversation about appropriate behavior."

"I know what appropriate behavior is. How are you going to enjoy yourself?" she demanded as she leaned over the edge of the buggy. "You're not—oh!"

Eliza stepped into the creek, silencing her cousin completely. The water was cool and clear, and the granite rocks provided stepping-stones to easily take her out into the center of the creek.

At the creek's center was a flat rock three times the size of Mama's fancy dining table that sat almost a foot above the water. Eliza sat down and stretched out her legs as she watched Justine trying to decide what to do.

As a child she had come out here with a picnic lunch and dined as she made up stories of being a mermaid or being lost on a deserted island. Sometimes her brothers or Wyatt would join her, though most times it was just her.

It all seemed so silly now. So bittersweet given what happened to Wyatt. Next time she would come here at the end of their adventure so she could share that experience with Justine.

"Come back here," Justine demanded.

Eliza reached down to cup water in her hand and then tossed it in Justine's direction. "No, you come and join me."

The girl screamed and then sat back, her eyes wide. Eliza ignored her to kick up water with her toes and watch a school of tiny silver fish hurry into the weeds at the creek's edge.

After a few minutes, Justine called to her. "I'm afraid."

"Would you be afraid if I carried you?" a distinctly male and somewhat familiar voice asked from somewhere behind the trees and brush.

Eliza froze. She'd foolishly left the rifle secured under the buggy seat, but she did have her knife in her pocket.

She reached for the weapon, then thought better of the idea. Any man who'd gotten on to Gentry land was probably allowed there. Papa was adamant about that. So whoever was out there probably was employed by the ranch or had permission to visit.

Still Eliza remained on guard as she called out, "Who's there?"

A moment later, the security detective she now knew by the name of John Brady made his way through the thicket. "What are you doing here?" she demanded.

"I heard a scream." He looked over at Justine and then back at Eliza. "I thought I ought to investigate. Mr. Gentry said he's been plagued with bobcats out here recently, so I thought maybe—"

"What is a bobcat?" Justine asked, wrapping her fingers around the ends of the ribbon tied at her waist.

"Never mind," Eliza told her. "Why are you here exactly, Mr. Brady? And by that I don't mean here at the creek but here at my father's ranch?"

The detective was dressed all in black from his hat to his boots, with only a row of silver buttons on his vest to add a change of color. His beard was trimmed short, and his eyes were shaded by the hat he wore low on his head. He had a gunfighter's stance and a way about him that told her he was capable of using the guns strapped to both hips.

To cover the fact that his even gaze made her slightly nervous, she picked up a pebble and skipped it across the water. It was a poor attempt, but she managed four skips before the pebble sank in the middle of the creek.

Justine immediately smiled. "I remember you from New Orleans. You're that nice man who follows people."

CHAPTER 11

That man who follows people.

Leave it to a child to sum up his entire career in five words.

"You have a very good memory." He turned his attention to Eliza. "That looks like a fine use of a creek on a summer morning."

It was an idiotic thing to say, but she was a beautiful woman wading in a creek without a care in the world, and he didn't run across that every day. Then there was the recollection that he'd often ditched his own boots to wade in that creek with her.

A lifetime ago.

Then there was the realization that Eliza wasn't much older than the little girl tagging along with her the last time he saw her.

Wyatt slammed the door shut to that memory and turned to the girl in the buggy. "I'm glad you remember me." He paused. "Justine, is it?"

"Yes. You have a very good memory too, Mr. Brady."

"In my line of work, it's a necessity."

Wyatt turned to Eliza. Even though the thought of her in a ball gown was still fresh in his mind, he preferred this version of her in stable boy's clothes over that one.

She'd picked up another pebble and was about to toss it, a sure sign he made her nervous. Or at least it used to be.

"To answer your question," he told her, "I have a meeting with your father, but I'm early. I heard a scream and—"

"And you thought a bobcat had gotten us," the girl supplied. "What is a bobcat?"

"Never mind, Justine," they said in unison.

Eliza grinned in his direction, and Wyatt clamped his mouth shut. He had no business here. He'd promised Mr. Gentry he would avoid Eliza, and now here he was courting trouble.

The problem was, he would rather face her father's wrath than leave Eliza up to her ankles in the creek. However, good sense quickly prevailed.

He looked around. "Looks like you're safe," Wyatt told the girl. "I don't see any bobcats."

She looked unsure. "How can you be certain?"

Eliza gave him a look that told him he'd created the problem and he could certainly fix it. So he gave it a try.

"See, those bobcats, they're particular about who they spend their time with. They don't like people much, but they can be a problem when they decide they want to bother the cattle and chickens. So if there's one around you, it's usually because you're a cow or a chicken." He paused to give the girl a serious look. "Which are you, a cow or a chicken?"

"I'm neither," she said with a giggle.

"Well, there you go. I guess you'll be just fine out here, so I'm going to get on back about my business and you can do the same here. Just watch out if you start to moo or grow feathers though."

She giggled again, and his heart warmed to her. He knew the story of this one. Her mama was that dangerous combination of pretty and high-strung that caused her to chase whichever man offered the most interesting distraction.

Mr. Gentry had him check on his wife's sister, Eugenie,

occasionally just to make sure the young widow was still alive and worthy of being mama to Justine. His contacts always found her alive, but in Wyatt's opinion her worthiness as a parent was a whole other thing.

If the Lord ever gifted him with a wife and children, he certainly couldn't imagine abandoning his duty to them to go off pursuing whatever made him happy. He did, however, know plenty who did exactly that, and not just Justine's mama.

"Mr. Brady," the girl said. "I think I want to go in the creek now."

He looked over at Eliza, who seemed to be watching them closely but didn't appear interested in joining the conversation. "Then you ought to jump on it. I'm sure the water must feel good. Does it, Miss Eliza?"

"It does," she told him. "Come on and join me, Justine. I've just seen some tiny fish. And maybe I'll teach you to skip rocks if you want to learn."

Justine leaned down to take off her shoes and then rolled up her trousers to just below the knee. Then she beamed up at him.

"All right. I'm ready, Mr. Brady."

"Have fun, ladies," he told her as he turned his back and made his way toward the thicket.

"Where are you going?" the girl called.

Wyatt stopped and turned around. "Off to a meeting."

"You said you were early," she told him. "And you asked me if I would be less afraid if you carried me. So I want you to carry me."

His memory was good, but unfortunately, Justine's was better. He had said both of those things.

"All right," he said as he moved back toward the buggy. "Climb on my back, and I will take you to the creek so you won't have to walk on the grass."

He leaned close enough to allow her to climb onto his back. With

Justine practically choking him with her arms around his neck and her legs wrapped around his middle, Wyatt crossed the distance to the creek.

"Okay, let go. You're at the water."

"No. That's the problem. I don't want to go into the water."

She shook her head so hard she dislodged the silly sunbonnet she'd been wearing. It tumbled toward the ground, but Wyatt caught it and handed it back to her.

"Don't be silly," Eliza called. "There's nothing to be afraid of."

Wyatt disentangled himself from her and then set her down and turned around. "She's right. And besides, the first step to becoming a grown-up is to conquer your fear."

"Is it?" She shrugged. "Then I guess I should do it, but would you just at least take me as far as the rock where Eliza is standing? Once I'm beside her, I know I will be fine."

He looked down at his boots and then at the water level to determine whether he was willing to risk soaking the footwear he'd had made to fit the last time he was in Paris. It was possible he could deliver the child to Table Rock, as the children used to call it when he lived nearby, without getting them wet.

Possible but not guaranteed.

Then there was the problem of keeping his word to Mr. Gentry. He'd promised to stay clear of Eliza, and here he was practically being invited to wade in the creek with her.

It was an innocent mess he'd wandered into, yet still a mess.

But if he could help a little girl conquer her fear, then maybe Mr. Gentry would understand if he caught him here. And if he didn't, that was a risk Wyatt would have to take.

After all these years, the boss ought to know him well enough to trust him.

"All right, Justine," he said slowly. "But I'm going to have to take my boots off to do it, so just give me a minute."

He walked back over to the buggy and made short work of depositing his boots and socks inside where they would be safe. Then he returned to the bank and looked down at Justine.

"Ready?"

"Ready." She reached to try to climb onto his back again.

"Not this time." He nodded to the creek and then offered his hand to her. "I am going in first and you're going to follow. As long as you walk in my footsteps, you will be fine."

"Oh, I know about that," she said as she looked up, eyes wide. "That's like what my last governess told me about Jesus. Just follow where He walks, and we will be fine."

Wyatt smiled. "That's a real good lesson to learn. Your governess was a smart lady."

From his research, he knew that the governess had been fired because she was too smart. Watching what went on with her boss, she'd reported Eugenie to the police for child neglect and offered to take in Justine as her ward. That hadn't set well with the girl's mama, but Wyatt had to believe the governess was on the right track, even if she might have gone about things the wrong way.

She took his hand and looked up at him, half scared and half brave, and his heart twinged just a little. "All right. Miss Eliza, here she comes."

He took two steps and looked back. She was clutching his hand with all her strength, but the girl had managed to follow him despite the fact she was staring down at the water like it could swallow her up at any moment.

"Stick your toe in the creek," Eliza told her. "It's not cold at all."

"Go ahead," Wyatt echoed. "See, I'll do it."

She watched him do as he said he would and then grinned and did the same. Her squeal of delight once again put him in mind of

Eliza at that age.

"I like it," she said with a grin. "Now take me to Eliza. I want to stand on the big rock."

"To the big rock it is."

"Hurry, Justine," Eliza said. "The fish are back."

Justine pushed past Wyatt. "Oh, I want to see the fish! Are they pretty?"

Wyatt moved out of her way and his foot slipped off the rock, sending him tumbling into the creek. He landed with a splash that soaked both of his companions.

Justine squealed with delight, but Eliza's response wasn't quite as gleeful. She shrank back from the edge of the rock and swiped at the trousers that were now dotted with creek water.

His eyes met hers. She affected an irritated look that he remembered all too well. Oh, but then he spied the slight quirk of her lip, the mischief in her eyes.

And then he laughed, not because the current situation was funny, but because of all the nights he'd lain alone on his bedroll in the middle of nowhere, counting stars and asking the Lord to let him spend just a few more minutes with Eliza Gentry. To laugh with her just one more time.

He climbed to his feet and moved slowly toward the ladies, who were now watching him closely. Holding his dripping wet arms out wide, he roared.

"And that," Eliza told Justine, "is what a bobcat sounds like."

Justine looked up at him and grinned, then adjusted her bonnet. "Moo."

He pretended to lunge for her, and Justine kicked water at him. Before long they were all soaked, even Eliza, who stayed out of the game but didn't bother to try to move out of the way.

Finally, Wyatt held up his hands. "All right, Madame Cow, the bobcat gives up. May I sit on the rock with you?"

"You may," Justine told him. "But go sit by Eliza. You're scaring the fish away."

"You're fine over there with Justine," Eliza said in what sounded like a teasing tone.

He compromised by stretching out on a spot halfway between the two of them to let the sun dry his clothes. Eventually he would have to leave the ladies and this creek and go meet up with Mr. Gentry. Until then. . .

Wyatt groaned and reached into his vest pocket. The paper that Bryant had retrieved from the counterfeiters was nothing but a soggy mess.

"Was that important?" Eliza asked.

It was. Very. He'd planned to take the sample paper to Mr. Gentry and alert him to what he suspected Ben Barnhart was doing now. Without the evidence, he could still speak with Mr. Gentry, but it wouldn't be the same as showing him what was found at a place that Bryant was known to frequent before it was raided.

He let out a long breath and tossed the soggy mess into the creek, then watched the current take it out of sight. "Just a piece of paper I was going to show your father," he told her.

She looked past him to Justine and then back to allow her gaze to collide with his. "I'm sorry."

"It's fine," he told her as he leaned back on the rock and closed his eyes. "I have an excellent memory."

Eliza smiled. "Well, good. I'm glad our adventure didn't ruin things for you."

Oh, but it did. The entire remainder of the day was now ruined because nothing would be as good as this moment. Nothing.

He'd been worried Eliza would recognize him when she saw him in New Orleans, but she hadn't. That had been a disappointment and a huge relief all rolled up into one complicated bundle.

Of course, the last time she'd seen him he was barely fourteen years old. He'd changed since then. He'd grown a beard and about a foot in height. He'd traveled the world and dined with kings, two sultans, and more than one president, and all of them thought he was a decade older than his actual age.

Wyatt wasn't the skinny kid she'd known. Yet deep inside, under the layers of whatever it was he'd put between him and the life he had before Wyatt Creed was buried alongside the Chisholm Trail, he was still that skinny kid.

The skinny kid who'd had it bad for Eliza Gentry.

"If you fall asleep, we'll soak you again," the object of his thoughts said with a lilt of teasing in her voice.

He opened his eyes and saw her looking down at him. She grinned and disappeared from sight. Wyatt sat up and found her back on her side of Table Rock wearing an innocent look.

On the other side of the rock, Justine lay on her stomach with her face inches from the water. "There are so many fish in the water," she exclaimed when she noticed him watching her. "And they're all so very pretty. I had no idea."

"This creek has always been a favorite place for my brothers to fish," Eliza said.

Wyatt almost chimed in to agree but caught himself at the last minute and turned in her direction instead. "Do you do this often?"

"This?" She shook her head. "You mean sit on Table Rock in the middle of the creek?" Her laughter held no humor. "Hardly. Mama would never approve of this much fun."

She never did. He kept that to himself too.

"I miss it." Eliza looked away. "I had such a happy childhood, for the most part anyway. Then everything changed." She returned her attention to Wyatt. "What about you? What was your childhood like?"

"I don't remember," came out of his mouth as easily as it had for years. That had been his answer each time he answered questions about his past. Wyatt worked hard to make that answer the truth.

Most of the time.

The two exceptions were staring down the gun that was supposed to kill him and his memories of Eliza.

"Wait a minute. The man with the excellent memory cannot remember his childhood?" She gave him a sideways look. "Why is it I am having a hard time believing that?"

"I don't know." He offered a half grin. "Are you usually this skeptical?"

"No." Eliza shifted positions to lean over to trace circles in the water with her index finger. "There's something familiar about you. I feel like I've known you forever."

His heart jolted. *Time to go.*

Chapter 12

Eliza's finger stilled, but she made no move to look back at Wyatt. "Thank you for what you did for me at River House. I did allow Ben to court me for a time, but he didn't want to listen when I told him that time was well and truly gone."

"I was just doing my job."

"You do it well." She paused. "I'm still undecided what I do well. Other than change my mind, apparently."

He'd never known stubborn Eliza Gentry to change her mind once it was set on something. The only answer was she hadn't set it on who she wanted to court her. Wyatt could have told her that, but of course, he would not.

But then, Ben Barnhart never knew her as well as he did. If Wyatt had anything to do with it, he never would.

Wyatt retrieved his pocket watch to check the time and realized he'd ruined it in the creek. He ought to be upset. The watch was a reward given to him by a grateful sultana after he foiled an attempt on her husband's life last fall.

Per his timepiece, time had literally stood still while he'd been with Eliza. He tucked it back into his pocket and decided he would never get it fixed.

"I would like to apologize for making your job more difficult." She sat back up and turned toward him as she spoke. "I wasn't considering anyone but myself when I took off from River House on that horse."

"Apology accepted," he said. "You and that man you were arguing with seemed to know one another well."

"Well enough. We were children together. I thought I loved him." She shrugged. "He was correct when he said I kept changing my mind. I think part of the attraction was that my father and his despised one another."

"And the rest of it?" he asked, then wished he hadn't.

"A married woman makes her own decisions," she said. "Ben is handsome, charming, and persistent."

"And off-limits as far as your father is concerned." Wyatt's fingers curled into fists. "I should tell you that my assignment was specifically to keep him away from you."

Her eyes met his. "I know. But he never tried to see me, did he?"

"Not until the night of the party."

Eliza let out a long breath. "I was an idiot. I just reached a point where. . ." She shook her head. "Never mind. A lot of things have changed since then."

"It's only been a few weeks," he said.

She tucked a red curl behind her ear. "It seems longer. There isn't much to do here except tolerate my mother's excursions into town and count meteorites when I see them."

Once again Wyatt almost gave himself away by jumping into the conversation just like he had in their youth. "So you enjoy looking at stars?" he said instead.

"Not just looking at them. I've studied them for years." She paused. "Well, I've read lots of books about them. My parents believe university studies are wasted on a woman."

"I see."

"That's what I always liked about Ben. I could talk to him about my dreams, and he listened. He didn't tell me I couldn't become an astronomer."

The statement stung. Likely Ben just wasn't paying attention when she talked, but he kept his silence on that opinion. "Is that what you want?"

Another shrug. "It is what I think I want. Or maybe my parents are right and I should stop dreaming and secure a future for myself by marrying well and setting up housekeeping with a man who can take care of me."

"No. Don't do that." Her brows rose at the tone of his voice. Wyatt amended his tone. "Maybe you're the one who is supposed to discover constellations we didn't know existed or map out a new comet's path."

Her eyes widened slightly. "Are you interested in those things too, Mr. Brady?"

"I once had a friend who was, so I know a little about it. Now, much as I would like to stay, I have to go," he said as he stood. "I don't want to be late."

"You're not late yet, Brady, and it looks like I'm just in time too."

Wyatt turned to see William Gentry standing next to the buggy. His heart sank. It didn't take a genius to know the man was not happy. Not that he blamed him.

"Eliza, Justine, what are you doing?"

"Watching fish." Justine scrambled to her feet and tucked her bonnet ribbons over her shoulder. "And having an adventure with Eliza. We have a picnic basket, only it isn't time for eating yet."

"That explains the two of you." He turned his attention to Wyatt. "What's your excuse for sitting in bare feet in the creek with my daughter?"

"That's my fault," Justine told him. "He thought a bobcat was after me."

"Was it?" he asked her.

"No." She adjusted her bonnet. "But I made a loud noise because Eliza was going to get water on me, and I was a little frightened."

Wyatt made his way toward the bank. "I was riding toward the stables to look for Red since I had some time before our meeting. I heard a scream and thought I better make sure they were safe."

Mr. Gentry had his hands on his hips and an expression on his face that Wyatt had seen only a few times in his life. "Which apparently they were." He gave Wyatt a sweeping glance. "Your clothes are wet."

"That's my fault too," Justine said. "I wanted him to take me to the rock where Eliza was, and I was afraid of the creek water, which I am not afraid of now, and then he said he would be, then I said—"

"That's enough, Justine." He looked past Wyatt to his daughter. "You're awfully quiet, Eliza."

"Nothing to say," she answered. "Mama left for town without Justine. She was bored and apparently afraid of the creek water. Mr. Brady saved us from potential bobcats, and here we are."

"There is no need to take an attitude with me," her father snapped. "You can imagine how this looks."

She shook her head. "It looks exactly as I said. What is it you're thinking, Papa?"

"With all due respect, sir, all is well here, so maybe we could speak elsewhere?" Wyatt reached the bank and walked past Mr. Gentry, retrieved his socks and boots, and slipped them on. "If you'll let me, sir," he added.

All he got out of the statement was a sideways glance from Eliza's father.

"Eliza," William Gentry called. "See that you watch Justine closely. I wouldn't want any more bobcat scares."

"Stop teasing, Papa," she said. "We're fine. Besides, your security detective probably has his employees hidden in trees all over the ranch to watch us."

He shook his head, turned his back on the creek, and made his way out of the brush at a brisk pace with Wyatt a step behind. They rode in silence until they reached the ranch house.

Once inside, Wyatt followed him into the book-lined library that served as the office for ranch operations. Maps of Texas filled the empty spaces on the walls, each of them hung in elaborately carved wood frames. Behind the desk the brand of the Gentry Ranch had been burned into a piece of oak and was hung in the same kind of frame.

"Sit down," Eliza's father said none too kindly.

Wyatt quickly complied by finding one of the two leather chairs flanking the desk and taking a seat. It had been years since he'd been inside the Gentry ranch house, and back then he'd been a guest of the Gentry sons and not an employee of the owner.

He sat here now a different man. Literally.

Wyatt focused on the map of the Chisholm Trail that held pride of place over the fireplace at the end of the room, waiting for Eliza's pa to be seated at the desk.

The older man rested his palms on the polished wood but said nothing more. His eyes studied Wyatt. His silence spoke volumes.

Finally, he sat back in his chair. "Did you tell her?"

"No."

"Were you tempted?"

After he thought about it a minute, Wyatt had his answer. "No, sir. Ultimately I was not."

Mr. Gentry shook his head. "Ultimately?"

"It came down to whether my word is my bond and my promise means anything." He shifted positions but kept his eyes on the ranch boss. "It is and it does. Much more than the possibility of having my friend back."

A moment passed. Then he gave Wyatt a curt nod. "But did she recognize you?"

Again he had to consider the question before he answered it. "She did not."

"You're certain?"

"I am." He paused. "And the way Justine told it wasn't the best, but it happened just as she said. I had no intention of stopping at the creek until I heard the child scream. It was instinct that sent me there. The child was afraid of the water. I thought I could help, and I did. I was leaving when you got there." Another pause. "That's all of it. Nothing more or I would tell you."

A nod and the matter was settled. Or seemed to be.

"Your telegram said you had something to discuss with me in regard to the Barnhart boy," Mr. Gentry said. "He hasn't come after Eliza again, has he?"

"I've been tracking him, and he's living in a room at the Driskill Hotel," Wyatt said.

"So he hasn't been coming around here?"

"No," he said. "And it's not in regard to your daughter than I wanted to speak with you. My investigation has turned up evidence that he was associating with counterfeiters in New Orleans."

The older man's red brows gathered. "Whatever for? Judge Barnhart has more money than good sense, and that apple doesn't fall far from the tree. He'd have no need for more, would he? Is he being blackmailed?"

"Again, I don't know. The information came to light when we were keeping tabs on him in New Orleans while your family was there. He frequented a warehouse near the river as well as an apartment house. The building was raided just before we all left. The police confiscated plates, ink, and paper of at least two types."

"But not Barnhart."

"No," he said evenly. "Not Barnhart."

"What about that apartment?"

Wyatt met his gaze. "It belonged to a woman. Apparently they were close. Suffice it to say her affections could be bought."

Crimson climbed into the older man's cheeks, matching the strands of red that remained among his gray hair. After a moment, he let out a long breath.

"Is that all?"

"Just fair warning that I'm going after him, sir." Wyatt paused. "I'm doing this on my own time. I wanted you to know because it might get ugly."

"It might," he agreed. "But it'll be worse if he knows a dead man is chasing him."

He lifted one shoulder in a slow shrug. "Then he won't know."

"Ben isn't stupid," he told Wyatt. "He's going to wonder why the man I hired to protect my family in New Orleans is here at the ranch. I've never had the need for security here and never will. You'll need a reason to be here."

"Let him wonder," he told Mr. Gentry. "He knows what I do for you. Maybe that will be enough to keep him away from Eliza."

"Was it enough in New Orleans?"

"No," Wyatt said. "But to be fair, we tracked him there, and I got her out of the situation. He never made another attempt."

"That we know of."

"No." He looked the older man in the eye. "It didn't happen. He was under our surveillance the entire time."

"Then I will expect that surveillance to happen again." He paused. "And for that, you can put yourself back on the payroll. I may not need protection, but I won't be caught unaware if Ben Barnhart comes calling on my daughter."

Wyatt shook his head. "No. With all due respect, sir, I intend to do that for free."

Eliza heard the low hum of male voices, but owing to the thick walls and solid wood door that closed off Papa's office from the rest of the home, she couldn't make out a single thing they were saying.

"You're not doing it right," Justine whispered, causing Eliza to jump. "You have to put your ear to the door."

Mr. Brady's abrupt exit had caused her cousin to decide she too needed to return to the house. Her excuse was that she needed a wardrobe change for the picnic part of their adventure.

Eliza had complied only because she was curious what Papa and Mr. Brady might be discussing.

"Hurry and change," Eliza told her. "I'm getting hungry, and if you take too long, I'll bring the picnic basket in and we will eat at the kitchen table."

That caused Justine to hurry up the stairs and disappear into her room. Eliza was left to decide what to do until she returned.

The talking continued. Her curiosity continued as well.

A glance up the stairs confirmed that Justine was not yet about to return. Eliza walked over to the door and pressed her ear against it.

A moment later, the door opened and she tumbled into John Brady's arms.

He caught her, held her, and stared into her eyes. She looked up and there it was again. Something. A memory?

"Eliza."

A word and a warning all rolled up in her name. Mr. Brady swiftly set her on her feet but held her shoulders to steady her. Had he not, she might have tumbled yet again.

What was wrong with her?

This was the same security detective who had kept her safe in New Orleans. Who had raced her home from River House and who had abated Justine's fears and ended up being soaked in the process.

But those eyes. . .

A tug at her sleeve caught her attention. Justine was standing just out of view of the men, shaking her head. The nine-year-old had exchanged her trousers and shirt for a pink day dress with lace trim.

The ribbons in her braids, still damp, remained in place, but she'd elected not to wear the pink bonnet. Instead, she had tied a multi-colored headscarf around her hair.

Justine stepped into view and offered the security detective and Papa a broad grin before turning her charm on Eliza. "I'm ready now. We can go have our picnic. Goodbye, Uncle William and Mr. Brady. Please go on with your conversation without us."

As the girl led Eliza away from the still-open door, she leaned over to whisper, "I repeat. That is *not* how it works when you're listening to grown-up conversations. First, you never, ever put your ear on the door if you think the people inside might be leaving, and second, you especially never ever get caught."

"But you said to put my ear on the. . ." Eliza shook her head. "Never mind. Get in the buggy and let's go have a picnic."

"Fine," Justine said as she flounced ahead, her braids bobbing. "But you and I are going to have a serious conversation about appropriate behavior."

CHAPTER 13

June 18
Austin, Texas

Justine sat on a stool at the end of the counter at Alexander & Cornwell's Drug Store on Sixth Street enjoying a milkshake as if it was the last one she'd ever be allowed to consume. Because Mama supervised her clothing choices today, the girl wore a somewhat subdued frock in pale blue sprigged with pink roses and finished at the sleeves in pink lace.

She'd insisted on wearing her hair in a single braid, which she coiled at the back of her head. It was likely that Mama had not yet spied the pair of silver forks from the pantry that the audacious nine-year-old had artfully inserted into the whole arrangement.

Standing nearby, Miss Maddie Trawick, Mama's well-to-do spinster friend, was busy telling Mama all about how a certain acquaintance of theirs had resorted to sending her daughter to the Reed School for the Cure of Stammering in Detroit.

"It worked, it surely did," Miss Maddie said as her head bobbed and the black feathers on her hat danced. Miss Maddie was in perpetual mourning for some relative or other, so Eliza had never seen her in any color except black.

"I don't know, Maddie," Mama said. "It seems a little suspect to make that kind of claim, don't you think? And to send a child all that way."

"I don't know about all that, but I do know that once the fix was made, not only did their daughter not stop talking, but they then had trouble with her speaking her mind far too much. I told her they might ought to send her back and see if the training could be reversed."

Miss Maddie fell into fits of laughter. Mama looked across the distance between them and shook her head in Eliza's direction.

Eliza seized the chance to indicate to her mother that she would be stepping outside to take a walk. It wasn't unusual for Eliza to slip away from her mother to stroll down to Gammel's Old Book Store on Third Street in hopes of finding a new book.

She stepped out into the early afternoon sunshine and then turned toward the bookstore. Traffic was busy as usual on Sixth Street, and the sidewalks were full of people darting in and out of the businesses that lined the thoroughfare.

As she passed the Driskill Hotel, Ben Barnhart stepped out of the shadows with a paper-wrapped package under his arm.

He fell into step beside her. "Good afternoon, lovely lady."

Though she did slide him a sideways look to show her irritation, Eliza otherwise ignored him. Apparently Ben failed to notice. Instead, he measured his steps to hers.

"Warm today, isn't it?" he said. "But it is June, so it is to be expected."

When the topic of the weather failed to incite any response, he moved to a discussion of the quality of food in the Driskill Hotel dining room and then what he planned to achieve in the next legislative session.

Finally, he stepped in front of Eliza and thrust the package into her hands. "You won't find what you're looking for at the bookstore. I bought them all."

"Why do you think I am going to the bookstore?" she said as she tried to hand the package back to him.

He took a step back and shook his head. "I have no use for those."

She examined the package. "What's in here, Ben?"

"Everything Gammel's had related to astronomy," he said with a shrug. "The clerk told me you'd already read the rest of them."

There was a moment's indecision, but she shook her head. "I cannot keep these. If you won't take it back, I will leave it on the street."

He shrugged. "Then I'll have it delivered."

Eliza's temper flared. "Look, Ben. Thank you for this kindness. I just cannot accept it." She paused. "Even if I wanted to, my father wouldn't allow it."

Ben moved closer. "It wasn't so long ago that you didn't care what your father would allow. We were engaged to be married, Eliza."

"Quiet," she said, acutely aware that anyone who passed might hear and rumors would fly.

"No, Eliza, I won't be quiet," he told her. "We were engaged. I still want to marry you. I tried to say that in New Orleans, but it didn't come out right."

"It came out just fine." She set the package on the ground and walked away. Once again, he caught up to her, and this time he had nothing in his hands.

She let out a long sigh and picked up her pace, slowing only when she reached the next intersection.

"I'm having the package delivered," he said, "in case you were wondering."

"I wasn't."

"And I am going to marry you, Eliza Gentry."

She stopped short and faced him. "No."

He leaned forward to press a kiss against her cheek. "Soon. The arrangements have already been made."

Eliza's temper flared. "You never have understood that you don't always get what you want, Ben Barnhart."

"And you don't understand that I always do."

Eliza turned around and brushed past him without comment. The idea of spending time at the bookstore had been replaced by the need to get away from Ben. The need to go home.

She walked three blocks before she dared to take a look behind her to see if Ben was following her. He wasn't, but John Brady was.

"Did my father send you, Mr. Brady?" she demanded as she waited for him to catch up.

Wyatt offered a nod to Bryant, who was stationed across the street, to continue tailing Barnhart, and then he looked down at Eliza. "No, he did not."

She sighed. "I'm sorry. I shouldn't have assumed."

Crimson colored her cheeks. Whatever Barnhart said, she didn't like it.

He shrugged. "No harm done. I don't know where you're going, but I would be happy to walk you there."

"Thank you. I'm headed back to Alexander & Cornwell's Drug Store on Sixth Street," she said. "Justine is having a milkshake, and Mama was deep in conversation with a friend when I left them."

He measured his steps to hers and walked along in silence. At the next intersection he encountered another of his employees. True to his training, his man made quick eye contact and then moved on without acknowledging him.

The pair would follow Barnhart and report back. In the meantime, Wyatt had the best job of all: accompanying Eliza to wherever she was going.

When they reached the buggy, he waved away Mrs. Gentry's driver to lift Eliza up inside. "Do you care to join me?" she asked him.

"I think it would be better if I stood right here on the sidewalk," he said. "I've already had to explain my intention toward you to your father twice."

She shook her head. "Twice?"

"There was the horse race back into the city from River House, and then the adventure at the creek a few days ago." He paused and tried not to recall how good she felt in his arms when he caught her eavesdropping at the door. "Although you likely had some explaining to do as well. Was our conversation interesting enough to be worth it?"

Eliza slid a red curl away from her face and smiled. "I never heard a word, so no. It was not."

"Trust me, you didn't miss anything."

"Oh, didn't I?" She met his gaze. "Then why don't you enlighten me? What did you and my father talk about behind closed doors?"

"You know I can't tell you that." He shook his head. "Where would my security company be if the detectives didn't keep their meetings private?"

"Fair enough." Eliza pressed her palms onto her knees. "I'm sure you have other things you need to do besides babysitting me. I'll be fine here until Mama finishes her chatting and Justine tires of her milkshake."

"I'm sure you will, but I'll be staying anyway." He paused. "I couldn't help overhear you and the Barnhart fellow talking about an engagement. Was he pressing you again?"

"*Pressing* isn't the right word, but yes, he did bring that up." She looked around before returning her attention to him. "I don't know what he thinks he will accomplish by continuing to hound me about this. Or why he has to insist that I am meant to be his wife."

"He's been doing that since he was a child."

As soon as the words were out, Wyatt longed to reel them in. He'd been so careful not to let any of his former life cross his lips in

Eliza's presence. And now this.

She'd heard him, but her expression told him nothing.

"I do my research," he finally said.

"Then you are thorough. Because he has. I ignored it when we were young, but now it is different." She paused. "I wish my brothers were still on the ranch."

"Where are they?"

"Zeke has his own ranch on my grandparents' land east of San Antonio. He's married with three little ones."

"And your other brother?" At her look of surprise, he reminded her, "I do my research, remember?"

"Then you ought to know he's on a clipper ship to the Orient but has promised Papa once he returns he'll come back to work with him at the ranch." She paused. "I miss them both, but I especially miss Trey."

"Do you think he will become a rancher?"

Her grin was wistful. "The voyage he's on will take more than a year, possibly two depending on how many ports they visit. I think he'll obey Papa's wishes and come back for a while. Whether Papa will make him stay and become a rancher? That remains to be seen."

Wyatt had done his research, but that research had been limited to Eliza, not her brothers. He had never imagined Trey as a sailor off on an adventure to the Far East, and he'd certainly not expected Zeke to go off on his own.

"There you are," a woman's voice called. "Oh, and Mr. Brady is with you."

He looked over to see Mrs. Gentry heading their way with Justine in tow. When she arrived at the buggy, Wyatt helped her up and smiled down at the child. As he lifted her up to sit beside Eliza, he noticed she had two pieces of Mrs. Gentry's silver stuck in her hair.

A glance at Eliza told him she'd seen it too. They shared a smile, and he stepped back from the buggy.

"Thank you for entertaining our Eliza." Mrs. Gentry tapped on the back of the driver's seat, and they were off.

Justine swiveled to wave, and he returned the gesture. When he turned away from the street, he found Ben Barnhart watching him. A glance past the judge's son assured him that Bryant was still in place.

"She's mine," Barnhart said when he'd closed the distance between them. "Don't assume you have a chance with her, Brady." He paused. "If that's your name, which I doubt."

Men like Ben Barnhart had never been able to intimidate him. Rather, he found the attempt amusing.

"I don't see you having much luck with her either." He grinned. "And that would be based on what she just told me."

His mocking expression wavered slightly. Just as quickly as it disappeared, the sneer returned. "Of course she did. We're keeping things private until it's all done. I'm sure you can understand considering you're one of her father's employees. I'm not his favorite person, but I will be once the grandchildren start arriving."

If ever Wyatt wanted to punch Ben Barnhart, it was now. Instead, he shook his head and walked away.

"Brady," the judge's son called out, "I know you've got men following me. Just so you know, they're not invited to the wedding and neither are you."

Wyatt rounded the corner and then waited for Bryant to join him. "Where has he been?"

"Courthouse, a bookstore on Third, Driskill Hotel, and then he found Miss Gentry and followed her. That's where you picked up the trail and conversed with him."

He nodded. "Go see what he was up to at the courthouse and then catch up to the man following him now and report back. He's up to something."

June 26
Gentry Ranch

The night was dark with no moon to dim the stars overhead. Eliza waited until Mama and Papa went to bed and then slipped out to make her way across to the stables, where she found Red waiting for her.

By agreement, the ranch foreman went along on her excursions to see the stars from a remote part of the ranch ever since he caught her trying to go by herself last fall. She never knew whether he'd made the offer because of Papa or in spite of him, but she was glad to have him along.

Red threw a blanket in the back of the wagon and waited until Eliza climbed aboard to light the lantern. He eased out of the barn and down the path to the clearing at the top of the next hill. There, he stopped the wagon and silently tossed the blanket in the back, then picked up his rifle and doused the lantern.

On these nights when the new moon allowed every star in God's creation to blaze, Eliza climbed into the back of the wagon and lay looking up at the heavens until she tired of it. Or usually, until Red cleared his throat indicating he was tired of it.

Tonight no comets or meteorite showers were expected, but that didn't matter to Eliza. As long as she could remember, she'd loved to take in God's heavens and give back thanks that He allowed her the good sense to appreciate them.

Red made a sound. Not his usual signal, but still a noise she figured meant it was time to go.

"Just a few more minutes, please," she whispered.

Silence.

"Red, do you mind terribly?"

Still no response.

Though it was tempting to take his silence as agreement, Eliza sat up and turned around. Though the night was dark, she could see the outline of the ranch foreman as he sat slumped over on the bench.

She scrambled over the seat and fumbled for the lamp, all the while calling out his name. The lamp finally blazed. Eliza had to close her eyes to shield them from the burst of light.

When she opened them, she saw that she and Red were not alone. The man who stood beside the wagon wore the clothes of a ranch hand but the pale, freckled skin of a man who spent his days indoors rather than out under the Texas sun. A shock of fair hair stuck out beneath a hat that was obviously borrowed, for it was a size too big and tilted at an odd angle when he moved his head.

Eliza snatched up Red's shotgun from the floor of the wagon and aimed it at the stranger. "I don't know you."

"Don't matter," he said, "you're coming with me." Straightening his hat, he glanced at Red. "Looks like your friend is dead."

"He's not," she exclaimed, her heart racing. "He's just suffered some sort of—"

"Look, lady, I've seen dead men, and he's dead." He shrugged. "Saves me from shooting him and attracting attention."

Her finger pressed against the trigger. The only shooting that would happen tonight would be from her rifle.

Eliza held the gun steady. "Why would you expect me to go with you when I could shoot you where you stand?"

"Because we have your brother Trey. You don't want him to end up like your pal here, do you?"

CHAPTER 14

June 27

It wasn't yet full daylight, yet William Gentry was pacing the confines of his office like a caged panther when Wyatt arrived. Mrs. Gentry sat quietly dabbing her eyes in a chair beneath the map of the Chisholm Trail. Neither looked as if they had slept in quite some time.

"I got your message," Wyatt said. "Something happened to Red?"

"Close the door," was the boss's immediate response as he paused behind his desk.

Wyatt complied and turned to face Mr. Gentry. "How can I help?"

"Where was Ben Barnhart last night?" he demanded.

"In his room at the Driskill where he's been every night this week. If he had so much as sneezed, I would know about it." Wyatt paused. "Why?"

A look passed between husband and wife. "Eliza is missing," Mrs. Gentry said, her voice so soft he wasn't sure he'd heard correctly.

"One of my men was out on patrol out on the western range and found Red. Thought he was dead, and he was close to it, but the doc says it was some sort of apoplectic episode. All I could get out of him was that he drove Eliza out in the wagon to look at the stars. That's all he remembers."

"Where is he?"

"Doc's with him in the bunkhouse. I tried to bring him up here and set him up in a nice room, but the old coot just wanted his own bunk." Mr. Gentry chuckled, though there was no humor in the sound. "That's not true. He didn't want his bunk either. It took the doc giving him a dose of something to make him sleep in order to keep him from joining the search party."

That sounded like Red. The man was not only ageless but also the toughest cowboy he'd ever met.

"Did Miss Gentry give any indication that she might leave before last night? Was there an argument of any kind?" His gaze went from Eliza's mother to her father. "Anything?"

"Nothing." He shrugged. "I knew she'd be out last night. I doubt she realized I kept such close tabs on her, but after Red came to me to say he'd caught Eliza taking a wagon from the barn after midnight last fall, I figured it was easier to let her do what she would do but put Red in charge of keeping her safe. He said she didn't seem to mind."

Wyatt shook his head. "So there was a regular arrangement? Something that anyone who was watching would know to expect?"

"Every new moon, so yes, just about the same time each month. Red said they rarely said a word. She'd show up at the barn and he'd throw a blanket in the back of the wagon. When they got to that hill over at the western range, he'd sit there with his rifle at the ready and she'd climb into the back of the wagon and do whatever it is she did."

"She counted falling stars," he said. "And looked for whatever new constellation she'd learned about in those books she reads."

Mrs. Gentry smiled. "You always did know her better than any of us."

Wyatt let that statement settle deep inside, tucking it in with the other thoughts that had no business surfacing. "She was a good friend to me."

"Speaking of books," Mr. Gentry said abruptly. "There was a delivery for her yesterday afternoon. A fellow from Gammel's in Austin brought it."

"That's a long way for a bookstore delivery," Wyatt said.

"I thought so too, so I opened it to see what was inside." He nodded to the stack of four books on the corner of his desk. "It was more of those astronomy books Eliza likes."

"May I inspect them?"

At the boss's nod, he walked over and picked up *The Heavens* by Amédée Guillemin, the volume at the top of the stack. The spine was black, the cover dark blue leather the color of a night sky. Across the top was a comet falling from the sky depicted in gold leaf. Below, a rising sun, also in gold, spread its rays over the water. In between a moon and golden stars danced across the sun's rays.

Immediately he was transported back to a time when he'd swept floors for a month in order to earn enough money from old Mr. Gammel to buy this book. He'd told Eliza it was to make amends when he'd given it to her before they left for the trail, but the truth of it was he'd given it to her to keep his pa from throwing it into the fire as he'd threatened to do.

Wyatt opened to the flyleaf where an illustration of Donati's Comet from October 4, 1859, decorated the page and then looked up at Mr. Gentry. "She already owns this book."

The older man's brows rose. "How do you know this?"

"I just do," he said. "Why would she buy another one?"

"Maybe she was replacing a lost copy." Mrs. Gentry rose. "I'll go check and see if she still has it on her shelf."

"Yes, thank you, dear." He waited until his wife was gone and the door closed behind her before speaking again. "Turn to the last page. There's an inscription."

Wyatt thumbed through the pages until he reached the end of

the book. There on page 524 in the margin next to an appendix titled *"Very Unequal Stars"* was a note written by what he would guess from the penmanship was a masculine hand.

"Tonight under the stars. Tomorrow as my wife."

It was signed *"BB."*

Ben Barnhart.

His blood ran cold, but he kept his expression neutral as he looked up at Mr. Gentry. "What do you make of this?"

The older man's shoulders sagged. Before he spoke, he sank into the chair behind his desk. In that moment, he appeared older than he'd ever looked.

"I think she ran off with him."

Wyatt closed the book and replaced it on the stack. "Is there anything else in the other books?"

"Nothing." He leaned forward and rested his palms on the desk. "I haven't told her mother. I don't know how."

He let out a long breath. "One of my men followed Barnhart into the courthouse last week. Considering his father is a judge, it didn't raise any concern for me. When he told me he didn't go into his father's office or his courtroom, I just figured either my man was mistaken or father and son met elsewhere in the building."

"But now it's possible he could have been swearing out a marriage license," Eliza's father said on an exhale of breath.

"It is possible," Wyatt agreed.

The door opened and Mrs. Gentry stepped inside with a book in her hand. "You're right. She does have a copy of this book, and it appears to have been well loved." She stopped short. "What? Something's wrong. Tell me what it is, William."

Wyatt met the older man's steady gaze. "I'll just be going now. I'll investigate this thoroughly and report back as soon as I know anything."

Mr. Gentry rose and stepped around the desk to offer his

outstretched hand. "You're a good man, Wyatt Creed. Thank you."

Wyatt Creed.

He hadn't heard his full name spoken aloud in almost ten years. Unable to respond, he settled for a nod of his head and a polite good-bye to Eliza's mama.

Once outside, he stepped into the golden sunrise of a new day. Like the drawing on the cover, the rays reached up to where the last reminder of the night appeared in the form of a few errant stars. There was no sliver of moon, but there would be tomorrow.

And the next night. And the next until the moon was full. Then it would reverse the process to disappear once more.

Why he considered all of this as he swung his foot over the saddle, Wyatt couldn't say. Perhaps thinking about the things Eliza enjoyed would make her absence less real.

For as much as she was gone from her home today, he knew in his heart that she was gone from this family as well.

He'd seen her performance at River House. Watched her rebuff the repugnant judge's son. But he'd also seen her meet him just last week on the street outside the Driskill. Barnhart had a package with him. She had accepted it then returned it to him.

Was that so she would know what to expect when it was delivered?

Wyatt thought on that as he decided to bypass the bunkhouse where Red was recuperating. He could speak with the ranch foreman another day. First he needed to find Ben Barnhart and have a word with him.

Barnhart was at his usual table in the Driskill dining room. Built as a showplace for the cattle baron Colonel Driskill, no expense had been spared in the hotel's construction. The room, where more deals were made than on the floors of the state capitol down the road, was as elegantly furnished as any restaurant in Paris, London, or New York. The difference was the patrons: a mix of Texas elite and plainly dressed ranchers who were wealthier than any of the finer folk.

When Wyatt walked in, the man had the audacity to grin. He'd obviously been expected.

"Care to join me, Brady?" he said. "That is what they call you now, isn't it?"

Wyatt's senses were already on alert. The comment made him slowly press his palm to the revolver strapped to his side.

"Do you actually plan to shoot me here in the dining room of the finest hotel in town? I never figured you had a flair for the dramatic, but maybe you're different now." The judge's son laughed. "It wouldn't be the first thing about you that has changed."

"You always did talk before you knew what you were saying, Barnhart."

A shrug. "Sit down. Or do you want the governor to wonder what's going on over here?"

He looked over in the direction that Ben had nodded and found Sul Ross sitting at a large table with a half dozen associates. Most were deep in conversation, but the governor was watching them closely. So were the three men whom Wyatt easily identified as security detectives.

Ben gave the older man a nod, and it was returned. That was enough for Wyatt. He sat and put on a cordial face. It was better to be assumed a friend of this man than to be removed by the governor's security men as a threat, even if it galled him to be associated with a Barnhart.

As soon as he sat down, a waiter came over to offer coffee. "Nothing for me," Wyatt said, waving him away.

"He'll have what I'm drinking," Ben told him. "And privacy after that."

The waiter hurried away with a nod. Wyatt returned his attention to Ben, allowing the fool a minute to speak in case he had a mind to do so.

"I assume you're looking for my bride. She's indisposed."

Wyatt managed not to wince at the statement. Several responses rose up. "No, but her father is," he said instead.

"I see. And you aren't? That's interesting." He paused while the waiter returned with a cup of coffee and quickly walked away. "I thought you'd be pining away for the woman you can never have. And yes, I know all about your deal with her father."

Wyatt's hand curled around his revolver under the table. If he kept his expression neutral, it was a miracle.

Barnhart smiled. "You're wondering how I knew it was you." He shrugged and gestured to his neck. "The scar. I believe your father's explanation was that if he'd been aiming, you'd be dead, but he was just trying to teach you a lesson."

Pausing, he seemed to be waiting for a response. Wyatt refused to give one.

"Does she know?" Ben finally asked him.

"Where is she?"

He sat back, unable to hide his disappointment that Wyatt hadn't taken the bait. A moment later his cordial expression returned. "I told you. She's indisposed. And if you're here on behalf of her father to haul her back home to the ranch, it's too late. She's mine now."

"Yours." He leaned back in his chair. "How do you figure? You call her your bride, but the woman I know never would have willingly married you."

A smile rose. "And yet she did. This morning before dawn, actually."

"You're lying."

"Believe me or not, but it's the truth. You'd be surprised what the son of a judge can get done at the courthouse when he's in a hurry." He shrugged. "Besides, you know I was there last week, and I would wager a guess that your man told you I didn't go there to see my father. What do you figure I did?"

"She despises you."

"Because of that scene she made at River House?" He chuckled. "You don't know her like I do. She's been that way for years."

Anger told him to argue. To explain to this idiot that Eliza Gentry was not that way at all. But to argue was to give in and break the promise that had kept him alive.

He'd never do that.

"No," was all he could say without allowing the torrent of words he wanted to add.

"Then why did she marry me? Tell me that."

He shifted positions and sorted through the many reasons he shouldn't shoot this man right here in front of the governor. "She didn't," he said once good sense won out.

"We're talking in circles now. I say she did. You say she didn't." He shrugged. "I guess it will all come down to what my wife says when she—" He looked up. "Oh, there she is now."

CHAPTER 15

Eliza walked into the dining room at the appointed time and then stuttered to a halt. What was John Brady doing having breakfast with Ben?

She sucked in a deep breath and let it out slowly. Her brother's life depended on how well she conducted herself in public this morning. So she squared her shoulders and smiled, then walked across the Driskill's half-filled dining room as if she owned the place.

"Miss Gentry," someone called, and she looked over to see Governor Ross motioning her toward him.

"Good morning, Governor," she said when she reached his table.

After a few excruciating minutes of pleasant small talk, Eliza returned to her path to the table where Ben and Mr. Brady were waiting.

She tried not to look around. Ben had told her the kidnappers had planted a man in this room to watch her. If she failed to convince him, her brother would be lost to her forever.

"Mr. Brady," she said with what she hoped would be a smile. "Ben didn't tell me you would be joining us this morning."

"I've come from your father's ranch," he told her, green eyes watching her far too closely for comfort. "Your parents are heartbroken."

Eliza let out another long breath and toyed with the napkin on the table in front of her. Tears threatened, but somehow she held them back.

"Red and Papa knew one another before he married Mama, so of course he would be devastated to lose him," she finally said.

"Red is going to be fine," the security detective said.

Eliza closed her eyes and gave thanks, then opened them again. "I'm so very glad to hear this. He looked like he was dead. His eyes were closed, and I didn't have time to check to see if he was breathing, but—"

"Why is that?" the detective asked.

She shook her head. "I'm sorry, what?"

"Why didn't you have time to check on a man who was like a second father to you?" He leaned back in his chair. "You must have had to leave in an extreme hurry."

"Good news on old Red," Ben interjected. "He never liked me much, but I couldn't find fault with him on the trail. He always treated me like everyone else." He paused. "What was the problem?"

"Apoplectic episode of some kind is what the doctor thinks. He's supposed to get better." Mr. Brady's gaze collided with hers. "Was it always the plan to have Red drive you out to the far side of the ranch and then leave him there to run off with this man, or did that just evolve in the moment?"

"Do not answer him," Ben snapped, pounding his fist on the table.

Eliza gasped and several diners looked over in their direction. A waiter came running. "Is there a problem, Mr. Barnhart?"

"I think our guest was just leaving," he said. "The only problem will be if he doesn't."

"Then there won't be a problem." Mr. Brady pushed back from the table and stood. "You can always go home, Miss Gentry."

"That's Mrs. Barnhart, isn't it, dear?"

She looked up into those kind green eyes—those familiar

eyes—and she knew she couldn't fool him. Yet she tried.

"As of this morning, yes."

Ben's triumphant expression lasted until the security detective had disappeared out into the lobby. Only then did he wipe the smile off his face.

"Excellent performance, Eliza." He reached over to take her hand and then lifted it to his lips. "Anyone who was watching would see how very much in love we are."

Her stomach turned a flip but she kept her smile in place. "Who is watching, Ben? Have you figured it out?"

"Not yet, but my men are on it. The only way I was able to negotiate on your behalf was to convince them I was your husband," he reminded her. "If your father had agreed to their demands, you wouldn't have been the next one kidnapped and we wouldn't be sitting here now."

"That doesn't sound like something Papa would do, Ben. I'm not sure I believe it. He loves us so. Why would he possibly jeopardize the life of the son who is named after him? It just makes no sense."

Ben released her hand and shifted positions. "Darling, I can't speak for what your father would do. I can only tell you what I was told he has done."

"I suppose so." She offered him a smile. "I don't know how your men managed to stop the kidnapping, but I am grateful."

"As am I." Ben squeezed her hand. "I cannot imagine a world without you in it, my love."

"How long will we have to pretend?" she asked.

"As long as it takes," was Ben's cryptic response. "Now, I have some things to attend to. I've arranged a suite for you next to mine. There's a door between them so you can easily find me if you need me."

"Why would I do that?"

He chuckled. "All right. Well then, there's a door between our suites, and that ought to convince anyone who wonders why a newly married husband and wife would have separate rooms."

Eliza relaxed a notch. "As long as it is only the kidnappers we are trying to convince. I would be horrified if anyone actually thought we were married."

His expression fell. "I'm going to try not to take offense, Eliza. Would being married to me be the worst thing in the world?"

"No, of course not," she said. "The worst thing in the world would be to lose my brother. I would do anything to save him."

Ben's smile returned. "That's what I'm counting on."

❧

Even on a swift horse, the ride back to the Gentry ranch seemed far too slow. When he finally arrived, Wyatt found the ranch swarming with activity. The sheriff had come and gone, leaving a man behind just in case.

Wyatt made his way through the gamut of cowboys and lawmen who milled around on the lawn. "You there," someone called, and he saw it was Red.

The older man waved him over, and though he wanted desperately to speak with William Gentry, he honored the ranch foreman's wish and detoured to the porch adjacent to the bunkhouse.

Red was seated in a rocker that had obviously been brought over from the main house. A bowl of soup sat beside him, and coffee steamed in one of Mrs. Gentry's fine china cups.

"What's the news on Miss Eliza?" he asked, his eyes alert but his voice slow and measured. "And stop staring to try and figure out what kind of palsy I've ended up with. Doc says other than the fact I might not be able to smile even and the ladies will think my left eye is winking at them, I'll be just fine."

"I'm glad to hear it. I just came from speaking with Eliza." At the older man's surprised expression, he continued. "She's alive and well, and when I left them she was having breakfast with Ben Barnhart at the Driskill Hotel."

Red looked away and muttered a string of words that he never would have said in front of a female. Then he looked back at Wyatt.

"Did he take her?" Wyatt asked.

"His wasn't the voice I heard. That belonged to someone else. Doesn't mean he wasn't behind it though." He paused, his expression pained. "If I could've just stopped them. I was there, but—"

"Don't, Red. It couldn't be helped."

"I heard that man tell Eliza it was good I'd died of natural causes because otherwise he was going to have to shoot me." He looked up at Wyatt. "I'd have shot him first if I'd had the chance."

"Wasn't supposed to happen that way." Wyatt nodded toward the ranch house. "Have you spoken to the boss?"

"Not since I finally convinced the doc to quit pestering me and go home." He shifted positions. "Don't plan to until that circus over there goes home. Will has his hands full already. He don't need me underfoot. Go on and tell him what you know."

With a nod, he bid Red goodbye and headed for the ranch house. The sheriff's deputy met him at the door and refused to allow him inside.

"He will want to see me," Wyatt told him.

The deputy returned a few minutes later and motioned for Wyatt to follow. He found Eliza's parents in the parlor with Justine. Mrs. Gentry rose but remained in place as her husband stalked over to Wyatt.

The girl ran across the room to launch herself into his arms. "Did you bring Eliza back?" she asked, her eyes wide beneath the brim of a straw hat that was meant for a much older person. "I miss her terribly."

"No, Justine, I'm afraid I didn't."

The child slid down and ran back to her aunt. Then she buried her face in Mrs. Gentry's skirt and began to wail.

"You have news." A statement, not a question, from William Gentry.

"I have."

He glanced over his shoulder. "Excuse us, dear."

Wyatt followed the rancher into his office and waited once again until the door was closed and the older man was seated behind his desk. "Did you find her?"

With anyone else, he might have given a gentle answer, but Wyatt knew this man too well to do that. "She's with Ben Barnhart at the Driskill Hotel. They were having breakfast when I left."

The color in his face drained. "Barnhart wanted to be sure he was seen with her."

"They claim to be married, sir."

He leaned back in his chair and closed his eyes, dropping his hands into his lap. After a few minutes he opened his eyes again. "Do you believe them?"

"I haven't decided."

He swiped at his eyes with the back of his hand. "Did she look happy?"

Wyatt had to think about it. "Not particularly. But that might have been due to the circumstances. She did run off. That has to make a person a little bit nervous. She was relieved that Red wasn't dead."

Mr. Gentry let out a long breath. "How did this happen?"

Wyatt shifted positions and studied his hands. Finally, he looked up. "I've tried to piece it all together, and I don't know yet. It just doesn't add up."

"No, it doesn't." He shook his head. "I don't know how I will tell her mother."

"Why don't you hold off on that, sir? Keep her home and don't let anyone come to the ranch who might pass on gossip." He shrugged. "I have a feeling all the facts will come out if given time."

A knock at the door interrupted any response. The same deputy who had escorted Wyatt in walked over to Mr. Gentry and whispered something.

"Put a hat on him and hide his face as best you can. I'll speak with him out there." He gestured out the window to a table and chairs on the back porch. "Whatever you do, do not let my wife know he is here."

Once the deputy was gone, Mr. Gentry turned to Wyatt. "My men intercepted Ben Barnhart at the gate. He wants to see me."

"And you're meeting him outside there," Wyatt supplied as he looked over the situation.

The window was flanked by curtains that were currently open to allow sunlight in but could be closed. The windowpanes were thick, but the sash could be raised to allow anyone in the office to hear what was happening on the other side clearly.

"I'll expect you to be listening," Mr. Gentry said. "Now tell me how I need to handle this and what you think I need to ask him."

"What is it you want from him?" he asked out of habit.

"I don't want a thing from him except my daughter," he snapped. "I just want Eliza home again."

"You understand they very well may be married," Wyatt said carefully. "How will you handle that if it's true?"

The older man's expression went cold. "I will always love my daughter, but if she has chosen a Barnhart over this family, then I don't know how I will forgive her." He paused. "Or if I can."

"Are you sure about that, sir?"

He shook his head. "You were there, son. You know the kind of man Ben Barnhart is. He killed your father, and you yourself said he's very likely involved with counterfeiters and who knows what else. Would you have me welcome him into my family?"

Wyatt took a deep breath and set aside all the reasons he agreed with William Gentry to offer a word of warning. "She is your daughter, sir. Your flesh and blood. What if she realizes she has made a mistake and wants to come home?"

He looked over at the map of the Chisholm Trail. "Sometimes living with your mistakes is the best way to learn. Now what else do I need to make sure I say or do?"

By the time Wyatt had finished briefing Eliza's father, the deputy had returned. "They're bringing Barnhart around to the back so the missus doesn't catch sight of him. Want me to have someone keep an eye on him while he's with you?"

"I want to speak with him privately," he told the deputy, "but it wouldn't hurt to have eyes on Barnhart from a distance. If you'd do that yourself, I'd be much obliged."

The deputy nodded. "I will, sir."

Once the lawman had departed, William Gentry walked over to the window and opened it, then focused his attention on Wyatt. A look passed between them. No words of instruction were necessary. He knew what to do.

Eliza's father stepped around the desk to walk toward the door. Then he stopped short and turned around.

"Something wrong?" Wyatt asked.

Mr. Gentry pressed past him to return to his desk and leave his pistol there. A look passed between them. Then Eliza's father shook his head and walked toward the door.

CHAPTER 16

Wyatt closed the curtains and took his place on the floor behind the desk. Even if a stiff wind blew through and lifted them out of place, there would be no evidence he was there.

The office door opened, and Wyatt held his breath. No one was supposed to come in here without the boss. That was an unbreakable rule in the Gentry house.

He palmed his pistol and waited for the intruder to show himself. Light steps moved toward the desk and halted.

A moment later Justine peered around the edge of the desk. Though she'd been dressed like a normal nine-year-old when he saw her in the parlor earlier, now she wore a pale green ball gown several sizes too large that was very likely borrowed from Mrs. Gentry or Eliza. White gloves covered her hands, and a bridal veil tucked into her ponytail completed the ensemble.

"What are you doing here?" she whispered.

"I could ask you the same thing." He slid out of his hiding place and stood. Turning the girl around, he marched her to the door. "You are not supposed to be in here when Mr. Gentry isn't here."

She halted just before the hallway and looked up at him with a suspicious expression. "Neither are you."

"That is where you're wrong. He asked me to wait for him here while he had a meeting."

Her expression went solemn. "I know. He's meeting the man Eliza married. I don't like him."

"That seems to be a popular opinion around here."

She shrugged. "I told Trey not to trust him with that necklace. I bet he stole it."

"What necklace?"

Justine gestured to her neck. "The one Trey always wore since he was young. I heard them talking the night before Trey went off on that ship to sail to China for a year. He said he didn't want anything to happen to his prize possession so Ben ought to give it to Eliza for him."

Wyatt glanced back at the window to be sure no one had arrived on the porch yet and then turned back to Justine. "Why didn't he just give it directly to Eliza?"

"He tried, but she wouldn't take it. She said he had to keep it because then every time he wore it he would think about home and family and he wouldn't want to stay gone too long. I asked her where it was the next time I thought about it, but she said Trey was wearing it. We argued about that, and she didn't believe me."

It made no sense that Ben Barnhart would want a basically worthless shark's tooth that Trey had been wearing since he was ten. "If Eliza didn't believe you, why should I?"

Justine didn't look the least bit bothered by the question. "Because it happened and I heard it. After Eliza and I went up to bed, I heard Trey talking to that man outside on the porch. That's what they said."

Who knew what Ben might be doing with Trey's necklace? Probably nothing, but with a Barnhart one never knew.

Wyatt mentally filed away the information for future use. He'd learned that any given random fact could potentially be what broke a case wide open.

"Thank you for telling me this, but you must leave now." He moved her out into the hallway. "I have to wait for your uncle, and you probably should put that ball gown and veil back where you found them before Mrs. Gentry sees them." He paused for effect. "They're her favorites."

Justine's eyes widened. "Are they? I didn't think she would notice."

He glanced past her, then looked down at the girl again. "Oh, trust me. She will notice. Now scoot."

She took off running, holding the dress up with one hand and her veil with the other. This time when the door shut, Wyatt made sure to turn the key and lock it. He barely made it back to his listening post before he heard several sets of boots scuffling across the wood planks of the porch.

"Thank you, Deputy. I'll signal when it's time for you to escort him off the property," Mr. Gentry said.

One set of boots walked away and left the porch, followed by the sound of chair legs scraping over wood. Finally, there was silence.

The wind lifted the edge of the curtain, revealing a slice of blue sky off in the distance. Wyatt shrank farther down out of the way and waited for the men to begin speaking.

"Before you say anything," Eliza's father began, "I want you to know that the deputy over there believes you're not worth the bullet it would take to shoot you, but I told him I'd look the other way if he changed his mind."

Ben's chuckle finally split the silence that followed. "You're good at looking the other way, aren't you, old man?"

A scrape of boots, a soft thud, and then the sound of a chair turning over followed. Ben laughed again, but this time his laughter held no humor.

"I don't suppose your deputy friend would admit to seeing you punch me just now."

Another scrape of boots and William Gentry was presumably back in his chair. "Frankly, I don't care if he does or he doesn't. And you can go ahead and brag to whoever you'd like that Eliza's pa gave you that black eye."

"I'll mention that to your daughter when I get back to the hotel." Silence fell between them.

"Look," Ben finally said. "I didn't expect you'd be happy to see me, so I won't hold that punch against you."

A chair squeaked, and Wyatt assumed the older man was shifting positions. "I don't care if you do. Did my daughter send you?"

"She has no idea I'm here." Ben paused. "Although she will probably figure out where I've been when she sees me."

"Oh, come on, Barnhart. I can't be the only man who wants to punch you. Just get on with whatever brings you here so you can leave again. I only have so much tolerance for sitting here being civil."

"I could argue civility with you, sir, but I won't." The sound of paper rustling drifted toward Wyatt on the breeze. "I'll just leave you with a look at this."

"What is it?"

"The license authorizing my marriage to your daughter."

For a moment, silence fell between the men on the porch. Wyatt shifted positions and waited.

"It's legal," Ben added.

"Why'd you do this?" William Gentry asked, his voice rough. "I let you get away with murder when you were just a boy, and this is how you repay that? You steal my daughter away in the middle of the night and would've killed Red if the good Lord hadn't seen fit to make it look like he was already gone."

"Don't you see, old man? That's exactly why I had to marry her."

"I don't follow."

"You weren't there when Creed was shot. You didn't see me pull the trigger, and yet you think you let me get away with murder. How do you know it wasn't Wyatt? His pa beat him all the time when he was drinking, and everybody in camp saw he was drinking that night."

"Because Wyatt Creed didn't do it. If he was going to kill W. C. Creed, he would have done it long before that night, and he sure wouldn't have done it on a trail ride with a dozen and a half others nearby. You, on the other hand, were and always have been possessed of a shortage of temper and good sense."

"You have it all figured out, don't you?"

"WC probably said something you didn't like, so you shot him. That's what I believe." He paused. "Why involve Eliza nine years down the road?"

"Because Wyatt Creed isn't dead. I sat across the table from him at the Driskill Hotel this morning." He laughed. "You look surprised. Did you think I wouldn't know it was him? That scar on his neck gave him away. Well, that and the way he makes moon eyes every time he's around Eliza. And that is why I had to marry her. She doesn't know yet, but she will figure it out eventually."

Wyatt's fingers curled. It took everything he had to remain in place.

"You're talking nonsense," Mr. Gentry told Ben. "Pure nonsense."

"Am I? You're treading dangerous ground encouraging Creed to spend time around Eliza. She's a smart girl. It wouldn't have taken long until she figured it out too. Or he told her."

"He wouldn't have. In exchange for his life, Wyatt made a promise to me, and he's kept it."

"But you didn't keep your side of the deal, did you, Gentry? When you hired him to watch your wife and daughter in New Orleans, you were hoping Eliza would recognize her old friend, weren't you?"

"No, I didn't think she would. But I knew how to find him. I always did. I made him promise that too. And when it came to hiring someone to keep you away from Eliza, I couldn't think of anyone better suited for the job."

"Yet he failed."

Three words that struck Wyatt in the gut. He had failed. He'd bet that keeping tabs on Ben would keep him away from Eliza, and he was wrong.

"But see," Ben continued, "I had to marry Eliza because if I hadn't, he would have. She might not know who she was really marrying, but she would have married him. Then eventually his secret would have come out. They always do between husbands and wives. Once that happened, where would that leave me? You know your daughter. Do you believe for a minute that she would allow the man she loves to remain accused of a crime he didn't commit?"

"No," Eliza's father said. "She wouldn't stand for it."

A chair scraped across wood. "Now that she's married to me, I hope you don't go entertaining any thoughts of telling the story of what happened out on the trail that night. I've got a campaign to run, and it would be a pity if I had to claim that I had no idea my wife's father let a murderer get away."

"But I did," he said. "You."

"You're hardheaded but you're smart, Gentry. Just let it be. Stay away from my wife, and I won't say a word about who Detective John Brady really is. Nor will I mention that you, Wyatt, and my wife conspired to cover up a murder."

"You wouldn't."

"I would," Ben said. "And the word of a state senator will be taken more seriously than the word of a man who helped his daughter's friend get away with murder. You'd all go to jail, Eliza included. Is that what you want for your precious daughter?"

"You're not a senator yet," William Gentry snapped. "And if I have anything to do with it, you won't be."

"Oh, that's too bad. I would think you had more concern for your future grandchildren than to see their mother in jail."

Wyatt heard paper crumpling. "Take this license and go," Eliza's father told him. "You've made your point."

"I hope I have." Ben paused. "I realize there's nothing I can say to Eliza to keep her away from her family, so I will leave that up to you."

"What do you mean?"

"If you love your daughter and want the best for her, you will figure out a way to convince her that she's better off with me than you."

"And just how do you expect I will manage to tell her mother she's lost the only daughter she has?"

The anguish in William Gentry's voice was heart wrenching. Again Wyatt had to force himself to remain in place when everything in him wanted to go after Ben Barnhart.

"Does she know what happened on the trail nine years ago?"

The curtain rose and fell on a breeze, once again allowing Wyatt a glimpse of the sky above. He waited to see how Eliza's father would respond.

"I told Susanna everything."

"Then it's your fault my wife can't see her mama. You'll explain it just fine, I'm sure."

"Deputy," he called, "escort this man out while he's still walking. I won't be responsible for what happens to him if you don't get him out of my sight immediately."

CHAPTER 17

Eliza paced the confines of her suite at the Driskill Hotel with a nervous energy she could not seem to rid herself of. Even the beautifully appointed room and the lunch Ben had sent up before he left to meet with the kidnappers had not settled her restlessness.

Before he left, Ben had assured her everything would be fine. Trey would be returned safe, and she could go back to her life at the ranch.

Now she wasn't so certain. Something was wrong. Something she couldn't quite put her finger on.

She went to the window and lifted the sash. The sounds from the street four floors below rose up to greet her.

"Are you considering jumping? It's a long way down."

Eliza gasped and turned around to see Ben standing in the doorway that connected their rooms. "That door was locked."

He retrieved a key from his pocket and held it up. "I assured management it must have been some sort of mistake when I couldn't get into my wife's bedchamber from my own. They were kind enough to give me a key."

She sank down to rest on the windowsill, her heart still beating rapidly. Ben's having a key to her suite was completely unacceptable, but if she would be leaving today for home, it meant nothing.

"Tell me everything that happened," she demanded. "Have they released Trey?"

"Trey is fine." He moved into the room and pocketed the key once more. "He'll be home eventually."

Eliza took in his casual stance. The expression on his face that told her something else was going on. Something she had not been privy to.

"Eventually?" She shook her head. "What does that mean?"

"Stop worrying, Eliza. I have it all under control. Everything went exactly as planned." He walked over to lift the silver cloche covering her plate on the lunch tray and then looked over at her. "You didn't touch anything. Are you ill?"

She shrugged. "I wasn't hungry. If everything is under control, I suppose I ought to go back home. There's no more need for me to pretend we're married if the kidnappers have been handled."

Ben replaced the cloche and walked toward the door that divided their suites without a response. Just before he shut the door, she called to him.

"Answer me," she demanded as she stood and headed in his direction. "Is it safe for me to return home now?"

"No, Eliza. According to your father, you can never return home."

Eliza stalled in her steps. "What are you talking about?"

"It's easier to show you. Stay right there." He disappeared into his suite and returned a moment later with a piece of paper that looked as if it had been crumpled and then flattened again. "Now that we're married and you're a Barnhart, your home is with me. He was clear about that, and I agree with him. So I've been looking at properties near the governor's mansion that should be satisfactory for us."

"Wait, what?" She shook her head. "Are you joking?"

"I'm quite serious. My campaign is launching soon, and I'll need to be settled soon. It would help if there was a baby on the way, but these things do take time."

Her temper spiked. "That's enough, Ben. Where is my brother, and no more games and deception."

He placed the paper on the table next to the door and shrugged. "Your brother is fine. We are legally married. You are a Barnhart. That's about as plain as I can make it. No games or deception. Just the facts."

"No. Our marriage was a farce, Ben. I agreed to pretend to be married to you so you could negotiate with the men who were holding Trey hostage. There was no real marriage."

His smile caused her stomach to churn. "Beautiful Eliza," he said gently. "There were no kidnappers. Trey is still off on his adventures to the Far East, or at least he was as of the last letter I received from him. He's a good friend, you know, so when he asked me to keep his cherished shark's tooth necklace safe for him while he was away, of course I agreed."

"You said that necklace was the kidnappers' proof he was taken."

"I said what I had to say at the time. What matters is we are married, just as you told that detective Brady this morning. See, you didn't lie to the detective you like so much. That should make you feel better."

Eliza sank onto the nearest chair, her knees weak. "You made all of this up? How is that possible? I was kidnapped by a man I've never seen before, and Red might have been shot if he hadn't had that apoplectic episode."

"We'll have a good marriage if you allow it to be."

Again her temper rose. "That is your response? We don't have a marriage, Ben. Stop saying that."

"Oh, but we do, and there's the proof." He nodded to the paper still sitting on the table. "You signed it yourself, dear. There will be a brief mention of it in the *Statesman* tomorrow. I asked them to hold off for a few days to give us time to inform our families of the happy news."

"No," she said again. "There is no happy news. I did not sign anything."

"You're overwrought. That's understandable."

He moved closer, pinning her to the chair as he stood over her. His hand cupped her jaw. His smile was beautiful and deadly all at the same time. Had she not known this man from childhood and been acutely aware of what he was capable of, she might have thought him handsome.

"Back away," she told him through gritted teeth.

"Rest, dear. In time you'll get used to the idea." He paused to lower his lips to touch hers. "Our children will be beautiful, Eliza. Just like you."

She slipped out from under his arm and stormed out of the room without a backward glance. Once she was down in the lobby, good sense caught up to her and she made her way back up to her suite.

The room was empty and the door to Ben's suite still open. She looked inside to find it empty as well.

Glancing down, she spied the crumpled paper on the table and snatched it up. Whatever Ben Barnhart was up to, he would not get away with it.

Her first stop that afternoon was the Travis County courthouse where she would determine whether the paper in her hands was legitimate. If it was, then she would lodge a complaint that her signature had been forged.

After waiting a few minutes, the clerk ushered her into his office. The room was a tiny space just bigger than the maid's room at the home in New Orleans, and it held only one small window with a view of an alley behind it.

Immediately Eliza felt claustrophobic. Ignoring the desire to bolt and run, she sat down across from the older man who took the chair on the other side of the desk. He looked over the license and then set it down on the desk between them.

"How can I help you?" he asked.

She decided to keep the question simple and direct. "Is this a legitimate license or is it a forgery?"

"I am only going on what I see in front of me, but I assure you this indeed appears to be a document issued by this office. The Travis County clerk uses a particular type of paper for marriage licenses and the watermark is showing right there in the center, so that would settle the question for me. You cannot just walk in off the street and buy this paper anywhere."

"Where could it be purchased?"

"Nowhere that I know of. We order straight from a paper supplier in. . ." He shook his head. "Never mind about that. It's not for sale in stores, I can assure you. Is there a problem, Mrs. Barnhart?" he asked, his expression kind and his gold wire-framed spectacles perched on the end of his nose. "And congratulations on your recent marriage."

"This document is a forgery." She handed him the marriage license. "I am not married. I did not sign it. And that is the problem."

"But you did," he said after adjusting his spectacles to examine the paper again. "Right there. It says your name."

"It does, but I didn't see this until an hour ago. Someone signed in my place."

Eliza waited for a response, but the clerk seemed preoccupied studying the paper. Finally, he handed the document back to her. Still he said nothing.

"Well?" she said as she placed the bogus license on the desk between them. "Are you going to do something about it?"

He sat back in his chair and regarded her with an unreadable expression. "I knew your daddy well before you and your brothers were born, and I've been acquainted with the judge and his wife since before they were both knee high to a grasshopper, as was I. So I say this with respect to both families."

"All right," she said slowly.

"I cannot find any fault with that document other than someone crumpled it, and the thing ought to have been treated with more respect considering what it is. Beyond that, it looks legitimate, and I have to consider it so."

"But it isn't," she said, her voice rising. "I told you. I did not sign this. My supposed husband presented it to me an hour ago."

Crimson climbed into his cheeks the same way it did in papa's when he was irritated. She didn't care.

"And furthermore," Eliza continued, "if you will hand me a paper and pen, I will show you that my signature looks very little like that one."

"Very little?" One brow rose. "So you're saying it's similar."

She glanced down at the paper on the desk between them and back up at the clerk. "Yes, I suppose there's a similarity, but I did not sign it."

"So you said." He leaned forward and rested his palms on the desk. "Mrs. Barnhart, the deed is done. Any remorse you have over your choice of husband is best served by setting it aside and determining to be a good wife to the man you've got."

Several responses occurred. Eliza bit them back and leveled an even gaze at the man. "Is that your final answer on my complaint, sir?"

There was a brief pause and he nodded. "It is."

"That is unfortunate."

Eliza rose, her back straight and her shoulders square. She snatched up the forgery and offered the clerk a curt nod. Then she departed the office and, a few minutes later, the building.

She walked five blocks as quickly as she could until the capitol was in view. There she stopped to catch her breath and determine her next move.

Home. Yes, tomorrow she would go home. Papa would know what to do.

Returning to the hotel, Eliza stopped at the front desk and asked for a porter to be sent to her room. She went up to wait, relieved that Ben was gone.

When the porter arrived, she opened the door and let him in. "I'll need you to move that dresser in front of the door," she told the young man.

The porter looked perplexed. "But ma'am, if I do that, the door won't open from the other room into this one. Whoever's adjoining this suite can't get in."

Eliza smiled. "Exactly."

June 28

If Ben had returned to the Driskill last night, he hadn't bothered to try to open the door between their suites. So far this morning all was quiet, causing Eliza to give thanks as she slipped out of the hotel.

With no transportation of her own, Eliza arranged with the livery to borrow a horse and buggy to make the trip out to the Gentry Ranch. The horse was skittish and tried to bolt several times, but despite that, she arrived at the ranch safely.

Red met her on the porch of the ranch house. The red-haired gentle giant looked pale but much better than he had when she'd been forced to leave him for dead in the wagon.

"They ain't here," he told her from his perch on the porch rocker. "But I sure am glad you are."

"So am I, Red."

The ranch foreman rose with difficulty and leaned on a cane as he shuffled toward her. She crossed the distance between them to envelop him in an embrace. Then she pulled away to hold Red at arm's length.

Evidence of his apoplexy showed on his face, but even a partial smile from this man warmed her heart more than she could adequately explain to him. So she returned that smile and gave thanks to the Lord that he was still standing on this earth.

"I thought you were dead," she said, tears springing to her eyes. "I was so afraid you were gone forever."

"I thought I was too," he admitted. "I was sitting there keeping watch and praying the Psalms like I always do on those occasions, and next thing I knew I was flat on the floor of the wagon with my arms and legs ignoring me. Couldn't speak neither. But I could hear. And I heard what that man said. He was going to shoot me. And he took you. All I could do was pray because I couldn't sit up and shoot him and I couldn't call for help. There's only been one other time in my life when I felt so helpless, and I don't care to feel that way again."

He straightened and took a step back, leaning heavily on his cane. His expression told her he felt he'd said too much.

"Where're Mama and Papa?" she asked him.

"Gone," he said. "Don't expect they'll be back anytime soon."

She shrugged. "I can wait."

"No, Miss Eliza, you can't." He studied the ground for a minute. When he looked back up at her, he had tears in his eyes. "They lit out for New Orleans in a hurry. Mr. Gentry, he was plenty upset. So was the missus and that little girl. He told me to give you something if you were to come looking for them."

Red turned to walk back toward the porch, and Eliza fell into step beside him. "I don't understand, Red," she said. "What happened to make them leave like this?"

He kept walking, his pace slow and uneven. When he reached

the porch steps, Eliza was tempted to help, but the ranch foreman seemed determined to do it himself. When he finally reached the porch, he veered off toward the chair where he'd been sitting instead of going inside.

"Sit a spell," he told her. "I need to rest up."

Eliza joined him on the porch, her heart pounding. Panic threatened, but she took a deep breath and forced it away as she exhaled.

"You've got to go home to your husband, Miss Eliza. Get what you need out of the house. I'll look the other way while some of the boys load things up for you. I'll even loan the wagon for the trip back into Austin and not mention it to your pa. But I can't let you live here anymore."

She opened her mouth to speak, but the words froze in her throat. "But this is my home," Eliza finally managed. "Where will I go?"

"You'll go back to your husband and make the best of the situation you've found yourself in," Red said. "And if you're thinking Zeke and his wife will take you in, I ought to warn you that your pa has sent word he's not to do that. You know Zeke. He'll listen and do whatever his pa tells him to do, so I wouldn't advise putting him in a situation where he has to turn his own sister out on the street."

"Is it that bad, Red?" Tears threatened, but she blinked them away. "I only went along with Ben because I thought I was saving Trey's life."

His brows rose. "What's this now?"

"Ben told me Trey had been kidnapped. He showed me his necklace as proof. I was supposed to pretend we were married so Ben could negotiate with them as my husband, but oh Red, I feel so stupid."

"You're anything but, Miss Eliza," he told her. "I wish I could fix this for you, but I just can't."

"No, I created this mess, so I'm going to have to be the one who fixes it."

"That ain't true." Red shifted positions to look directly at Eliza. "Ben Barnhart created this mess. He calculated it all to happen just as it has."

Red was right, but she wouldn't allow herself to get off so easily. "I could have said no."

"You wouldn't have, and he knew it. You love your brothers, and you'd do anything for them. I'm sure Ben Barnhart has been sitting on this idea for a while." He paused. "I mean no disrespect, Miss Eliza, but I couldn't stand him as a boy, and my opinion of him has only gotten worse since then."

"I'm not feeling any kindness toward him right now either."

She pressed her palms against the arms of the porch rocker and stared out at the land that made up the Gentry Ranch. She'd grown up here, had skinned her knees climbing trees, and had looked up at the stars from just about every corner of the property.

With one stupid choice, all of that was lost to her.

Or was it?

"I'm going to make this right, Red, but I need some assistance."

Red shook his head. "I done told you I am not the man to do the fixing in this situation. You're going to have to find someone else to do that."

"That is exactly what I intend to do." She stood but motioned for him to remain seated. "I need to get in touch with a man Papa does business with. Where would I find that information?"

He thought a minute. "Most of that information I'd say Will carries around in his head."

"Oh."

"But he does keep a ledger in his office where he records such things. You may find your information there."

CHAPTER 18

Eliza planted a kiss on the old man's cheek then hurried inside. Three steps into the house, she halted as a wave of sadness rushed over her.

Everything was so quiet. Too quiet. The people who made this house a home weren't here. And they were gone because of her.

She would fix this. Eliza shook off the melancholy and hurried down the hall to Papa's office, where she went directly to his desk.

The drawers were locked, but she'd long ago learned how to use a hairpin to open them. Sliding out the center drawer, she retrieved Papa's ledger book and placed it on the desk.

It took only a few minutes to find the information she needed. Less time than that to write it down on a piece of Papa's writing paper. While she waited for the ink to dry, Eliza stood and walked over to the map of the Chisholm Trail hanging on the wall.

Her heart had been broken on that trail. Completely and forever broken.

Someday she would ride that trail again and make a happy memory. It was the least she could do for Wyatt. Remembering him as she did now, a boy who never did get to grow up to be a man, wasn't how it ought to be.

They'd looked up at the stars, counted meteorites, and made each other laugh more times than she could count. Eliza pressed her finger to the place on the map where the trail ended for Wyatt. Someday, once she fixed this mess she was in, she would go back and honor him where he lay.

But that was a task for another day. She went back to the desk and blew on the paper to be certain it was dry, then folded the page and tucked it away in her pocket.

Eliza stepped out into the hallway and looked up toward the stairs. Her room was there, as were the rooms where her rambunctious brothers had slept. Poor Justine had been assigned Zeke's old room, and she claimed it still smelled like old leather and cows most days.

Unlikely, but the thought made Eliza smile at that moment.

She ought to gather some clothes. That idea took her as far as the staircase, where she stalled. Better to pay one of the maids to pack them and send them into town. She couldn't imagine doing that herself today.

With the beginnings of a plan forming and the information on how to get started in her pocket, Eliza retraced her steps to emerge into the afternoon sun. Red was still sitting in his rocker, and now his eyes were closed. Had he not been snoring, she might have worried.

Instead, she tiptoed across the porch boards and took her seat next to him again. He awakened a few minutes later, shaking his head when he saw her smiling in his direction.

"How long have you been there, Miss Eliza?"

"Long enough to know you snore."

Red waved away the comment with a sweep of his hand. "Aw, any cowboy in the bunkhouse could tell you that. I reckon you're wanting to go, so I'll go fetch what your pa left for you."

He stood and walked past her into the house and returned with a letter that he handed to her. She smiled and opened it to find a folded piece of writing paper from Papa's desk containing two lines in his masculine scrawl. One said: *"I'll always love you."* The second line had the address of Central Bank of Austin and the same address she'd just copied out of his ledger.

She hurried out, hugged Red, and returned to the buggy. "Will you promise to come see me in Austin?" she asked him.

"I don't see why that wouldn't be all right," Red said. "You'll let me know soon as you're settled where I can find you."

"I will. I promise."

Tears threatened as she turned the buggy away from the house. This was just temporary, she told herself. What she'd made wrong could be made right.

It had to be.

Eliza's first errand after returning the horse and buggy to the livery was to walk over to Central Bank of Austin. "My name is Eliza Gentry," she told the banker. "My father left a message that I should inquire here, possibly about an account."

He nodded and went off to check, returning with a frown. "Is there another name?"

She let out a long breath. "Barnhart," she told him. "Eliza Jane Maribel Barnhart."

This time the banker offered a smile when he came back to the window. He slid a folded paper toward her.

"This is the current balance, Mrs. Barnhart. The account is only in your name. Is there anything else I can do for you?"

Her eyes widened, and tears sprang up when she took in the number on the paper. "You're certain?"

"Quite," he said. "Your father was insistent that you be settled and independent. Those were his words. I took care of opening this account myself. There is also a safe deposit box assigned to you should you wish to put your valuables away."

She smiled. Papa had thought of everything.

Eliza withdrew some cash, returned to the Driskill Hotel, and marched up to the desk to demand a new suite. "Something that does not attach to another room, please. And I am to have the only key, no matter what Mr. Barnhart might tell you. He is not paying for this room. I am."

Though the desk clerk raised his eyebrows at the request, he dared not argue with the new Mrs. Benjamin Barnhart. Of course, the generous tip she left might have helped too.

Later, when Ben got wind of the fact she'd not only moved to another suite but gone out to the ranch and sent a maid back with all her clothes, he pounded on her door and demanded to be let in.

"I'll just go down and get a key," he threatened.

"Go ahead, but you won't be successful. And you wouldn't want me to make a scene on the day before our wedding announcement appears in the *Statesman*, would you, dear?" Eliza asked sweetly from the safety of the other side of the locked door. "How would it look to the voters?"

Ben went away, but he came back a short time later. "You are requiring an apology," he said, his voice sounding sincere. "I can either give it through the door or come inside."

"Through the door, please," she told him.

"All right. I apologize."

"For what?"

She heard muffled cursing. "Eliza, just please open the door so I can do this without an audience. We have things to discuss. I've bought us a house."

Not close to an apology. She considered telling him that, then decided to just let it go.

The last thing she wanted was to see Ben Barnhart again, but if her plan was to work, she had to. "Slip the address under the door. I'll meet you there tomorrow morning at nine o'clock."

More cursing. "I don't have anything to write with."

Eliza went to the table and retrieved pen and paper, then slid them under the door. A minute later, the pen came rolling back. The paper slid into the room right after it.

June 29

The next morning at promptly nine o'clock, she arrived in front of a two-story home bricked in limestone with porches wrapping around to the left on both floors and a turret spanning three stories on the right. Ben was waiting for her at the door.

"Well?" he said with more enthusiasm than she'd expected. "What do you think?"

She turned to look to her left, focusing on the capitol building nearby. "It's lovely."

"Come in and see what it looks like."

Eliza returned her attention to Ben. "I'm sure it's fine. Ben, I need to take a trip. I will be gone a week at most."

"Running home to Mama and Papa?" he asked, his voice a sneer.

"No. I tried that. It didn't work."

Was that relief she saw on his face? "Then where are you going?"

"Ben," she said slowly, "you worry about your new house and your campaign, but don't worry about me. I'll be fine."

"I have my campaign to think of, Eliza."

"Where I am going will not affect your campaign. I'll be back in a week." She turned and walked to the train station.

June 30
Galveston, Texas

The next morning, Eliza awoke in the grand Tremont House hotel on Galveston Island. From her fourth-floor room she could see above the buildings of the city known as the Wall Street of the South all the way to the sparkling Gulf of Mexico.

Eliza took breakfast in her room, then left to find the address that Papa had wanted to make sure she had. The address she'd already looked up herself.

Even at this early hour, the morning was already warm. The salt-scented air felt nice as she struck out. The concierge had explained the best route to take—Twenty-Fifth Street then cross at Avenue O and continue down Twenty-Seventh—and she stuck to it. Less than ten minutes later, she stood in front of her destination.

The home of the John Brady Detective Agency was a lovely one-story cottage with a white picket fence all around and pink roses climbing a trellis that arched over the front gate. A porch wrapped around the front and disappeared along one side. Floor-to-ceiling windows flanked both sides of the front door, their dark green shutters held open against the sea breeze.

Numbers posted on the gate declared this to be the correct address, yet Eliza paused, her hand on the latch, to look for a sign that this might indeed be the home of the Brady Detective Agency.

There was none. No indication at all that this was anything other than a tidy cottage on a tidy street in a lovely seaside town.

For the first time since she had walked away from Ben's new home—she could never consider it her home—she felt nervous. What if this wasn't the right address? What if the agency had moved?

Worse, what if John Brady wouldn't help her?

Eliza turned on her heels and began to retrace her steps to the hotel. A few blocks away, she passed a lovely church just as the bells rang, announcing services were beginning.

Hurrying inside, she took a seat in the back pew and listened to a sermon based on 1 John 3 about living as God's much-loved children. She left feeling not only uplifted but also secure in the knowledge that her current troubles had not escaped the Lord's notice.

Eliza stood for a few more minutes debating whether to move forward or go back to the hotel and take a nap. Yes, perhaps a nap would help. She'd slept poorly on the train and had only enjoyed a few hours of fitful rest last night at the Tremont House.

She would try again tomorrow to approach John Brady's house with her troubles. After all, Ben wasn't expecting her to return for a week. And while getting John Brady involved would likely make things worse, doing nothing was not an option.

CHAPTER 19

July 1

Wyatt's heart thudded to a stop when he saw Eliza Gentry standing on the sidewalk in front of his house. At first he was certain he'd been mistaken. He had the bad habit of seeing her often in crowds. Of catching a glimpse of what he thought was her and chasing a red-haired stranger until he realized he was wrong.

But this time he was right. And she seemed uncertain about whether to knock on the door. Before she could make her escape, Wyatt opened the front door and stepped outside. "You've come all this way. Do you plan to finish the trip by coming inside, or are you leaving?"

He held the screen door in one shaking hand while hiding the other behind his back. He might have spoken with the bravado of a man who wasn't surprised to see his visitor, but inside he felt the exact opposite.

Eliza didn't answer him.

Another minute passed, and Wyatt tired of waiting. "Either open the gate and come in or leave me in peace. I'll give you to the count of ten."

He got to four and the gate opened. She still stood on the other side of it, but she had made progress.

Wyatt shook his head. "Oh, for crying out loud, Liza Jane, get inside the fence and tell me why you're here."

She gave him the oddest look. "What did you call me?"

What *had* he called her? Wyatt was so busy trying not to look like a fool that he'd probably just acted like one.

He squared his shoulders and took the porch steps two at a time. When he reached Eliza, he held the gate open and nodded toward the porch.

"Welcome to the Brady Detective Agency, Miss—" He shook his head as his heart sank with the reminder of what he must call her. "No, I'm sorry, Mrs. Barnhart."

"You of all people should just call me Eliza." She gave him a sideways look. "But that's not what you said."

His brow furrowed. "What did I say?"

"You called me Liza Jane." She searched his face, and her gaze collided with his. "Nobody has called me that for years."

Wyatt froze. Old habits as well as old identities certainly did die hard.

"If I did, I apologize," he managed through a clenched jaw.

She offered a smile that nearly did him in. "Actually, it's a nice reminder of a better time."

For both of us.

"Since we've waded in a creek together, what do you say we use first names, John? Or am I being impertinent?"

"I have a feeling you've been accused of being impertinent before and it hasn't bothered you a bit."

Eliza laughed, and his stupid heart soared. "You've been speaking with my father." Then she sobered. "It has just occurred to me that I can't do that anymore."

"Come inside unless you're just passing through," Wyatt said as casually as he could.

She brushed past him, leaving the scent of lavender and roses in her wake. Eliza walked straight and tall, her braid brushing the small of her back beneath her straw hat. Oh, how he wanted her to come in and stay, and yet he also wanted to get rid of her as quickly as possible.

He ought to talk with her on the porch and then send her on her way. Yes. That would work.

Wyatt allowed her to reach the wide steps that led to the porch before he caught up to her. His housekeeper, Janie, opened the door and welcomed his guest inside.

Plain and yet pretty in her own way with deep brown eyes and thick black hair that she wore tucked into a bun at the back of her neck, Janie had been housekeeper to the previous owner. When Wyatt purchased the home from the elderly Seaborn widow, it was made clear to him that Janie came with the deal. Mrs. Seaborn wouldn't sell the house unless she knew her valued employee remained employed as long as she wished to be.

The situation had worked out fine for both of them. He paid Janie full-time wages for what was barely part-time work, and in turn, she kept his home neat and brought over the occasional meal from her brother's restaurant on Twenty-Fifth Street when she knew he was in town.

She rarely spoke, and she minded her own business, two things he appreciated in hired help. And people in general.

"May I get you some tea or coffee?" she asked Eliza.

"Tea would be lovely. Earl Grey if you have it."

From Eliza's expression, he knew she wondered just who this woman was. Had he been inclined to do so, Wyatt couldn't have given an answer. The previous owner told him her husband had been killed in a dispute over property in Nacogdoches County some ten years ago that had left her penniless.

He'd asked her once if he could investigate that situation and help, but she declined his offer. He'd never brought it up again.

"You have a lovely home." Eliza smiled up at him. "And your friend is very nice."

"Housekeeper," he told her, though he wasn't sure why it mattered so much that she understood theirs was a working relationship and nothing more.

"Oh." A nod. "I see."

Wyatt realized he was still standing in the doorway holding the screen, so he stepped inside and let it close behind him. "Come on in here and sit down. I assume this isn't a social call."

"No," she said as she removed her hat and smoothed down the top of her braid. "It is not. I need your help."

Anything almost came out of his mouth. "I'm listening," was what he said instead.

Because as much as he wanted to help Eliza, he also wanted to keep her safe. He had no doubt that Ben Barnhart would make good on his threat to turn them all in—including Eliza—as murderers. He also had no doubt that the Barnhart family had the connections to produce witnesses who might not otherwise ever set foot on the Chisholm Trail. What a Barnhart stated as fact soon became gospel whether it was true or not. Which brought him back to the beautiful redhead standing there wondering what was wrong with him.

Wyatt escorted Eliza to the parlor and waited until she took a seat in the chair next to the window. He settled opposite her and waited for her response.

"I've been duped into a false marriage, and I want to get out of it."

He let out a long breath and leaned back, crossing his arms over his chest. "That's not what you told me at the Driskill."

Eliza braced for the statement. She'd been preparing an answer all the way from Austin. As she sat here in front of the security detective, that answer evaporated and only the plain truth remained.

"I lied."

He said nothing.

"Did you hear me, John? I lied about being married to Ben Barnhart. I had a reason, which I now feel incredibly stupid and gullible for. Ben told me I would be saving Trey's life if I pretended to be married to him while he negotiated with what turned out to be non-existent kidnappers. Then there is this." She pulled out the marriage license and handed it to the security detective. "I did not sign that."

The detective studied the paper and handed it back to her. "All right."

"All right?" Eliza shook her head. "That's all you have to say about this?"

He shifted positions and regarded her with an unreadable look. "I believe you."

"Then fix this, please. You've always fixed things for my father. Do it for me," she snapped.

"How?"

The housekeeper returned with a tray filled with an elegant blue-and-gold Sèvres teapot and two matching cups. Eliza watched her slow and careful movements as she set the tray on the table and then stepped back to look over at John.

A moment passed between them, and Eliza felt an odd twinge of something akin to jealousy. Ridiculous, of course.

Eliza thanked her but continued to watch as the housekeeper stood waiting for a word from John. His attention was elsewhere, but hers was focused on him. Finally, he noticed her standing there.

"That will be all, Janie. You can go home for the day," he told her without looking in her direction.

She watched Janie's expression fall. The housekeeper turned hard eyes on Eliza before she made her way out of the parlor.

John Brady might be oblivious, but that woman had set her sights on him.

"Let me see that paper again," he said when the housekeeper was gone.

Eliza handed it back to him and watched as the detective ran his hand across the page and turned it over to study the back. He looked up at her.

"Have you shown this to the clerk in Travis County?"

"Yes. He wasn't helpful," she said.

"How so?"

"He examined the document and said it was legitimate. Something about the paper only being available from a certain supplier and this being that paper." Eliza waved her hands. "I don't know exactly except that I was told the license was legitimate. He refused to consider my complaint that my signature was forged."

Eliza sat forward and poured a steaming cup of tea. John was still studying the paper, so she took the opportunity to look more closely at her surroundings.

The room was simply furnished but with pieces that were anything but simple. From the rosewood sideboard and matching parlor set to the paintings on the wall, everything was of a quality that Mama would have demanded. The paintings on the wall looked to be museum-quality originals except for an antique map of the Republic of Texas that had been hung over the fireplace.

The grandfather clock in the corner ticked off the seconds in a beautifully carved cabinet that was decorated in ebony and gold leaf. A closer look at the clock's face revealed that it not only told time but also indicated the phases of the moon.

She took a sip of tea and returned her attention to John. "You see something in that, don't you?" she finally asked.

Her voice seemed to break the spell. He jolted his attention toward her. "I'm just being thorough. What else have you done?"

"I went to see my father. He was gone. Mama and Justine too. He left a note for me with Red." She paused. "He told me he would always love me."

"Of course he would," John said. "He's your father."

"He left me two addresses. One was the Central Bank of Austin and the other one was yours."

John's expression told her this information had taken him by surprise. She waited for a response. When he said nothing, she continued. "I need help with this, John. You've worked for my father for years. Obviously he has endorsed you as the only one who can help me now." She paused. "And he has given me the funds to hire you. Name your price."

"For what, exactly?" he said slowly.

"For righting this wrong," she told him. "I want to be free of this nightmare. I want my family back. And I want Ben prosecuted for this forgery."

"That's a tall order," he said.

"If my father didn't think you could deliver, he wouldn't have said so in his message."

"I can deliver. What I haven't decided is whether I should. You've married a dangerous man with extensive connections in politics and elsewhere."

"Are you afraid of Ben Barnhart, John?"

"Never have been and never will be," he snapped.

She'd hit a nerve. It didn't take much to know these two had some sort of shared history. Something that caused John Brady's temper to flare.

"It's your safety I'm concerned with, Eliza. You have no idea what sort of mess you're stepping into if you pursue this."

"So you just want me to forget everything and go on with

pretending I'm married to Ben Barnhart? Is that your advice? Better yet, is that the advice my father would have given you if he was here?"

"Your father is not here, Eliza. Did you stop and wonder why he left the ranch with your mother and Justine? Could it be because he knew you would be safe with Barnhart as your protector but he feared for their safety if you decided to fight this marriage?"

She hadn't considered that. "But why?" she managed.

"I've already told you. Barnhart has powerful friends. He wants to win an election. To do that, he needs to make up for his age by showing the voters his respectability. That's where you come in. He needs a wife. Now he has one."

"Why me though?" One look into the security detective's eyes and she knew he had the answer to that question.

"You're asking the wrong question," he told her. "Why not you?"

"No. You know exactly why I was chosen for this." She placed her cup back on the saucer and sat back. "But you won't tell me, will you?"

"Why do you think I know?"

"Because you're a security detective, and you're paid to know everything about the people who employ you. My father would have briefed you on me and Mama before he sent you to follow us around New Orleans. What did you discover that will tell me why Ben Barnhart went to such trouble?"

"Because he's always said he would have you for his own. Always. On that last trail drive, he told everyone who would listen to him that someday he was going to marry you. When he gets an idea in his mind, he's on it like a starved dog on a bone. He wanted you. He got you. If I had to guess, that is the real reason the judge sent him on that trail drive. He wanted to forge a relationship between the two of you that would end in marriage. What he didn't count on was creating a monster who would do anything to make that happen."

The vehemence with which John Brady spoke surprised Eliza.

"How did you know about that trail drive? No one was supposed to know he was there. Afterward, the judge made sure we didn't talk about it, and he denied Ben had been there when rumors started to. . ."

No. She would say nothing further. No good would come from dredging up those memories.

He lifted one shoulder in a casual shrug. "Like you said, I'm a security expert and I'm paid to know everything about the people who hire me."

She almost believed him. Almost but not quite. There was something personal in this for John Brady.

When she said nothing, he continued. "So the real question here is do you want to get out of this false marriage situation, or do you want your family out of danger? Let me know which of those you want help with."

CHAPTER 20

W hy can't I have both, John?"

Wyatt sighed. Eliza Gentry might be a beautiful, intelligent, sophisticated woman, but deep down she was still the same spoiled and pampered girl he remembered. "Eliza, it is one or the other."

She sat very still and seemed to be studying her hands. Slowly she looked up at him with tears shimmering in her eyes. "I refuse to believe that."

He stood. "Then I cannot help you."

Her voice rose, but Eliza remained in her seat. "Papa gave me your address. He provided the means for me to find you and to pay you to help. Why would you refuse?"

"Because one of us has the good sense to know this is a situation with no good solution."

Eliza was on her feet in an instant. "And one of us has the good sense to know there is always a better solution to a situation than just walking away from it."

He took a step closer and looked down at her. "Which of us is doing that, Eliza?"

Crimson climbed into Eliza's cheeks as she stood there staring up at him, eyes narrowed. After a minute, she opened her mouth to speak and then clamped it shut again.

It was killing him not to pull her into his arms and tell her he would make everything right. That he would fix what was wrong and give her back the world that had been taken from her.

"How do I get my family back?"

The question took him by surprise. The answer hurt worse than anything else so far.

"You go home to your husband and convince him not to hurt them."

"I'm not legally married to him," she said.

"That paper you showed me says otherwise."

Tears welled up in her eyes, and Wyatt's knees went weak. If she stayed a minute longer, he would do something stupid. Or worse, say something stupid.

Like tell her who he was and why she should walk away from everything Ben Barnhart could give her to stay here with him.

But he couldn't do that. Wouldn't do it.

He'd loved Eliza Gentry as long as he could remember. Definitely as long as he'd had any sort of idea what the word meant. And in all those years, he'd never felt like he ought to give up on that love.

Not when he had to walk away from that trail ride a dead man at the age of fourteen. Not when William Gentry called him out of the blue to guard his wife and daughter. And not when he heard Ben Barnhart's story of how he had claimed Eliza for his own.

But standing here looking at her, he knew that remaining in her life would only put her and her family in danger. She could never fall in love with a dead man, and this dead man could never fall out of love with her.

"You don't need me or this agency to fix what happened." He took her by the shoulders and aimed her toward the door, snagging her hat to fit it atop her head just before he opened the screen. "Go back to your husband. Then the rest of these problems will solve themselves."

"But. . ."

"Go home." Wyatt led her out the door and onto the porch then closed the door behind her.

Before the screen had time to slam shut, he opened it again. "Liza Jane, come back."

Eliza turned around and smiled. John Brady didn't look nearly as happy as she felt, but he would get used to the idea that helping her was the best choice.

"I know you're teasing me with that name," she said. "But I kind of like it actually."

John's expression remained neutral. "Sit, please." He pointed to the steps. "You will listen, and I will do the talking."

She nodded and complied, not because Eliza intended to do as he said during the remainder of this investigation but because she felt so relieved that he would be helping her.

John eased down beside her and stretched out his long legs, then gave her a sideways look. "Show me the license again."

Retrieving the vile document, Eliza handed it to him. This time when John studied it, he held it up to the light for quite a while.

"The clerk said there was only one supplier of this paper," she told him. "That's how he knew it was legitimate."

He set the page on the step in between them. "And that's how I know it isn't."

"I don't understand."

"I can't tell you more than that right now." He picked up the license and held it up in front of him again. This time, instead of studying the document, he tore it down the middle and gave her half.

"John, that's not the fix I was thinking of. You can't just tear up the marriage license and call it done."

Folding the paper, the security detective stuck it into his pocket. "That is not my intention, but I need this half." He paused. "I'm sorry. Were you considering framing it?"

Eliza opened her mouth to tell him just what she thought of the question. Then she noticed the twinkle in his sage-green eyes.

"You're incorrigible."

His laughter surprised her. "I've been called a lot of things, but never incorrigible." His expression sobered. "Every instinct I've ever developed in my career as a detective is telling me not to do this."

She sat very still and quiet. For once, she had no good argument. No trick of humor to divert him. "There's more you haven't told me," she said instead. "You knew this would happen, didn't you?"

John shook his head. "No. There was no indication of this. My men were following him, and yet somehow. . ."

"He had help," Eliza told him. "The man who came for Red and me was no one I had seen before." She shook her head. "Wait. Why were your men following him? Had he made threats against me or my family?"

"The fact he draws a breath makes him a threat," John said.

Eliza turned to face the gate she'd walked through just a short time ago. The beautiful pink roses still bobbed in the salt-scented breeze, and the sun still shone in a bluebonnet-blue sky. Nothing had changed.

Yet it was about to.

"John," she said slowly, keeping her attention focused away from him, "there's something I need to tell you. Something important that may help you understand Ben Barnhart's motives."

She dared a glance in his direction and found him watching her closely. "All right."

"When I was twelve, I went on a trail drive with my father. My mother was against it, but Papa won out and I was allowed to go. Have you ever ridden on a trail drive on the Chisholm Trail, John?"

His green eyes went misty. "I have," he whispered. "It was some-thing to see when all those cattle and horses go heading off in the same direction. Or at least you hope they're all going the same way."

"Yes. There's mostly nothing but prairie except for that suspen-sion bridge at Waco over the Brazos, and a great big sky full of stars at night, and it is just the best thing in the world." Eliza sighed. "Or it was."

Eliza expected the detective to prompt her for more information. Instead, he sat quietly and waited.

"I think about that trail ride a lot," she continued. "There was a meteor shower last Wednesday—"

"Encke's Comet."

"That's right. You told me you know about astronomy."

He offered a faint smile. "A little."

Eliza studied him for a moment longer, then returned to her story. "The last trail ride I went on was in the spring. In April. I couldn't wait until bedtime when everything got quiet and my brothers fell asleep. I would lie on my back and look up at the heavens to watch for falling stars. I would count them." She smiled at the recollection. "Sometimes it became a friendly competition with Wyatt. He was my best friend."

A sob tore through the remainder of her words. "I miss him so much," was all she could manage on a ragged exhale of breath.

Wyatt leaned in to gather her into his arms. At fourteen, he'd thought of her as a child. A girl who irritated him and made him laugh. Who challenged him and made him wonder what she would be like when she was grown.

He'd been a kid then, hardly old enough to imagine holding Eliza Gentry in his arms. Even as an adult, he couldn't have imagined it to be nearly as good as it felt to wrap his arms around her and feel her head resting on his shoulder.

Abruptly she lifted her head to look up at him. "Did my father tell you what happened on that trail ride?"

"I know," he said, not exactly answering the question she asked but still telling the truth.

"I never believed Wyatt did it." She swiped at her eyes with the backs of her hands. "He was the sweetest, kindest person I'd ever met. He would never harm anyone. So how could he possibly have done what Pa said he did?"

Wyatt bit back a response. There was nothing he could say. Not that the right words would have come anyway.

"What did your pa tell you?" he finally managed to ask.

"I was a child," she told him, "so he told me very little. It's more what I remember about that night. Zeke, Trey, and I were in the wagon. A gunshot woke us up, and I ran to see what had happened. Later, when Papa sent us back to camp, I had to stay with Cookie in the wagon." She paused to look up at him. "He was our cook, and he was always so wise. He told me I'd be sorry if I defied Papa. That's the only time I can remember that he was wrong."

"Why?" came out as a hoarse croak. Wyatt cleared his throat and tried again. "Why do you regret staying in the wagon?"

"Because I never got to say goodbye to my best friend." She paused. "I hope he knew how much I loved being his friend, even if he did get me in trouble with my parents."

Wyatt gave her a sideways look. "So you're blaming him for your troubles?"

Eliza smiled. "He loved to tease me. And he was always daring me to do things that I shouldn't do. That time he convinced me I could jump off the springhouse and land in the saddle of my horse was almost the last straw for Mama. After that, she was determined I should be trained up as a lady instead of spending my time with the horses and on a trail ride. Or, I suppose, with Wyatt Creed."

"You never said whether you tried to jump into that saddle."

"No, I was terrified, so it didn't take much to let my mother win that battle. I never admitted to Wyatt that I was scared though. As far as he knew, I was just as brave as he was."

"Maybe Wyatt was a little bit scared too."

She looked away. "He might have been, but he never showed it to me. He always seemed fearless."

"He wasn't."

Eliza looked sharply in his direction. "How would you know?"

A moment of panic and then he shrugged. "A man wants to look brave in front of the girl he cares for, whether he's full-grown or just a kid. I promise he was just as scared as you most of the time."

"Not when he died."

The words came like a punch in his gut. "You weren't there."

"No, but Red and my papa were there. Papa is the one who. . ."

"You don't have to tell me the rest," he supplied when he saw she was struggling again.

"I want to." Eliza shifted positions to turn toward him. "I have never trusted anyone with this story before, John."

John.

Wyatt kept his expression neutral as guilt rose. Eliza was opening her heart to him, telling him something deeply personal about a lost friend. Meanwhile, her lost friend was right here in front of her.

"I heard Red and my father talking after everything got quiet again and the cowboys were sleeping. They had Ben with them, but he didn't say much."

"Papa was telling Ben he ought to come clean to his father. I couldn't hear it very clearly, but I felt like Ben had done something wrong too. No one actually witnessed the shooting, so. . ."

Again she paused. This time she shook her head and then

continued. "I know it's easy to say that my beliefs about my father are colored by the fact that I love him dearly. But I do not believe my father had it in him to shoot Wyatt Creed. I also do not believe Wyatt would have given my father a reason to shoot him."

"But you heard him and Red talking about it," Wyatt supplied.

"Other than what he said to Ben, everything I heard between Papa and Red was about what a good man Wyatt was and how he would never be like his father. They talked about him like he was alive but told us he was dead and buried next to his father."

Silence fell between them. Wyatt shut down thoughts of that night. Remembering would do no good. He walked out of that camp a scared kid but a different man, and that man still lived.

Wyatt Creed did not.

"Eliza," he said softly as he carefully avoided her gaze, "I appreciate that you shared this with me, but maybe you ought to let it go."

For a minute she said nothing. Wyatt looked straight ahead, watching the roses sway in the breeze rather than brave a look at the woman beside him.

"Why?"

Wyatt chose his words carefully. "Because no matter what happened that night on the trail, it's done and can't be changed."

Eliza didn't react. He tried again. "Eliza, let's go back to talking about what we're going to do about the situation with Barnhart."

Her eyes flashed. Somehow he'd struck a nerve with just that simple statement.

"Yes, let's talk about Ben. There is no one on this earth I would less like to be associated with than him." Her laughter held no humor. "You're wondering why I reacted so strongly."

"I am curious," he said.

"He wasn't even supposed to be on the ride. The story was that his father begged Papa to let his son come along. Papa was against it but gave in because of his friendship with the judge. After everything happened, Papa sent Red to take Ben to Waco and we went on to Kansas with the herd. We were told that Ben's father would be coming to get him in Waco. Papa and the judge never spoke after that. Before, they had been good friends. Something just doesn't add up. The cowboys said Ben was just there when the two Creeds argued. I think he had something to do with it and that's why Papa sent him home."

"You think he knew something?"

Eliza nodded. "I know he did. I think that's a good place for you to start your investigation. It would be like Ben to use whatever happened on the trail against my family."

She was getting too close to a truth that would be dangerous for her to discover. Time to distract her.

"Where is Ben now?"

"Austin, I suppose." Eliza shrugged. "I told him I had to do something and would be gone for a week."

"And he didn't have anything to say about that?"

"I don't know." Another shrug. "I didn't wait for a response."

Surely Ben hadn't let her leave alone. Wyatt glanced around, looking for the person sent to follow Eliza. Though he didn't see anyone, that didn't mean Barnhart's man wasn't nearby.

Wyatt stood and reached down to help her to her feet. "Where are you staying?"

"The Tremont House," she said as she arranged her skirts. "Why?"

"You can't go back there."

"Why not? All my things are there."

"I'll get them for you. I'll need to get Bryant here. In the meantime, we're going inside."

He led her back into the house and shut the door and latched it. "Stay right here. If you hear any kind of scuffle, I want you to head out that door and don't stop until you get to the house across the street.

Tell Mrs. McDonald you're with me, and she will let you in and protect you better than any man I know."

"Mrs. McDonald," she repeated. "All right."

Wyatt offered a smile, then palmed his revolver and stepped into the kitchen. Unless Janie had locked the door, which was unlikely, this would have been an easy entry point into the home while they were seated out front.

A glance told him the lock had not been set. He went back toward the entry to find Eliza watching him. She said nothing and had not moved, both good signs.

He cleared the parlor and then stepped into the hall. Two bedchambers were on this end of the home. One was where he slept, and the other was where he ran the business side of the John Brady Detective Agency.

Bypassing the office, where he always kept the door closed when Janie was cleaning, he went into the bedchamber and found it empty. A check of the armoire had the same result.

Wyatt stepped toward the office door, stopping just close enough to reach the knob. With his right hand on the revolver and his left on the door, he took a long breath and let it out slowly. Then he opened the door.

One shot rang out, blazing past and grazing his left arm. It stung, but Wyatt ignored it.

The shooter came around the door so quickly that he knocked Wyatt down. Rolling up into a seated position, Wyatt aimed his revolver and fired.

The shooter, a light-haired man in workman's clothing, fell and didn't move. Wyatt stepped close enough to kick the gun away from him and pick it up.

"Eliza," he called.

Silence.

CHAPTER 21

Wyatt rounded the corner and saw the door standing open. He ran out onto the porch and saw the gate was open too. Good. Eliza had followed his instruction.

After surveying the area to be sure there were no other shooters, he ran across the street, pausing only when he reached Mrs. McDonald's porch. He found the older lady waiting for him just inside the door.

"Where is she?"

Her eyes were wide, and her ample girth blocked him from entering. "Who?"

"Eliza Gentry. Red hair and a pale yellow dress. About this tall." He held up his hand just below his chin. "I told her to hurry over here if there was trouble."

"And there was?" the widow asked.

"Yes, but I handled it."

"I see." She remained at the door, her hand on the knob. "Well, I am glad you've handled your trouble, Mr. Smith."

Mr. Smith?

He'd known Greta McDonald ever since the day he moved into the home across from her. She'd made it her business to watch every person who came in and out of his gate.

She certainly knew his last name wasn't Smith.

"Thank you, ma'am." Wyatt looked her in the eyes to let her know he got her message. "You'll let me know if you see her, won't you?"

"Certainly." She cut her eyes to the left and then looked at him. "I will be looking for her."

He gave her a curt nod and took a step back. Without drawing attention to what he was doing, Wyatt looked into the window to the left of the door. From his vantage, he could see no one in the room.

The door shut. Wyatt retraced his steps off the porch. Other than the usual traffic on Twenty-Seventh Street at this time of day, nothing seemed out of order.

An idea occurred. Wyatt returned to the front door and knocked. "I'm sorry to bother you again, Mrs. McDonald, but remember I mentioned having a need to reach my roof to repair shingles? I wonder if I might borrow that ladder now. Is it still in the shed, or have you brought it into the carriage house?"

Her face offered no expression. "No, it's still in the shed. And yes, you may borrow it. Just be careful of the door. It can stick and sometimes that is painful."

"Thank you. I'll watch out for that."

Wyatt offered her a smile and managed to keep that smile in place until he walked around to the side of the house. Thick oleanders grew against the building, obscuring most of the windows on the first floor.

He knew the floor plan well enough to know that the first two windows belonged to the front parlor. The second window was a smaller family parlor, and the last two windows belonged to the dining room and kitchen.

All of the windows were open on this warm June morning, and as far as he could tell, none of the rooms were inhabited. He opened the small gate that allowed him into the fenced yard behind the McDonald home.

When he had first moved into the neighborhood, the couple had had a massive dog that roamed the yard. In quick succession both the dog and Mr. McDonald died. Now the yard was empty, though the remains of the doghouse still leaned against a tree at the edge of the property.

The structure was big enough for an adult to fit, but only if that adult was willing to fold herself into the small space. The possibility that Eliza would do that willingly was very small.

Wyatt glanced behind him at the back door. The big wooden door was open, but a screen door remained closed. The room was dark, making it impossible for him to see inside.

Two other structures sat on the property: a shed filled with Mr. McDonald's tools and the carriage house next to it where a buggy in need of repair was kept. Though the carriage house was the logical spot for Eliza to be hidden, Mrs. McDonald seemed to indicate otherwise.

Thus, Wyatt detoured around the carriage house, arriving at the back of the shed rather than the front where the window and a door were located. He stopped just short of turning the corner and listened for any sound that could indicate Eliza was nearby.

Silence.

He gave thanks for the recent rains that had softened the ground that now muffled his footsteps as he progressed toward the door. Just before he reached the door, Wyatt spied Mrs. McDonald pass by the kitchen window. Someone—a man—was following her.

Wyatt ducked out of sight and, after a moment, looked again to see that the kitchen was empty. If there was at least one man inside, there could be more. Then there was the fact that Mrs. McDonald indicated he should go to the shed. Of course it was also possible she gave that answer because the ladder was indeed inside the shed.

He cocked his pistol and rushed the door of the shed. The space was dark and smelled of damp earth. It was also completely empty.

Something was very wrong here.

⁂

Eliza dusted off her skirts and stepped around the creaky old buggy to peer out of the carriage house's side door. She'd heard muffled footsteps, but they'd stopped nearby and now all was quiet except for her furiously beating heart.

She'd done as the security detective had asked and hurried over to the home across the street once the shooting began, but now Eliza regretted following his directions. As soon as she had time, Eliza planned to give the grumpy old lady a piece of her mind for slamming the door in her face. For now, however, she had a much more important mission: finding John Brady.

Eliza opened the door slowly and looked both ways down the narrow gap between the carriage house and the tool shed. Seeing no one, she set out to retrace her path back to John's home.

The old lady was watching from the kitchen window. Though Eliza was tempted to give her a look that told the woman exactly how she felt about her behavior, she chose to ignore her instead.

Out of nowhere, John Brady caught up to her and grasped her elbow. "Where are you going?" he said in a hoarse whisper.

"To find you. Thank you very much for sending me to that old woman's house. She slammed the door in my face and left me standing on the porch. I almost went back to make sure you weren't shot too."

"I wasn't. And I will deal with Mrs. McDonald later."

He picked up his pace and pulled her along until they reached the street again. There he turned to the left and continued walking with her at his side.

"I need to get to the telegraph office and the police station. But first I have to be sure you're safe."

Eliza looked up at him. "I'll come with you."

"No. We don't know how many men Ben sent after you. I need reinforcements and a police report regarding my dead visitor." He paused. "Look, just cooperate with me on this. I'm going to put you somewhere safe while I send the telegram. Then I will come back for you and we will go to the police together. This just may be the way to get Ben Barnhart to back down."

"Why do you think that? You don't know him like I do. Ben Barnhart never backs down. I think he has convinced himself we're married. Do you know he actually had a marriage announcement run in the newspaper in Austin? I mean, of all the nerve."

"He's always had a thing for you, Eliza. Don't you realize that?"

Her eyes narrowed. "I guess I knew he pestered me a lot. And he made a few comments on the trail drive that my father took exception to. But no, I hadn't really considered it, especially since there have apparently been a number of women he spent time with."

"Is that a guess, or do you have foundation for that statement?" he asked as he glanced back over his shoulder, then guided her across the street.

"While I was banished to New Orleans, I got a letter from Beatrice Cunningham, his Philadelphia fiancée. When I confronted him about her at River House, he claimed she misunderstood. Now, I can understand how a woman might misunderstand a man's attentions, but I cannot see how anyone would misunderstand a proposal and a wedding. Beatrice claimed there would be a wedding in Washington, DC."

"Do you still have the letter?"

She shook her head. "I gave it to Mama to read as proof I was well and truly done with Ben Barnhart. I doubt she kept it. Likely it ended up in the fire or the trash bin."

"I'll have my agent in DC check out the Cunningham situation and see what happened there." He nodded ahead toward a block of commercial buildings. "For now I am taking you to the safest place I know."

Ducking around the side of a two-story brick structure containing a hardware store, John guided her into an alley where delivery wagons vied with each other to find spaces to offload their goods, and discussions in several languages went on around them. No one paid any attention to them until they reached the middle of the block.

Here the air smelled of salt air and something delicious. A woman wearing all black sat in a cane chair, her head down, her attention devoted to shelling peas.

"Is there a restaurant on this block?" she asked him.

John grinned. "A favorite of mine."

He knocked on a door, and the woman looked up at them to smile a toothless grin. She said something to John in a language Eliza didn't understand. He reached down to kiss her on the cheek and then opened the door. The old woman's laughter chased them inside what appeared to be a very busy and very tiny kitchen.

Noise abounded, as did the activity of three men in dark clothing who all talked at once. One spoke English. The other two did not.

Chaos erupted when the men spied John. Then one of them saw Eliza and pointed her out to the others.

Instantly silence fell.

John stepped into the quiet with a firm announcement. "This is Miss Gentry. She's hungry and in need of a place to stay out of sight while I go to the telegraph office."

One of the men released his grip on his spoon, dramatically stepped away from the stove, and walked toward John. A quiet conversation ensued in a language Eliza did not understand. Occasionally a word that sounded very much like *Janie* would occur, but otherwise she could make no sense of the discussion.

Finally, the man nodded and called out, "Mama!"

The old lady came in from the alley and surveyed the scene. After another indistinguishable conversation, the woman nodded.

"You go, Giovanni," the English-speaking man said to John. "We will keep your woman safe."

The old lady spoke and the man translated. "And Mama says we will also feed her. She is too thin and the babies will not be fat and healthy until she is."

Eliza felt the heat of embarrassment rise in her cheeks as the woman studied her with what appeared to be a critical expression on her wrinkled face. What a thing to say to a stranger.

But apparently these people were not strangers to John. She gave him a look that told him she expected him to correct their assumptions, but he just shrugged.

"Don't feed her too much. We may be doing some walking after this."

He paused to whisper something in the old lady's ear. She frowned at Eliza. Then John was gone, leaving Eliza in a kitchen with strangers and no explanation as to who they were.

"Excuse me," she told them and then bolted out the back door. "John," she called to his retreating back. "Wait."

He stopped short and turned around. "Go back inside, Eliza. My friends will take care of you."

"But I don't know them. They don't know me." She paused. "And I don't think that old lady likes me."

"No, probably not, but she will treat you well because I asked her to." He shrugged. "She's been trying to get me to marry her granddaughter ever since I moved here."

"Janie?" Eliza asked.

"Yes. I guess you got that much out of the conversation with her brother and uncles."

"I got nothing out of it except her name," she said.

John's expression softened. "They are like family to me, but they're not welcoming of outsiders. That is precisely why I want you with them right now. I trust them."

"Why can't I just go back to the Tremont House and lock my door? I am certain I would be safe there."

"Oh, sure," he said. "Until your husband shows up and asks for a key. Do you think a hotel clerk would deny him that?"

"No," she said, thinking of the last time that happened and the surprise she had experienced at the Driskill Hotel.

"Or a man working for your husband who has no trouble lying about who he is in order to get into your hotel room does the same thing." John shook his head. "If you're going to work with me and my agency on this, you need to continue to do as I say. If you don't want to do that, that's fine. Go back to your hotel, but if you do, you'll need to have a plan regarding what to do when you are hauled back to Austin against your will to reunite with your husband."

"I don't have a husband," she snapped.

"Tell that to Ben Barnhart, his family, and the readers of the *Austin American Statesman*, Eliza. They all believe you do. Oh, and according to you, so does the Travis County Clerk's Office, and they are the ones who have the official say in the matter."

He had a point. "All right, but don't be gone long, please."

John shook his head. "Go back inside. And be warned. It doesn't matter that it's barely past breakfast. You'll be given a feast, and it would be impolite not to eat it."

"It does smell delicious," she admitted. "As long as the old lady doesn't poison it."

"She won't," he said. "I am certain of this."

"What makes you so certain?"

He turned to walk away, then glanced over his shoulder and fixed her with a grin. "Because I told her not to."

CHAPTER 22

John returned to a restaurant filled with the usual sounds of preparation for the lunch crowd that would descend on them in an hour. He'd sent telegrams to his agents in Washington, DC and Philadelphia and then contacted Jim Bryant.

Bryant would be invaluable in backing him up, not only on this case but in handling the other matters his agency had going on. The agent lived in Houston, so by late in the afternoon, he could reach Galveston by train.

Had this been any other matter, Wyatt never would have considered bringing in his best new agent to back him up. Bryant was better utilized elsewhere. But this was Eliza, and he'd have no other agent than his best working the case with him.

Just as he had in New Orleans.

On his walk back to the restaurant, Wyatt happened upon the police wagon making its rounds. He hailed the officer, a fellow named Stevens, and told him what had taken place at his home. Together they rode back to Twenty-Seventh Street, where Stevens examined the dead man, pronounced him as such, and then wrote down Wyatt's explanation of the incident.

"I'll be bringing a witness to the station as soon as I collect her," he told Stevens. "She did not see the shooting but heard it from where she was standing by the door."

"I don't recognize the fellow, but I'll see that he's removed from here as soon as I can locate the undertaker."

Wyatt had thanked him, and they parted ways. At least Eliza wouldn't be greeted with the sight of a dead man when they returned to his home.

If he decided to bring her there. That wasn't settled on yet.

Wyatt entered through the front door and followed the sound of singing until he found Eliza seated on a stool beside the counter where Janie's youngest brother, Anthony, was chopping garlic.

The red-haired beauty had obviously charmed the entire family, for the two uncles were currently singing a duet from the Italian opera *La Gioconda* while their mother was spooning meatballs into a bowl in Eliza's hands. She met his gaze across the distance between them and grinned.

Before John could even offer a greeting, he was hauled into the kitchen to help the brothers finish their song. Though his Italian was decent, his singing was not. By the time the singing was done, everyone in the kitchen had dissolved into fits of laughter.

Laughter was exactly what John needed. That and a bowl of what Eliza was having.

"He is hungry," Mama Rose declared, sending her sons into action.

Another stool was quickly found, and Mama provided another serving of spaghetti and meatballs for him. Before she stepped away, spoon in one hand and the steaming pot of meatballs wrapped in cloth in the other, she leaned in close.

"She is not our Janie, but I like her," she said in Italian.

"Me too, Mama," he told her, keeping to Italian out of respect, for he knew every person in this kitchen spoke English as well as he did.

"She will make for you a good wife, Giovanni." The old woman shook her head as if to ward off any protest. "You cannot see it yet, but I can. You believe there is no way. I say there is. And the good Lord, I believe He says so too. You just must ask Him."

Wyatt had asked Him a lot of questions over the years, but never that one. He nodded out of respect. "I will consider this," he told her.

And he would.

Mama patted him on the shoulder, then went back to the stove to scold Mossimo, the eldest, for his lack of garlic in the red sauce. He complained in turn and a debate ensued.

And so it went, the occupants of the restaurant kitchen falling back into their routine and ignoring Wyatt and Eliza completely. He leaned close to Eliza. "I see you're still alive."

She took another bite of the concoction in her bowl and nodded. "At this point, I don't care if this has poison in it or not. I've never eaten anything so delicious."

"I told you so. Now eat up. We have work to do."

Later, after they'd had their fill of food, Wyatt and Eliza managed to extricate themselves from the boisterous Italian family with promises to return soon. Eliza stepped out into the midday sunshine with a smile on her face.

"You enjoyed that," Wyatt said.

She looked up at him. "I did. It's refreshing to see a family who love each other so much. They remind me of my own family. Minus the copious amounts of food, the singing, and the debates about garlic in the sauce."

"You understood that?" he asked.

"The language, no. But it was easy to decipher the hand gestures." She shrugged. "Besides, Mama was right. There wasn't enough garlic in the sauce."

Wyatt laughed. "I guess you've decided she likes you now."

"I don't know about that," she said slowly, "but she likes you, and that's enough for me. I think we forged a truce based on that. Just be careful."

He looked down at her. "Why?"

"They want you married to Janie," she said. "Her brother told me, so no, I did not misunderstand hand gestures. I assured them I wasn't his sister's competition. That I have hired you for a security job." She paused. "We do need to discuss compensation for you."

Wyatt waved that statement away along with any suggestion that a romantic relationship was possible between him and the housekeeper he barely noticed when she was in his home. "They're good people." He sobered. "But we have work to do."

"All right, but just be careful that you don't give the wrong impression to them. Or to Janie."

He stopped short and frowned at her. "What are you talking about? She's a housekeeper. She picks up after me, launders my dirty socks, and provides a meal when she thinks I need one."

"Does that not sound like some men's description of a wife?"

"Not mine," he exclaimed.

Eliza gave him a look. "John Brady, for a detective who prides himself in knowing things, you are completely obtuse. Your housekeeper is in love with you. She does all those things because she adores you."

"She does all those things because I pay her to do them. I inherited her with the house, Eliza. Had I not agreed to take on the housekeeper, I never would have been sold the Seaborn home. It's as simple as that."

"No, it is not simple at all, John. That might have been the original arrangement, but that is not how things are now. Her family sees it. You obviously do not."

"And you do even though you have been an observer of this situation for less than half a day?"

"Yes," she said emphatically. "It didn't take me two minutes once I saw that woman in your presence."

"Well, you're all wrong." He shook off the ridiculous assumption and focused on the situation at hand. "Now about your situation. I have sent out telegrams to follow up on the jilted fiancée, and I've called for backup while we're here. Tonight I'll meet with Jim Bryant, my top detective. After that, we should have a plan in place. The only thing I haven't figured out is where you're sleeping tonight."

She shrugged. "That can be decided after our meeting with Mr. Bryant, can't it?"

"I wasn't intending to take you along."

Eliza shook her head. "But you will have to, won't you? I cannot go back for another few hours with that lovely family. I would not fit in the small amount of clothing I brought if I did. Speaking of, I really would like to know what to do about the things I left at the Tremont House."

"I'll send Bryant for them tomorrow," he said. "If anyone is looking for you or me there, they won't give him a second glance."

"I suppose I can sleep in my chemise tonight," Eliza said. "And my skin will survive a day without my rosewater lotion."

Wyatt immediately banished any thought of Eliza in her chemise from his mind. "Then it's settled. The body in my hallway should be gone by now. I happened on a policeman on patrol and reported the situation. He was going to call the undertaker and file a report. I told him we would follow up this afternoon."

"I'm glad I don't have to see that," she said. "When I heard the shot, my instinct was to go and see if you were harmed. But I didn't."

"And for that I am glad. In that small space, I could have hit you instead of the intruder."

She shuddered. "I never thought I would be the cause of a man's death. But if you count Red, who would have been killed had he not had a fit of apoplexy, that's two whose lives were threatened. And one taken."

Rather than comment that other lives would likely be threatened until Barnhart was stopped, Wyatt diverted the conversation. "The police station is in the new city hall on the corner of Strand at Market. It's a bit of a walk. Do you want me to find a buggy?"

"Don't be ridiculous," Eliza told him. "If I don't walk off this lunch, I will be miserable for the rest of the day."

Once they arrived at City Hall, Wyatt ushered Eliza up the curved exterior staircase to the second floor where the Galveston Police Department had their offices. Opened just last year, the building with all its turrets and grandeur was a bit fancy for Wyatt's tastes, but Eliza seemed impressed.

They were quickly ushered into a small office off the main hall where a pale, balding police detective with wire-rimmed spectacles and a suit that hung on his thin frame stepped inside. "Bit of trouble, folks?" he asked, clutching what was presumably the paperwork Stevens had filed earlier.

Wyatt filled the man in on the situation, then sat back and watched while he reviewed the paper he'd carried in. Eliza remained still and quiet, her eyes focused on the policeman.

Finally, the detective looked up. "So this fellow slipped in your back door while you and the lady were sitting on the porch, hid in your office, and then tried to shoot you while he was running off?"

"Actually, he didn't miss," Wyatt said as he lifted his arm to show a tear in his black shirt. "The bullet grazed my arm. It stung but nothing more than that."

"John," Eliza gasped. "You never said you'd been shot."

He shrugged. "I wasn't thinking about that when the man was heading your way with his pistol in his hand, and then I got busy and forgot."

"Got busy?" The detective gave him a look that Wyatt knew well. "Could you be more specific?"

Wyatt gave him the rundown of the rest of the events of the morning, culminating with his walk to the station. "So I didn't have time to check my arm."

"Would you like to do that now?" the detective asked.

He shook his head. "It's fine. I'd rather concentrate on the business at hand. Did you get an identification on the shooter?"

"No, the boys are working on that," he said. "I don't guess you knew him."

"I did not."

"And you, Miss Gentry?" the detective asked. "Did he look familiar to you?"

The written statement clearly said that Eliza had not seen the shooter. Wyatt found it odd but not completely surprising given the fact he would have asked the same question to see if he got the same answer.

"I never saw him," she said. "John told me to run if I heard gunshots, so I did as he said."

"Where did you go?" he asked.

"Across the street to his neighbor's home where I was told I would be welcomed." She paused. "I was not. The woman turned me away, so I went and hid in her carriage house until I heard John looking for me."

"Mrs. McDonald's behavior seemed odd to me," he told the policeman. "It is completely out of character for her to react that way. I saw there was a man following her through the kitchen when I went to the backyard to investigate."

"She allowed you access to her backyard?"

"She did," Wyatt said. "She even indicated, through my questions regarding borrowing a ladder—which were obviously meant to give her opportunity to tell me where Eliza had gone—that Eliza was in the shed when she wasn't. Again, I found her behavior suspicious but have not had time to speak with her."

"What's her name again?" When Wyatt told him, the detective wrote it down on the paper in front of him. "All right. I will have one of my men go speak with her. Maybe see if she's under some sort of duress. If she's a widow, that could be a reason she reacted as she did." He paused. "Or maybe she just took exception to a pretty girl running away from your home and asking her for protection."

His eyes narrowed. "I don't know what you're hinting at," he managed through a clenched jaw, "but we are the victims of a crime, not the perpetrators of one."

The detective moved his attention to Eliza. "Do you agree with what he just said?"

"Every word of it," she told him.

"So there wasn't some lovers' spat or disagreement between two of your boyfriends then?"

"Sir, I don't like what you're insinuating," she snapped.

"Then I'll say it more plainly. Did your two male friends disagree and shoot one another with the result being this fellow with a scratch on his arm and another fellow at the undertaker's?"

Eliza rose, crimson flooding her cheeks. "I am insulted that you would consider this as an option. I come from a good family and am a God-fearing woman. I will have an apology and the name of your superior officer immediately."

When the detective did not immediately speak, she gave him a curt nod and stepped out into the hallway.

"Where's she going?" the detective asked.

"My guess is she is doing exactly as she threatened," he said as he suppressed a smile. "Look, let me just say that what you've suggested, while it looks possible, isn't the case. She is a woman from a good family, just as she said. She approached me because I have done detective work for her father. I own the John Brady Detective Agency. We were conversing on the porch, because once my housekeeper left, it was more appropriate to hold our discussion outside rather than inside alone. And she won't tell you this, but Governor Sul Ross is an old family friend. I could name others, but suffice it to say you'd be outranked by all of them."

"Oh." And then his eyes widened. "Oh, good afternoon, sir."

Wyatt looked behind him to see the chief of police standing in the doorway with Eliza behind him. "I understand our department may owe Miss Gentry an apology?"

After that things moved quickly. The apology was issued, and Eliza charmed the chief into serving them tea and telling her stories of the early years of Galveston until finally the chief was called into a meeting and they departed.

"I would suggest we could get a bite to eat, but I'm not hungry yet. Are you?" he asked his companion.

She groaned. "I not only am not hungry for dinner, but I also expect not to be hungry for breakfast tomorrow. I may be ready to eat again by lunchtime tomorrow."

"I'll let Mama Rose know. She thinks you need fattening up."

Eliza laughed. "She's already doing a good job of it. Now that we know we're not dining again for a while, what else can be done on this case, Detective Brady?"

Wyatt sobered. "I hate to ask this, but there's one thing that you could do that would be helpful."

"Of course."

"It would involve taking a look at the intruder to see if you recognize him."

Her expression changed only slightly. "The dead man?" At his nod she continued. "Yes, all right."

Wyatt took her to the undertaker and then asked her to wait while he made arrangements with the owner. After assurances that the corpse would be covered except for the man's face, he led them into the back room where the man was laid out on a table with a blanket covering him.

Eliza took two steps forward and stuttered to a stop. "I know him."

"Who is he?" Wyatt asked.

"He's the man who kidnapped me and threatened to shoot Red. He definitely works for Ben."

Wyatt murmured a word of thanks to the undertaker and escorted Eliza out into the sunshine once again. She looked no worse for wear, but he knew it couldn't have been easy to do what she'd just done. He'd been at this a while and still never got comfortable with that part of his job.

After a glance around to see if anyone on the busy street seemed overly interested in the two of them, Wyatt led Eliza away from the undertaker toward an out-of-the-way spot on the other side of the street.

"Now that you can say with no hesitation that the man who shot at me is the same man who abducted you from the ranch, you have another decision to make."

Sometimes when she looked up at him, Wyatt was jolted backward to a time when life was much less complicated and a smile from Eliza was an invitation to make another memory.

"What's that?" she asked, diverting his thoughts.

"You've made a positive identification of the man on the undertaker's table. He's associated with the man who claims he's married to you. If we go back to the police station and give the detective that information, Barnhart will become directly implicated in this."

"He is implicated," she insisted.

"Of course he is." Wyatt paused. "But because Ben will say he sent that man down here to see what his wife was up to, you will then be implicated too."

"I don't understand. I'm innocent in all of that."

"But you can see how it would look like you're a runaway wife who didn't want to go home to her new husband so she found a way to stop the man who found her." Wyatt paused just long enough to let Eliza think about what he just said. "Let's examine the evidence. What proof do you have that this isn't what happened?"

CHAPTER 23

Eliza opened her mouth to protest. She had plenty of evidence. She'd been kidnapped by a man who brought her to Ben, who had then forged a marriage license and proclaimed them wed.

She sighed. "The man who might possibly corroborate my story of the kidnapping is dead and the marriage license has been confirmed as legitimate by the clerk in Travis County. Oh, wait. There's Red. He can confirm the kidnapping. I don't know if he saw the man who did it, but he was there."

"He can confirm that you were kidnapped. He cannot connect Ben Barnhart to the crime."

"The police chief liked me," she said. "He knew my grandfather. I could go to him."

"We may do that, but let's get a plan first." He glanced at his watch. "Bryant won't be here for several hours. I need a plan to keep you busy and away from any further harm."

"I am not a child, John. I don't have to be minded."

A thought occurred as he looked up at the cloudless sky overhead. "Eliza, have you been sailing lately?"

She smiled. "Not for a very long time."

He grinned and took her by the elbow. "Then I think it's time we remedied that. After we have a brief chat with Mrs. McDonald."

Once they arrived on the older woman's doorstep, Wyatt stepped in front of Eliza to knock on the door. She opened the door and smiled at her neighbor. Then she looked past him to meet Eliza's gaze and frowned.

"Why are you here again?" she asked Wyatt.

"To clarify a few things," he told her. "Miss Gentry tells me that when she came to you asking for help, you turned her away."

"I did," she said with not a bit of shame in her tone. "I'll not harbor your other women here, Mr. Brady."

"Other women?" Eliza said, incredulous. "Do I look like someone's other woman to you?"

"Apparently you do," Wyatt said before turning his attention back to his neighbor. "Miss Gentry is a client of mine at the detective agency. Were you aware there was a shooting at my home this morning?"

"I did hear a gunshot, yes. Two, now that I think on it." All the while that she was answering Wyatt, Mrs. McDonald was studying her. "Did she shoot you?"

"An intruder shot me," he said. "I killed him."

That got the old lady's attention. "You mean like a burglar of some kind?"

"Could be," he told her. "Miss Gentry and I were discussing business on the porch when I—"

Mrs. McDonald snorted. "Didn't look like business to me. I saw you pawing all over her."

"I was offering solace. My client has had. . ." He shook his head. "Never mind. I told her to run to you if she heard trouble. I thought she would be safe here."

She shrugged. "I guess I couldn't let her in. Janie warned me you had her over there. She's a good woman. Why don't you just marry her? You don't need these other women."

Eliza gave him an I-told-you-so look.

"What other women, Mrs. McDonald?"

"I guess it'd behoove you to know you have competition. There've been women about—yes, there have. Well, one for certain that I've seen." She looked over at Wyatt. "And it wasn't this redhead here, nor was it Janie."

"Janie is my housekeeper," he reminded her. "And I've been away on business for the better part of a month, so you would have to ask her who's been here recently. I wouldn't have any idea."

The old lady looked confused. "Well, I don't know then. I guess I'll have to ask Janie when she comes for coffee tomorrow. She's here every day just about. Unless she's needed at the restaurant. She brings me and Howard the best cannoli. Have you tried it?"

A look passed between her and Wyatt. "Who is Howard?" he asked.

"My new husband." Her smile rose. At least Eliza thought it resembled a smile. "He's a sailing man, so he's not here much."

"That would explain the man following you this morning. Just one more thing," Wyatt said. "When you sent me to the shed for the ladder, I thought you were directing me to Eliza. Why would you send me there? It was completely empty."

"It was?" She shook her head. "Well, I'll be." Then her eyes narrowed. "I think I know exactly what happened to that ladder and the rest of the late Mr. McDonald's tools. Howard," she shouted. "Come here now."

An older man shuffled toward her then stopped when he saw Eliza and Wyatt on the porch. Mrs. McDonald turned to face him.

"What did you do with the contents of that shed in the backyard?"

His gray brows rose. "I cleaned it out just like you asked, honey buns. It's nice and clean now. You ought to go see it."

"I don't need to. My neighbor says it's empty."

"Well, it is," Howard told her. "I thought you wanted it nice and clean, so I made it nice and clean. There's nothing cleaner than an empty shed."

"That is the most ridiculous thing I've ever heard."

"There's nothing ridiculous about it," Howard exclaimed. "Woman, you need to say what you mean if you're going to say anything at all."

"Mrs. McDonald," Wyatt said, "or whatever your name is now. If I could ask you some more questions about the woman you saw at my house, I—"

The old lady shut the door while the squabbling continued. Wyatt stepped back and looked over at Eliza. "I guess we have our answers about my neighbor."

"And a few more questions than we had when we got here," she said. "I don't think I've ever been called someone's other woman."

"I don't have anyone who could be called my other woman," he said. "So I have to wonder what Janie is telling her."

"We could go ask," Eliza said, "but I doubt she will want to talk to you with me there."

He looked as if he wanted to argue, then he shook his head. "Never mind. Let's go sailing."

A short while later, Wyatt caught the breeze and sent the sailboat skimming across the water on the bay side of the island. The sun glinted off the water, and birds scattered as the vessel cut through the channel.

Though the scenery was lovely, she was more entertained by Wyatt, who seemed completely absorbed in the work of keeping the vessel sailing in the direction he wanted it to go. Eliza sat beside him and tried to keep out of his way.

With the security detective intent on his task, he couldn't see that she was memorizing what she saw. That she was studying his profile and hoping she would never forget this moment. She glanced over her shoulder and saw that the island city was becoming smaller as the vessel sailed out into deeper waters.

Her companion smiled at her. "I'm going to lower the sails and let her drift for a while." With a few deft movements, the white sail slid down into a puddle and the boat slowed.

Wyatt sat back next to her, his attention on the horizon. Though the skies today had been clear and blue, a few wisps of cotton-white clouds now drifted past on the horizon. Other than the lapping of the waves against the boat and the sound of the gulls in the distance, all was quiet.

Eliza allowed a moment of pondering just what it would be like to have the ability to escape here whenever the need arose. To be able to climb into a sailboat and navigate a channel and then emerge into the Gulf of Mexico where the sun shone bright and any cares were left back at the dock.

She gave her companion a sideways look. She was also thinking what it might feel like to kiss him.

"This is lovely, John," she said on a long exhale of breath.

He nodded but otherwise kept still. "It's a place I go to think," he finally told her.

"Is that what you're doing now?"

Wyatt glanced at her. "I am."

"Anything interesting in those thoughts?"

Wyatt was thinking he wanted to kiss her. But this was not the time to be truthful. At least not that truthful.

"I was thinking how easy it would be to aim this sailboat for the horizon and never look back." He swiveled to face her. "Don't worry. I'm not going to do it. Mama Rose may have fed us well, but we would very likely get hungry in a day or two."

A pair of gulls chattered overhead as they dipped and then dove into the water just ahead of the sailboat. A swell of water broke, scattering them back into the sky.

"Is it awful that I truly don't care? Just point this thing for the horizon. I'll go where you go." She turned toward him. "I am so weary of fighting Ben Barnhart. It would be much easier if I could just walk away from it all."

He shook his head. "To walk away from Ben would mean you had to walk away from your family too. I know you don't want that."

Eliza looked down at her hands. When her gaze lifted, she had tears in her eyes. "No, I could never do that."

"Hey now, don't cry." Wyatt gathered her into his arms and held her. "We're going to figure this out."

"But I'm afraid Ben has already won," she managed before the tears fell harder. "I have all the truth, but he has all of the evidence. What I can't understand is why he's doing this. What is it that makes him so insistent that I have to be the wife who turns him into a respectable political candidate?"

"Eliza." Wyatt lifted her chin with his index finger then cupped her jaw in his hand. "You are a beautiful, intelligent woman who would be an asset to any man, not just a politician. Barnhart has been on this path since he was a child. Toward politics thanks to his father's insistence, and toward making you his wife."

She looked up at him, her eyes luminous. "You do know, don't you. That's exactly what he's like. It's flattering if you allow yourself to be caught up in it. But then there's this other side to all of that attention and all of that posturing to look and act a certain way, and it's a little frightening when you consider what happens if you fail."

"You? Fail?" Wyatt shook his head. "Any man with you for a wife would never fail."

Eliza leaned in slightly. "You say very nice things, John, but you don't know me."

"I do know you." He caught himself before he said more. Then he added. "I am a detective, remember? I am paid to know everything about people, and I am good at what I do."

She smiled then. "Funny, because I doubt you know what I am thinking right now."

"Try me."

"No," she said with a laugh, a tear still tracing a path down her cheek. "You're supposed to tell me what I'm thinking."

"Oh. I see." He swiped at her cheek with the back of his hand. "All right. Do you really want me to know what, in my professional estimation, you are thinking right now?"

"Yes," came out on a soft breath. "I do."

"I'm thinking that you want me to kiss you," he said, throwing caution to the salt-scented breeze.

"Detective," she said softly, "you really are good at what you do."

Wyatt smiled. "I am." Then he leaned down and gently kissed her.

He expected her to pull away or gasp and declare him a lunatic or something like that. Instead, Eliza leaned her head on his shoulder and sighed.

"Can you navigate this craft in the dark?" she asked.

Not the question he expected. "Not well."

She let out a long breath. "Did I officially hire you, John?"

He chuckled. "I think so."

"Then I would like you to sail toward the horizon just far enough to get us back to Galveston before dark."

Wyatt laughed. "That's not what you hired me to do, Eliza."

"No, but considering the day we've had and what has transpired since Ben decided I should be married to him, it does sound like a good solution."

He shook his head. "A good solution is to drift for a little while longer and then return to port, because we have things to discuss."

She lifted her head. "You mean the kiss?"

"Do you want to talk about the kiss?" he asked.

Eliza shook her head. "Not particularly. Except maybe to say that I'm glad it happened. And if things were different, maybe. . ." She paused. "No. That's all."

"That does sum it up," he admitted. "If things were different."

"I bet the stargazing is excellent out here," Eliza said after a while.

"I don't know about out here, but there's a place at the end of the island where I go sometimes. The light from the city isn't visible out there, so you get a pretty decent look at the heavens. It reminds me a little of being out on the trail."

She shifted positions to look up at him again. "That's right. You mentioned you've been on the Chisholm Trail."

"I managed the remuda on a trail ride when I was a kid," he said, testing the waters.

"So did my friend Wyatt."

"I know," Wyatt told her.

Eliza settled back beside him. "That's right. You've made it your business to know everything."

"Yes, I have." He let out a long breath and shifted positions to raise the sails again and turn the craft back toward the island.

"You know, John, if I needed to disappear for a while, I know exactly where I would go."

"Where?" he said as he concentrated on the sails.

"I would go on another trail drive. Do they still do them?"

"I believe so," he said, "but it's mostly done by outfits hired by the ranchers. Do you really want to go again? As I recall, it was mostly hard work and sleeping in bedrolls on hard ground."

"Sure," she told him. "It was also sleeping at night with nothing to do but look up at the stars. It's always a little chilly at night in April, but that's part of the fun too."

Wyatt shook his head. "You and I have different memories of the experience."

Eliza sobered. "But don't you see? I want that memory again, not the one I have of losing a friend. I just want to go one more time and make memories that are happy."

"Maybe I can take you someday." As soon as the words were out, he wished to reel them back in.

"I would like that," she said.

"So would I."

Eliza leaned against him again, and all was right with the world. "Someday when all of this has been put to rest and you're free to consider your future, I want to court you properly. If you'll allow it," Wyatt added.

"I would like that too."

Wyatt held her as long as he could, then shifted positions to handle the sails as he guided the vessel back to port. He didn't kiss her again. He would wait until she was able to consider him without the cloud of a false accusation of marriage following her.

But when that day came, and it would, Wyatt would be there.

And he would kiss her.

CHAPTER 24

July 2

Eliza woke up with the sunshine streaming through wooden blinds that she should have closed before she went to bed. After a meeting with Wyatt's employee, Jim Bryant, it was decided she should be hidden in plain sight at the Beach Hotel.

The vast structure with its many rooms facing the surf was a delight. From the circus-like atmosphere of entertainers on the beach—whom she had to settle for watching from the safety of her room—to the luxurious accommodations, the Beach Hotel had become a new favorite of hers overnight.

Without any firm plans for meeting with John or his associate Jim Bryant, Eliza could lounge in bed this morning without any guilt. She turned over in bed to avoid the blinding sun and closed her eyes again. Thoughts of yesterday's kiss in the sailboat drifted toward her on smooth waters, and she relived every moment of it again. And again.

Then came the knock at the door to her bedchamber. She bolted upright and wrapped a blanket around herself, then stopped just short of the door. "Who is it?"

"A delivery, miss," a masculine voice said.

"A delivery of what?" she asked.

"The box was sent over from the Tremont Hotel, so I don't know."

Eliza sighed. "All right. Just leave it right there, and I'll get it when I can."

"I'm sorry, miss, but I was instructed to get a signature to show that the delivery has been made."

She shook her head and gathered the blanket tighter around her. "All right. I'll open the door just enough to sign and no more than that."

"That's fine, miss."

One hand turned the crystal doorknob as the other reached into the space between the door and its frame to grasp the pen the deliveryman held. Instead, a hand grasped hers and pushed her backward to the floor.

A second later, the door slammed shut and Ben was on top of her. Eliza screamed, but the sound was quickly drowned out by his hand over her mouth.

"It's time to go home to Austin, Eliza," he told her, his face inches from hers. "Your beach vacation is over."

She squirmed and kicked and fought him until he slapped her. Then Eliza kicked harder. Ben pressed his hand against her mouth, and she bit him. When he moved away, she screamed.

"No one can hear you," he said. "The surf is too loud."

Eliza didn't care. She went to the window and stuck her head out, calling to the people on the beach four floors below. Ben was right. They couldn't hear.

And then his hand went around her throat and she couldn't scream. Couldn't speak. Couldn't breathe.

Something replaced his hand. A cloth of some kind. Then she could breathe but gagged when she tried to say anything.

Ben tied her hands together behind her back, turned her around, and led her to a chair beside the bed. He stood there and stared down at her. "Why are you so dramatic, Eliza?"

She glared at him. He continued to study her. Anger simmered just beneath the surface, but Eliza couldn't let it control her. If she was going to get out of this room alive, she would have to be smart.

"Did you think I would let this little visit with your old pal go on forever? You had to know I wouldn't. Now as soon as you're ready to be reasonable, we can get on our way back home. I've been asked to take part in the Fourth of July parade, and people will talk if my new bride isn't with me."

The idea of pretending to be his happy spouse was repulsive. Still, she showed no emotion.

"I saw you yesterday from the beach. You two were getting cozy. If I didn't know you were married to me, I would wonder why you were kissing another man. But you are married to me, sweetheart." He paused. "Yet you did kiss him. I would ask what you have to say for yourself, but you can't talk, can you?"

Her eyes narrowed. She seethed.

Ben moved closer, then lifted the chair next to hers into the air. Waiting for the blow, Eliza closed her eyes and cringed.

Instead, he set the chair directly in front of her and cupped her jaw very much like John had last night. She moved her head out of his reach, and he merely smiled.

"You don't like my touch as well as his, do you?" He shrugged. "It was always that way. I adored you, Eliza Gentry. I was the one who moved heaven and earth to go on that cattle drive just to be with you, and all you wanted to do was lie on a rock and look up at the stars with that idiot Wyatt Gentry. And now all you want to do is kiss him."

Eliza stared at Ben. He'd certainly lost his mind. There was no other explanation.

"Oh?" He sat back and crossed his arms over his chest. "He didn't tell you who he was, did he?" A smile rose. "Now that is interesting. All this time, I thought he'd surely told you by now. But he hasn't."

Her mind reeled. What was he trying to say? No, Eliza decided,

Ben was just trying to confuse her. She swallowed hard and then gagged with the effort.

"Keep it up and you'll choke," he said. "And don't think I haven't considered that I might get more votes as a grieving widower whose new bride met a tragic death, but unless it is an accident, there will always be a cloud of suspicion. Choking in a hotel room is not going to work in this scenario."

She sat very still but allowed her eyes to scan the room. Two windows opened to the back of the building where the surf pounded against the sand. There was only one exit door, and it was blocked by Ben.

The only way out was to go around him.

Until she had a plan to do that, all Eliza could do was pray. She closed her eyes, intent on some elaborate prayer. Instead, all she could manage was, *Father, help Your daughter, please. I am afraid.*

"You've probably decided that I am a monster, Eliza, but I'm not. If you let me, I would give you the world. But you ran off. Again. Just like you did when you disappeared to New Orleans." He shook his head. "I should have just gone through with the wedding to Beatrice. She knew how to treat a man, Eliza. She adored me. She would have done anything to become Mrs. Barnhart. But you?"

Ben shook his head and then held up two fingers close together. "I was this close to marrying her. We had a wedding date. I am certain she and her mother had it all planned out. Then she announced that we would be taking a European tour for at least half a year, and the other half we would live with her mother in Philadelphia. Does any of that sound like something I would be interested in doing?"

Eliza gave no indication of a reaction to his question. To do that would give him the impression she was participating in the conversation. Which she absolutely was not.

"She would have relented, of course. And I would have insisted we come back to Texas immediately. The judge and I have a plan, and it doesn't involve waiting until next year to begin my campaign."

He paused as if he was considering his words. Or perhaps reliving a memory. Either way, an unpleasant look crossed his features.

"Then I heard that Will Gentry had an old friend of ours looking after you. The John Brady Detective Agency was on the job." He paused to sneer. "I never did find out where he got that name, but it didn't matter. I could give you up for money and a wife who would do what I told her to do, but I sure wasn't going to let Wyatt Creed have you."

Her mind refused to wrap around that statement. Refused to consider the words of a madman.

"Oh, you still don't believe me." He shrugged, his voice cold and even. "All right, try this scenario on for size. There are two witnesses to a shooting on the trail, me and Wyatt. We tell different stories, but the gun belongs to Wyatt. Your father sends me back to Waco to face my father's wrath and then pretends to shoot Wyatt Creed and bury him next to his father."

Eliza shook her head. The lies this man spoke were unconscionable.

"Yes, Eliza. That is what happened. Wyatt Creed walked away from camp under cover of darkness. Will Gentry kept tabs on him and, when he needed him, called him into service to keep his family safe. The only problem is, Wyatt's presence anywhere near you is what ruined everything."

He paused. "You're wondering why."

This time she nodded. As long as he was going to spin a tale, she wanted to hear all of it so she could report back to John just how crazy Ben Barnhart was.

"Four people were there that night. Wyatt and me and your father and then Red." He held up four fingers. "I had Red handled until I heard he wasn't dead after all. Wyatt is easy to control. He's got a secret that cannot get out, so he steers clear of me. But you and your father, that's harder. See, the unfortunate truth is that William Gentry isn't afraid of anyone or anything. He only has one soft spot, and that's you and your mama and siblings. I like your brothers. They're friends of mine. Or were, though likely they won't want to maintain that friendship if they've spoken with your father about me."

He rose abruptly and went to the window. "I had to find a way to keep your father quiet. I knew you'd figure out that Wyatt still lived eventually. If either of you spoke out about what happened that night on the trail, I would lose all hope of holding public office. The people of Texas are funny about electing someone who's committed murder."

She gasped and then choked. Ben laughed.

"Oh, another piece of the puzzle you didn't know about." He shrugged and returned to his chair. "Yes, I shot the old man. He was talking out of his head. Saying things and. . ." He paused. "Never mind the details, but with you married to me, your father and you are both kept quiet about all that. William Gentry won't ruin the man who has fathered his grandchildren. And you, as the mother of my children, wouldn't dare hurt my career. Think of the shame our children would have to endure. So now we all get what we want. But only when you give up this adventure you're on and come back with me."

Ben leaned toward her. Panic rose. Her eyes widened.

"John Brady is Wyatt Creed. Your father allowed that to happen. No, he encouraged it. Your father has lied to you. Wyatt Creed has lied to you. I am the only one who has told the truth. So will you calmly walk out of this room with me and return to Austin, or do I need to send for the trunk I have waiting downstairs and have you carried out that way?"

He paused. "Look at me. You know I'm telling the truth and you know I'm right. Think about it. The eyes. The slash across his neck that healed wrong. The way he moons over you. The way your father trusted only him to watch his wife and daughter. It all adds up to only one thing."

His words sank in slowly. The absolute knowledge for most of her life that Wyatt couldn't have died on the trail had been attributed to grief. But maybe it wasn't grief.

She closed her eyes and recalled the memory of yesterday. Of John's profile. Of his face. Of. . . Eliza swallowed hard. Of the faint scar she recollected on his neck.

Then there was that moment at his gate when he called her Liza Jane. Only Wyatt Creed called her that.

Tears burned her eyes, but she refused to cry in front of Ben.

Ben was right. Papa had lied. Wyatt had lied. Even Red had lied.

But Ben Barnhart had told her the truth.

The woman seated across from him in his office on Twenty-Seventh Street was articulate, well-to-do, and hysterical. He'd invited her here this morning after a telegram reached him yesterday evening requesting time with the agency's owner this morning. The topic was Ben Barnhart.

Wyatt had quickly responded and then instructed Bryant to be there as well. Now he sat behind his desk, a half hour into an emotional monologue from Miss Beatrice Cunningham that involved broken promises, a ruined wedding, and a broken heart.

"So you see, I chose the John Brady Detective Agency specifically because I believe you can help me. I came to see you several times in the past month, but you weren't here. Your wife is quite rude."

"My wife?" He shook his head. "No, I am not married."

"Well, that's interesting. Your wife, Janie, is quite protective of you. She said I was to send a message through the post office box and you would pick that message up when you returned. I was to stay away from her home and you. She told me she did not allow other women here. Truly, I was only trying to hire you, but she was adamant. So was that neighbor lady who takes tea with her regularly. I finally stopped coming by and left a message in your post office box. And here we are." She paused. "So let me tell you again so you understand just what happened."

Then she was off again. She paused only to dab at her eyes and even then not long enough to let him or Bryant get a word in.

"Miss Cunningham," Wyatt finally said, interrupting a tearful story she'd already told twice, "please just let me see if I understand what the trouble is."

He looked past her to where Jim sat quietly taking notes and then returned his attention to the pale creature before him. "Ben Barnhart broke off his recent engagement with you and has disappeared."

"No." She dabbed at her eyes with a lace handkerchief. "He ruined the wedding when he suggested we elope. We did and then he was gone the next day. And no, he has not disappeared. He is here in Galveston."

Ben exchanged a look with Bryant. "How do you know this?"

"Mr. Brady, yours is not the only detective agency available for hire. I previously did business with the Pinkertons. They tracked Ben from Philadelphia to New Orleans and provided me with the information that led to you. A telegram reached me this morning that one of the agents had read in the *Austin American Statesman* that prospective candidate for political office Benjamin Barnhart and his wife were in Galveston on a belated honeymoon. Imagine the luck. Especially since he already has a wife."

"Imagine." He stood and nodded for Bryant to meet him in the hall. "Would you give me just a minute of time with my associate, please?"

Wyatt stepped around the desk and went into the hall. "I'm going to get Eliza and bring her here. The jilted bride is yours now. See if she has any more information on Barnhart that might help us."

"Boss, you can't go alone," he said.

"Yet I plan to. On second thought, set up a meeting with Miss Cunningham for tomorrow. Stall her somehow. Don't make her think we're not taking her seriously. Then meet me at the Beach Hotel."

Bryant nodded and returned to the office. Wyatt checked his revolver for bullets and headed out. Before he stepped outside, he lifted his eyes to the heavens and said a prayer that Eliza Gentry would be found safe.

Ben Barnhart? He'd have to work on that whole praying-for-your-enemies thing. For now he'd settle for praying that he didn't have to take the man's life. Let the hangman do it after a proper trial.

CHAPTER 25

In his haste to reach Eliza's suite on the fourth floor of the hotel, Wyatt took the stairs two at a time. He found the room empty. On the chair beside the bed, two strips of cloth that might have bound her hands and feet or perhaps served as a gag had been discarded.

Or maybe they weren't used for any of those things. He gave the room a thorough going-over, then went downstairs to find a clerk.

"Yes, sir, she has checked out," the clerk told him.

"Alone or with someone?" he asked.

"I believe the gentleman who accompanied her was her husband. I heard him tell the bellhop he needed transportation to the train station."

Racing out of the hotel lobby, Wyatt weaved around slow-moving guests and dodged folks who didn't have the good sense to get out of the way. He got to the station faster than he thought possible but not fast enough to stop the train headed for Austin with Ben and Eliza inside.

"What time is the next train to Austin?" he asked the station agent.

"Tomorrow morning at a quarter to five," the man told him.

He bought a ticket and went home to gather his things. Bryant was gone, and so was Miss Cunningham. He left a note on his desk for Bryant, letting him know what had happened, then packed a bag and returned to the station to wait.

"Awful early to be here," the station agent said when he saw Wyatt seated on the bench outside. "Might should go home and come back when it's closer to time to leave."

Wyatt waved him off and the agent shrugged and went back inside. He couldn't have slept at home anyway. Best to be here and ready to go.

Some time later, footsteps on the platform alerted him that someone was approaching. He must have dozed off because he jerked awake to find Bryant standing a few yards away.

"Didn't want to wake you up," he said. "I got your note."

He scrubbed at his face and then nodded. "Yeah, I've got to follow this thing through and see that she's okay. When we spoke last night, she was not of a mind to consider going back to Barnhart."

"Could she have changed her mind?"

"More likely Ben changed it for her."

Bryant nodded. "All right, well, any other instructions for me before you leave?"

"Why don't you share our information with Miss Cunningham. Let her know that her alleged husband has returned to Austin."

His employee nodded. "I'll do it. Just curious. Any particular reason I need to give her for doing that?"

"Tell her she ought to go to the newspapers down there and correct them on their false and misleading story. We've discovered Barnhart is not married, and she's still got a chance with him."

"That's mean, Boss."

"Mean to who, Ben or her?"

"Her," he said. "She's nice enough."

He sighed. "I'm sure she is. But if she raised a fuss about the legitimacy of the license it wouldn't hurt, would it? Especially since she's alleging she ran off with him first. Be kind. Don't get her riled up, and make the point that she needs to consult a police officer before she does anything else. Be sure she presents the marriage license she showed us."

"Will do."

"Oh, and I keep forgetting to give you this." He retrieved the folded license from his pocket and gave it to Bryant. "This is the marriage license he presented to Eliza. A clerk in Travis County said it was legitimate, but he based it on the paper it was written on and not on the signatures. Eliza swears that isn't hers."

Bryant held the half page up to the gaslight to inspect it. "This looks familiar."

"It ought to. I believe it's the same stuff that was stolen in New Orleans. Unfortunately, the sample you gave me was ruined, but you ought to be able to work your contacts and get some kind of confirmation, couldn't you?"

"I can do that."

"Thank you." He paused. "I'll book a room at the Driskill Hotel. You can send me updates there."

July 4

The parade snaked up Congress Avenue at a snail's pace. It was hot as blazes, and it was all Eliza could do to remain upright. Judge Barnhart and his wife had seen that the carriage carrying their son and his wife was festooned with the appropriate amount of ribbons and garland, and they'd commissioned a sign for the back that read A Vote for Benjamin Barnhart Is a Vote for Home and Family.

As the carriage reached the capitol grounds, the driver diverted them to a side street where Ben quickly jumped from the carriage. A uniformed coachman of some sort hurried to help Eliza down.

Her knees wobbled and threatened to give way. Ben pushed the coachman out of the way and caught Eliza before she fell.

"Do not embarrass me today," he hissed in her ear. "You will regret it."

"I already do," she said, not caring if it angered him. There was nothing he could do out here in front of half of Travis County, most of whom were voters.

Ben ignored her to fall in line behind other dignitaries who were gathering near the stage. At the appointed time, Governor Ross would address the crowd.

Then, finally, the farce would be over and she could go home.

After an eternity of waiting, the dignitaries were seated on the elevated stage and speeches began. Since Ben was not yet elected, his was the last name on the list.

When he was introduced, Eliza clapped politely but found she could not manage a smile. He spoke, but the words did not penetrate the fog surrounding her.

Then out of the crowd, a decidedly female voice shouted, "He's a bigamist!"

Ben's face went white, but he continued with his speech, a monologue on the importance of family and the promise of safety to the homes and hearths of his constituents. Ben had practiced in front of the mirror at the home near the capitol until Eliza could remember every word.

She sat very still and watched the crowd, hoping to catch sight of whoever had made the allegation. Then she heard the statement again, and this time she spied the person who shouted.

Beatrice Cunningham?

Eliza looked over at Ben. He was showing his nerves. He'd stopped midsentence and had to begin again.

Beatrice was making her way to the stage, a police officer in tow. "That's him, Officer," she said as she held up a paper for anyone who was near her to see. "Here's the marriage license, and that's my husband."

Everything that happened after that was a blur. Not the fog of the previous days but a whirlwind of activity that saw Eliza whisked off the stage and hurried into a much more discreet conveyance than the one in which she arrived.

Eliza allowed herself to be moved along from one place to another as if she were a sailboat floating along on the summer currents of the Gulf of Mexico. The police were the first to take a seat in the newly furnished parlor. She offered them coffee and answered their questions, and they moved along only to be replaced by other people.

So many people. She lost track of their names. Of who they represented and why they were there.

Ben arrived late that evening in a nasty mood. His father was with him, and between the two of them, the home was quickly filled with shouting. Eliza retreated to the small slice of greenery allowed to her in this city location, the back garden.

Last night she had discovered she could sit in a chair in a certain place in the garden and look up between the live oak trees to see the Little Dipper. If she moved to another spot, Orion came into view. She hadn't seen any meteorites, but then, she hadn't expected to.

Tonight she didn't care to look up to the heavens. Didn't even want to. Instead, she sat in her chair and stared off into the walled-in space that was her home.

Thoughts passed through her head and then evaporated. Others seemed just out of reach.

Ben had married Beatrice.

So he had lied too.

Just like Papa. Like Red. And like Wyatt Creed.

A tear slipped down and she swiped at it. If anyone saw her sitting here, they might think she was distressed at her husband's embarrassment in front of his constituents.

Tears were the appropriate response. But she wasn't crying for Ben or even for her. She was crying for what might have been.

And what never could be.

The sound of footsteps on the gravel path caused her to look up. Wyatt Creed approached.

Looking at him now, knowing who he was, it was impossible to believe she hadn't realized the man she kissed on the sailboat was the boy she had missed all these years. If he expected her to greet him, he would be disappointed.

Instead, she looked up toward the heavens and watched for something that she knew might never come.

He moved closer, keeping his silence until he'd taken the chair next to her. Even then, he didn't spare her a greeting.

Eliza continued to watch the stars pulse overhead, and then, to her surprise, a meteorite streaked past. It was small and disappeared quickly, but she'd seen it and that was what mattered.

Beside her came a single word softly uttered: "One."

"Do you still count them, Wyatt?"

"Every time."

He shifted positions. She refused to look at him. They sat in silence for so long she almost forgot he was there.

"I wanted to tell you," he finally said, his voice raw.

"But you didn't," was the only response she could manage.

Silence fell between them. Another star fell.

"Two," Wyatt said.

"Stop it," she told him. "You're trying to bring back a time that no longer exists. We aren't those kids anymore, Wyatt. There are too many lies between us."

"Is that how you see it?"

This time she spared him a quick glance. "That's what it is. You,

Red, Papa, and Ben. Every one of you lied. And you would all say it was to protect me." She pounded her fist on the arm of the chair. "Not one of you realizes I do not need to be protected."

"I see it clearly now." He stood and moved between her and her view of the sky. "I see you clearly now too."

"What does that mean?"

He looked away as if considering the question and then turned back to her. "Not a day went by from that night when I walked away from camp nine years ago until right this minute that I didn't think of you in some way or another. I looked up at the night sky and thought of you. I saw a red-haired woman across a room and had to make sure it wasn't you. You were everywhere." He paused. "You still are."

Eliza kept her mouth shut for fear she would admit that she could say the same thing about him. Her fingers gripped the arms of the chair, but she did not look away.

"But the woman I looked for, the one I saw everywhere? She's not who I was looking for. She was made of memories and imaginings and fashioned out of what I wished she had become."

"So you're disappointed in what you found?"

"The opposite, actually. I completely underestimated you in every way."

"Sit down, Wyatt," she said.

"You want me to stay?"

Eliza shook her head. "You can stay or go. That's up to you. But you're blocking my view."

He might have smiled. She thought she caught a glimpse of one before she turned her attention to the night sky.

"I brought you something." He slid a folded paper toward her.

"It's too dark to read this," she said. "Tell me what it says."

"It is a report that states your marriage license was printed on paper stolen from a printer in New Orleans. The one the clerk said they get their paper from. Two men in police custody in New Orleans have attested to the fact that they used the stolen paper to create marriage licenses for Ben Barnhart."

She turned toward him. "*Licenses* plural? As in more than one?"

"As in two." Wyatt paused. "One is yours. That was confirmed by the sample I provided when you allowed me to take half of your license. The other was confirmed this morning when Beatrice Cunningham delivered her license to the Austin Police Department." He paused. "Apparently a former Secret Service agent on the governor's staff was willing to come over to look at the document this morning before the parade."

"So he is a bigamist."

"No, Eliza," Wyatt said. "He's not married to either of you."

"I understand his reason for pursuing me and creating the false license. He's been chasing me for years. But why did he do that to Beatrice? And how did he do it? Was their license also from Travis County?"

"No, that's where it gets interesting. The printer provides this paper to a number of government entities, none of which are in Pennsylvania. He created a story that he wanted their wedding to be in Washington, DC, so they could be married in front of political dignitaries, when actually DC was the closest place that used the same paper."

Eliza shook her head. "Again, though, why Beatrice?"

"She told me that herself," he said, "when she came to see me a few days ago. She's the one who tipped us off that Barnhart had found you at the hotel. I wish I'd—"

"Stop," she told him. "It's not worth talking about."

"It is, but I will respect your request." He paused. "Beatrice told us that she would do anything for Ben. She would be a willing wife and a political asset. The only problem was Beatrice wouldn't leave

Philadelphia. That puts a damper on any Texas political aims. So he had to try again with a different wife."

"Why not just run for office up there?"

"And miss a chance to impress the judge up close?" Wyatt shook his head. "You don't see it, do you? Ben has lived in the shadow of a rich and important man. It's not enough to inherit what his father built. He wants to show the judge he can do it himself."

"And he is willing to do anything to achieve that," she said.

"Apparently." Wyatt paused. "Red told me there's a summer trail drive leaving out of Austin next week. Some of your father's cattle are going as far as Fort Worth with one of those droving outfits. There's room for you and a wagon for sleeping and stargazing if you want it."

"I might," she said.

They sat in silence for a while. Then Eliza slid Wyatt a sideways look. "You lied to me. I don't know what I'm going to do about that."

"Nothing you can do," he said. "Except maybe consider the circumstance and decide if you still feel like you did out on that boat."

"Oh, I do," she said. "I feel like I am drifting and bobbing and looking at dry land without aiming in that direction. Like I want to head off for parts unknown but I can't steer in the dark very well either."

"I'd go with you," he said.

"You can't."

"The offer is there anyway."

A popping sound alerted Eliza to the beginning of the patriotic fireworks display over in front of the capitol. Sparks of red, white, and blue shot up and turned the night sky bright with their glow.

Eliza watched in silence, wishing the noise and commotion would cease so she could see the stars again. After a few minutes the show ended. Only then did she hear the screaming.

She ran toward the noise with Wyatt on her heels. The front door of the house was open, but no one was inside.

Outside on the lawn, a circle of people had gathered. In the center was Ben Barnhart lying dead with a stain of red decorating the suit he'd purchased especially for the parade this morning. Kneeling beside him with a gun in her hand was Beatrice Cunningham, whom the papers would call Beatrice Barnhart in their morning editions.

Chapter 26

July 27
On the Chisholm Trail
north of Waco

The stars at night were big and bright, just as Eliza remembered. Unlike the utilitarian wagon she'd shared with Zeke and Trey, she'd somehow managed to be assigned to a much more comfortable sleeping arrangement with a brand-new wagon filled with plush pillows and blankets and a cover in case of rain.

Eliza suspected Red was behind the switch, although he denied it. He also denied asking the droving company to tag along in order to keep tabs on her, even though they both knew it was the reason.

She'd been hesitant to leave on this drive with Mama and Papa expected home soon. But their delay in traveling due to weather meant she had to choose.

And Eliza chose to go.

They had exchanged at least a dozen telegrams and letters since news of Ben's shooting arrived on their doorstep. Neither Papa nor Mama offered any comment on the affair other than to send their condolences to Judge and Mrs. Barnhart. There would be time enough to talk about Ben when the family was reunited.

Eliza settled onto the cot that had been provided for her and covered herself up to her chin, then looked up at the heavens. God's creation was spectacular, even more so out here far away from lights.

She had been on the trail for a while, and it was every bit as enjoyable and grueling as she recalled. Though she was a guest on this ride, she was still expected to do her part.

Just as she had all those years ago, Eliza volunteered her time helping the camp cook serve the meals. While he wasn't as old and wise as Cookie had been, he was congenial and made mealtimes interesting.

Often while she dished out beans and cornbread to the cowboys, the cook was dishing out advice. Or recipes. Or whatever knowledge he decided to impart to the captive audience that was the members of this cattle drive.

Tonight he waxed poetic about the types of beans and their benefits, weighing each one equally against the other. Eliza let him talk, pretending to listen as the men filed past.

When it was Red's turn, he shook his head. "Them cows don't chatter like this. Maybe you ought to swap jobs with one of them drovers."

She laughed. "Be nice, Red."

"It ain't about being nice. I'm being honest."

Eliza smiled at the conversation she'd had with Red tonight. And at the fact that he likely was somewhere near enough to keep watch or, failing that, likely paid someone else to do the same.

She sat up to look around, wondering who was next on the list of minders. Seeing no one, she rested her head on her feather pillow once more and resumed her watch of the heavens.

A meteorite streaked across the sky from east to west and a male voice said, "One."

Sitting bolt upright, she looked around to find the source. There could only be one person. Immediately her temper flared. He hadn't been invited on this ride, and she certainly hadn't seen him among the cowboys.

So it couldn't be Wyatt, could it?

She rested back on her pillow again. A few minutes later another falling star caught her attention.

"Two."

This time there was no mistaking who was counting stars.

"Wyatt Creed, where are you hiding?"

"I'm not hiding." A pair of sage-green eyes peered over the edge of the wagon. "I just thought it prudent to introduce myself slowly. I just joined the drive tonight. I'm here now and all settled in for my watch."

"Your watch?"

"Yep. Red's got me on night duty, so I'd be much obliged if you'd cooperate and go to sleep soon so I won't be troubled with having to talk to you all night."

Eliza suppressed a smile. As much as she was irritated with his surprise appearance, she had to admit his was a welcome face in a sea of strangers and cattle.

"I seem to remember there was a rock over there that had a good view of the skies. I thought I'd go over there and see if it still does." He paused. "I don't suppose you'd want to do that, would you?"

"I'm not sure that's a good idea," she told him.

"Suit yourself. I'll go alone then."

"No you won't. Not if Red told you to keep watch. You're a rule follower."

"You've got me there. Still, I bet I see more falling stars in an hour than you ever have. What's your highest amount?"

This was a familiar conversation. She easily responded with the familiar answer. "Why should I tell you? You'll just brag tomorrow about besting me with some made-up number."

Rather than take offense, Wyatt laughed. That had indeed been his plan.

"I'll be too busy to bother about that tomorrow," he told her.

"Too busy doing what?"

She was interested now. He could tell. So he took the opportunity to tease her just a bit more. "We've got a train stop coming up on the trail tomorrow. It wasn't there back in '80, but it's there now. I thought I just might get on that train and ride off to who knows where."

"Why in the world would you do that?"

He shrugged. "Maybe I feel like that boat bobbing out on the sea too. If I apply the rudder, everything just might go in the direction I want it to."

"Apply the rudder." She laughed at his poor attempt at a joke. But then, she always did.

"Do you think you can find the rock?"

"I know I can," he said. "I already did. Now put your boots on and let's get moving. Red will have my hide if I don't do my job properly and keep you close by."

With her boots on, Eliza jumped down from the wagon and followed Wyatt down the trail. Ten minutes later he shone his lantern on the rock. She recognized it immediately.

"Wyatt, there it is."

He helped her up on the smooth surface and joined her. "Best viewing spot on the Chisholm Trail."

She lay back against the cool stone and looked up into the skies overhead. "It truly is."

They lay there so long that Eliza thought Wyatt might have fallen asleep. Finally, he turned on his side and faced her.

"I can't think of the right words to say I'm sorry. I believe that's because they don't exist. None are good enough. What I did, lying to you about who I was when I ought to have come clean? That cuts to the bone. It doesn't matter why I did it or that I thought I was protecting you. There's no fix for it."

Eliza sighed. "No, there isn't."

"I wondered, though, if there's grace for it. And forgiveness. I would appreciate both of those in great measure."

"In great measure, is it?" She smiled, and his heart soared. "And why should I do that?"

"You shouldn't," he warned her. "I'm just a man. I am pitifully human and flawed. I cannot tell you I will not disappoint you. What I can tell you is there isn't a man on this earth who loves you like I do. Like I always have as long as I can remember. You were in every star I counted. You still are. If I have my way, you'll not just be in my past; you'll also be in my present and my future."

She leaned on her side to face him. "Wyatt, that sounds more like a proposal than a list of reasons I ought to forgive you."

"That's because it is." He climbed to his feet and helped her to stand. "Liza Jane, I am done with pretty words. I want to marry you and end all of this wondering whether I'm going to get to love you the rest of my life. Will you please cooperate?"

Eliza laughed. "That is your proposal? 'Will you cooperate'?"

"It is." He nodded. "You probably ought to just say yes because I am going to love you whether you are with me or not. I had nine years to try not to love you, but I never could figure out how."

"Wyatt, I don't know. It's crazy to just jump right back in where we left off, isn't it?"

"No crazier than letting your boat drift over the horizon, and you were all for that," he said. "And for the record, if you had insisted, we'd still be floating in that sailboat tonight."

"We'd be starving," she said with a half grin.

"Oh, I had that figured out. All we had to do was shoot up a distress signal and Mama Rose would send one of the boys out in a dinghy with some pasta."

"More likely she would send out Janie and a preacher to stop us from ruining her plans to bring you into the family."

He shook his head. "When are you going to believe me that I never had any interest in Janie?"

"Oh, I believed you the first time you said it. I just figured if Janie stuck around long enough, you'd give in and marry her."

"Well, that didn't happen, did it? Now can we return to the topic that's most important?"

"Sure. Three."

Wyatt shook his head. "Three? You saw one when I wasn't looking?"

"I did." She shrugged. "To the victor go the spoils. You'd better finish your speech before you get too far behind on counting."

He let out a long breath and then dropped to one knee. "All right. I'm going back to the original question. Liza Jane, will you forgive me, and will you also cooperate and marry me?"

She giggled. "I will." And then she added, "Four."

July 28

They'd remained on that rock long enough to count a half dozen falling stars last night, and this morning Eliza was paying for the lack of sleep. "You look lovely," Wyatt told her as he accepted his ration of breakfast.

"And you're not telling the truth."

"Oh, but I am."

She smiled and moved on to the next cowboy. Red brought up the end of the line. If he thought she looked extra tired, he said nothing. Instead, he grinned.

"You do decorate a campsite, Miss Eliza," her father's ranch hand told her. "I have enjoyed this ride. Didn't think I would."

"So have I."

Later, after the camp was cleared and the drive was on the move again, Eliza slipped to the back of the wagon to take a nap. When she awakened, the wagon was no longer moving. She climbed out to see what the cause of the delay might be and saw they had arrived at the train tracks Wyatt had described.

"Why not cross them and move on?" Eliza asked Red when she found him.

He'd been reading his Bible, and he looked up from it to regard her with an expression she couldn't quite decipher. "Because we're waiting for the train."

Eliza went back to the wagon and sat there until Wyatt rode by on his horse. "We're waiting for the train, apparently," she told him.

"I know." He nodded to a smudge of smoke off in the distance. "It'll be here soon."

"I assume you're not getting on it." She paused. "Considering our discussion last night."

Wyatt winked but said nothing. Then he rode away, leaving her to wonder what he meant by that.

Eventually the train approached, and to Eliza's surprise, it stopped right there in front of her. Over the hiss of the steam boiler, she heard someone calling her name.

"Mama?"

Eliza looked up to see her mother exiting the train, followed by Papa. She hurried to greet them. "What are you doing here?"

"We came to see you," her mother said.

"I've never seen the Chisholm Trail," Justine called from her perch on the train steps behind them.

She'd dressed in her best traveling finery, a pink floral ball gown that had been pinned up to keep her from tripping, a pair of opera-length gloves, and a straw hat decorated with red roses and white carnations that looked as if it belonged in one of the floats at the

Independence Day parade.

"Justine!" Eliza hurried over and the girl launched herself into her arms. "I'm so glad to see all of you."

The girl grinned. "Me too. And I have a secret that I can't tell you."

"Justine," Papa warned. "Do not say another word."

Wyatt rode up and climbed down from his horse. "I see everyone is here." He let out a whistle that sent all the cowboys hurrying toward them. "I want to welcome all of you to this auspicious occasion."

"What auspicious occasion?" Eliza asked.

"Our wedding."

"What?" She shook her head. "No one told me about a wedding."

"See," Justine said proudly. "And I haven't told her about the wedding dress you brought her to wear, Aunt Susanna."

"Justine!" Papa and Mama said together.

"I guess the secret is out," Mama said. "Wyatt asked Papa for your hand. He agreed. I brought my dress since we didn't have time to have one made for you."

Eliza looked up at Wyatt. "You arranged all of this? What if I refused to cooperate?"

He shrugged. "I guess I would have had to get on the trail and head off to who knows where by myself. It'll be a lot more fun this way." He paused. "Or we can call this an engagement party and then plan the fanciest wedding you want back at the ranch. Or in Austin. Or the cathedral in New Orleans. It's up to you."

"An impromptu wedding on the trail sounds good to me." She leaned toward him. "You have no idea what it would be like planning a wedding with my mother helping."

Wyatt laughed. "I think I do. Now go get dressed up so I can marry you properly."

"Wait," she said as a thought occurred. "We can't marry here. There's no minister."

Red stepped up, Bible in hand. "I guess you've forgotten I used to be a circuit rider before I came to work for your pa. I might be a bit out of practice, but I think I can still figure out how to marry up a couple legally."

Wyatt supplied the answer to her next question before she asked it. "And yes, I have a license. A real one. You'll have to sign it yourself though. I already have."

Eliza hurried inside, where she found the lone train car was filled with family and friends eager to attend a wedding. She spied Zeke and his wife and their little ones and ran to hug each of them.

"I'm so glad to see you," she exclaimed as she took turns hugging each of them.

"Are you glad to see me too?"

She turned around to see her brother Trey standing there. He was fit, tan, and wore his hair longer than she remembered. And he looked happy. "Trey! You're back."

Her brother gave her a sheepish look. "We were just about to set off from San Francisco when I heard what happened. I got here as quick as I could."

"You're just in time, Trey. Thank you."

She turned to the crowd. "Thank you all for coming to my Chisholm Trail wedding!"

"Let's get on with it then," Uncle Leo shouted from the front of the train car as the rest of the group cheered in agreement.

"All right," she called as she looked down at her buckskin skirt and blouse. "I'm not exactly looking like a bride right now."

Mama appeared in the doorway of the train car. "I can help with that."

A makeshift dressing room was arranged at the back of the dining car, and a few minutes later, she emerged dressed in Mama's beautiful wedding dress, ready to commit her life to Wyatt Creed.

As she stepped down from the train, the passengers clapped, and so did the cowboys. They all gathered around her and Wyatt as Red stepped up to read the vows.

"Before I start, Wyatt's got something to give you, Miss Eliza."

He reached into his pocket and pulled out something that sparkled in the midday sun. "What is it?"

"It's your wedding ring," he told her. "I had it made from the celestial comb I gave you at River House."

"That comb was from you?" She looked down at the ring. A star balanced in the center and a ring of diamonds resembling a comet's tail circled beneath it. "I thought it was lost."

"It was never lost. I had it with me all the time. Just like I had you with me." He slipped the ring on her finger.

"Hold on here," Red exclaimed. "I haven't said the vows yet."

"Hurry up, Red," Eliza said. "I'm ready for this man to kiss his Chisholm Trail bride."

And after making their promises and saying their prayers, Wyatt did exactly that.

AUTHOR'S NOTE AND BENT HISTORY:
The Rest of the Story

As a writer of historical novels, I love incorporating actual history into my plots. As with most books, the research behind the story generally involves much more information than would ever actually appear in the story. In truth, I could easily spend all my time researching and not get any writing done at all!

Because I am a history nerd, I love sharing some of that mountain of research I collected with my readers. The following are just a few of the facts I uncovered during the writing of *The Chisholm Trail Bride*. It is my hope that these tidbits of history will cause you to go searching for the rest of the story.

First and foremost, the Chisholm Trail was actually many trails that began in Texas or at the Red River—opinions among historians vary—and culminated at the railyards in Kansas. Those who believe the Chisholm Trail began at the Red River would tell you that the trails that led north from the ranches in southern Texas had various other names. The others would say there were a hundred or more feeder trails that led to one main trail across Texas, the Chisholm.

For the purposes of this story, I am taking the position that the Chisholm Trail originated somewhere near San Antonio (some say at Donna, Texas) and swept northeast to Austin, then straight north through Waco and Fort Worth. From the stockyards at Fort Worth, the trail continued north to cross the Red River at Red River Station, then on through Oklahoma to end at the railyards in Kansas.

In the early years of the Chisholm Trail, the cattle were driven all the way to Wichita, Kansas, but as new railroad lines were put in, the trail's end moved gradually south. By the later years of the trail, the use of which ended around 1887, the destination for the cattle was actually Caldwell, Kansas, which was just north of Indian Territory, now the state of Oklahoma.

Because trail rides could take months, ranchers who weren't keen to spend all of that time away from home began to allow trailing companies to take their cattle for them. The trailing companies would gather up the livestock—usually hardy Texas longhorns—and drive them north to the railyards for a price that was generally based on the number of cattle the rancher was sending with them. Tens of thousands of cattle would be moved at once, which is just amazing to consider, isn't it?

The history of the Chisholm Trail, blazed in part by Scots-Cherokee trader Jesse Chisholm and in use from the 1860s to the 1880s, is fascinating, and the story surrounding it is far broader than I can tell in this novel. Barbed wire and quarantines closed the trail by 1884, but during its heyday, it is estimated that more than a million mustangs and five million cattle were moved along its path.

I highly recommend doing more research on the subject. One book that I found particularly fascinating was *A Bride on the Old Chisholm Trail in 1886* by Mary Taylor Bunting. This is a true account of a young bride's trip up the trail with her husband on a cattle drive, and yes, it is still available for purchase.

The Waco suspension bridge opened to toll traffic across the Brazos River on January 1, 1870. At 475 feet long, the first major suspension bridge in Texas was wide enough for two stagecoaches to pass each other. Situated on the Chisholm Trail, the bridge also accommodated cattle with a charge of five cents per head. Today the bridge is only open to foot traffic and has been listed on the National Register of Historic Places. I highly recommend you visit Waco and see it for yourself.

I spied an advertisement for the Reed School for the Cure of Stammering in Detroit in the 1880 version of *Polk's Medical Register and Directory of the United States and Canada*. I bent history a little by having my characters mention it in 1889, but I couldn't resist.

Alexander & Cornwell's Drug Store at 219 East Sixth Street (also called Pecan Street during the 1800s) placed an advertisement in the June 13, 1889, edition of the *Austin American Statesman* newspaper stating that shoppers could find a complete stock of such items as toilet soaps, shoulder braces, fine perfumes, violin strings, chamois skins, and trusses. The ad claims their "soda water and milkshakes are unequaled in the city." My character Justine would agree. I should add that the building is still standing at that address.

Gammel's Old Book Store on Third Street was a real bookstore that placed an ad in the same newspaper. I have not been able to determine the exact address, but there were mentions of the store in newspapers as far away as Boston, so I assume they were quite successful during that time period.

The Heavens by Amédée Guillemin is a real book, and the descriptions I give are based on an 1871 copy that I found available for sale online. A scan of the entire book is also available for reading at archive.org. The illustration of Donati's Comet from October 4, 1859, is indeed on the front flyleaf, and the appendix titled "Very Unequal Stars" is on page 524.

The Driskill Hotel is a historic Austin hotel, and its exterior has changed very little since 1886 when cattle baron Colonel Jesse Driskill opened what the local newspaper called the finest hotel in the state. In 1887, the Driskill was the site of the inaugural ball of Governor Sul Ross, which established a tradition that carried on for many years. The hotel, now owned by a major hotel chain, takes up nearly an entire city block and is still a showplace. Busts of the heads of Colonel Driskill and his two sons were incorporated in the architecture of the building, with the colonel's facing Sixth Street and the boys aimed in other directions.

The home that Ben buys for Eliza is based on the Daniel Caswell house, a historic home in the Judge's Hill area of downtown Austin. Built by a prosperous cotton merchant, the Daniel Caswell house is currently owned by the Austin Junior Forum and now hosts weddings and other special events.

I found fictional Wyatt Creed's real-life Galveston home on a list of endangered historical properties at www.galvestonhistory.org. The two-story former beauty, built in 1886 by a well-to-do merchant, was originally a one-story home but was raised up after it survived the 1900 hurricane. At the time of this writing, the house is still standing and in need of a whole lot of love and work to make it a home again.

Encke's Comet is a comet that appears in late June every three years. Close approaches to earth usually happen every thirty-three years. It is also believed to be the origin of the Taurids and Beta Taurids meteor showers.

The Galveston City Hall, a French Renaissance Revival building with elaborate turrets and a grand curved double staircase leading to the second floor, was built in 1888 on the corner of Market Street and Strand Street. The police department was on the second floor, with the Galveston Market—reportedly a meat market—on the ground floor. Other city offices took up the third floor. Unfortunately, the building was damaged in the Great Storm of 1900, rebuilt, and then used by the city until it was torn down in 1966.

In a case of bending the facts or, as I like to call it, bent history, I could find no evidence that there was, indeed, a Fourth of July parade in Austin in 1889, so I created one for this story.

While fireworks have been around for centuries, I also found no evidence they were set off on the state capitol grounds on Independence Day back in 1889, thus another case of bent history.

Any other errors or mistakes are mine alone. Happy trails, y'all!

ACKNOWLEDGMENTS

As a tenth-generation Texan, I love writing fiction that weaves in the history of my home state. I want to thank the teachers who keep Texas history alive in the minds of children like me. What a wonderful legacy you are leaving. Thank you!

To the lovely ladies of the New and Improved Girls Loop, thank you for your support, your listening ears (or on a text loop I guess that should be *eyes*), and your encouragement as I raced to the deadline on this novel. I appreciate you!

To my husband who did laundry, cooked meals, and offered his support during the writing of this book, I love you, sweetheart. Oh, who am I kidding? He does that all the time, not just when I'm on deadline.

To my ultimate inspiration, my Father in heaven. This has been a year of trust, even in the face of great pain. Thank You for not giving up on me.

 **Kathleen Y'Barbo** is a *Publishers Weekly* bestselling author of more than one hundred books with over two million copies of her books in print in the US and abroad. A tenth-generation Texan and certified paralegal, she is a member of the Texas Bar Association Paralegal Division, Texas A&M Association of Former Students and the Texas A&M Women Former Students (Aggie Women), Texas Historical Society, Novelists Inc., and American Christian Fiction Writers. She would also be a member of the Daughters of the American Republic, Daughters of the Republic of Texas and a few others if she would just remember to fill out the paperwork that Great Aunt Mary Beth has sent her more than once.

When she's not spinning modern day tales about her wacky Southern relatives, Kathleen inserts an ancestor or two into her historical and mystery novels as well. Recent book releases include bestselling *The Pirate Bride* set in 1700s New Orleans and Galveston, its sequel *The Alamo Bride* set in 1836 Texas, which feature a few well-placed folks from history and a family tale of adventure on the high seas and on the coast of Texas. She also writes (mostly) relative-free cozy mystery novels.

Kathleen and her hero in combat boots husband have their own surprise love story that unfolded on social media a few years back. They make their home just north of Houston, Texas and are the parents and in-laws of a blended family of Texans, Okies, and two very adorable Londoners.

To find out more about Kathleen or connect with her through social media, check out her website at www.kathleenybarbo.com.